PRAISE FOR

original FAKE

"With a **sharply funny teenage voice, graphic panels bursting with life**, and a cast of characters as irrepressible as Uncle Epic himself, ***Original Fake* is 100% original: a subversive and timely story of the power of art.**"

—Kate Hattemer, critically acclaimed author of
The Vigilante Poets of Selwyn Academy

"*Original Fake* manages to be **grounded and trippy, thoughtful and tense, personal and epic**. What a good family we meet. What a great art adventure we go on. And, also, what? **It has pictures!**"

—Geoff Herbach, author of
the award-winning Stupid Fast series

ALSO BY KIRSTIN CRONN-MILLS

Transgender Lives: Complex Stories, Complex Voices

Beautiful Music for Ugly Children

The Sky Always Hears Me: And the Hills Don't Mind

ALSO BY E. EERO JOHNSON (ERIK T. JOHNSON)

Kozmo-Knot

The Outliers

original FAKE

KIRSTIN CRONN-MILLS

art by

E. EERO JOHNSON

G. P. PUTNAM'S SONS

G. P. PUTNAM'S SONS

an imprint of Penguin Random House LLC
375 Hudson Street, New York, NY 10014

Text copyright © 2016 by Kirstin Cronn-Mills.
Illustrations copyright © 2016 by Erik T. Johnson.

G. P. Putnam's Sons is a registered trademark
of Penguin Random House LLC.

Library of Congress Cataloging-in-Publication Data
is available upon request.

Printed in China by C & C Offset Printing Co., Ltd.
ISBN 978-0-399-17326-4
1 3 5 7 9 10 8 6 4 2

Edited by Stacey Barney.
Design by Ryan Thomann.
Text set in Chaparral with bits of Century Gothic
and the artist's hand-lettering.

*This book is for David Byrne, Laurie Anderson,
John Baldessari, and all the people who never said,
"But you're not a [poet/artist/writer/whatever]."*
—K.C.M.

*To all the kids who grew up but forgot to put down
their crayons, ink, paint, scissors and glue.*
—E.E.J.

HAVE YOU SEEN THIS GIRL?

SHE'S THE bENT N@JL to MY FLat TIRE.

THE LIGHTNING BOLT TO MY GOLF CLUB.

A THORN STUCK SO FAR IN MY SIDE I'M BLEEDING ALL OVER THE FLOOR.

SHE'S A PLAGUE. A MONSTER.

SHE HAS DEVIL HORNS UNDER ALL THAT HAIR.

SHE'S **MY SISTER.** *I CAN'T STAND HER.*

SHE'S DEATH AND I'M THE GUY DYING.

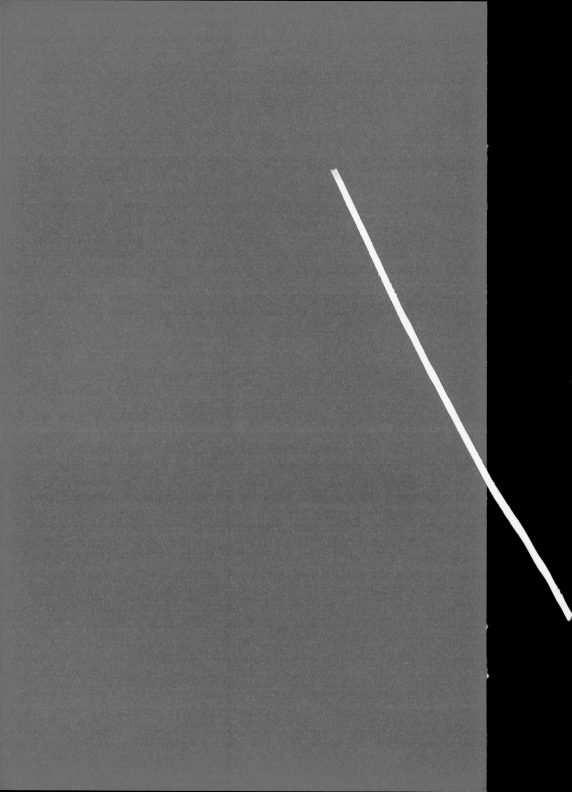

VANISH

If this door is locked, I'm in deep shit.

Lots of people go to school at six thirty on a Friday morning, right? Lots of those outgoing people, like speech geeks who have to practice for meets, or people like Principal Mackowski, who tells us every year at all-school assembly that he comes to school early to work when it's quiet, before all the "crazy loud people like you" get here, ha ha, big smile. Not introverted weirdos like me, but that's OK. I've practiced being invisible for a long, long time, so nobody will see me.

When I yank it, the door opens, and I slide inside. I'm following Brian the Custodian, who went in about thirty seconds ago. Thank god it didn't lock behind him. Custodians definitely get to school this early. He's down the hall, and I'm at the end of a bank of lockers, hoping my shoes won't squeak when I move fast. I let Brian get another thirty feet, and I start for the cafeteria, as casual as a rogue student can be in the early morning when they don't want to be seen. Then Brian veers off toward the gym, and I keep going to the caf, making sure my backpack doesn't make noise.

Finally I'm there, and the mural is in front of me. The ugly, stupid, dumb mural that I'm glad I'm not helping to paint. It's an idiotic scene of a lake and loons and farm fields and volleyball players and football goalposts and all sorts of other random stuff that's supposed to signify a high school in a Twin Cities suburb. Minnesota at its best, right? Go, Art Club! So freaking ugly. Sure, it's nice not to have all-white cafeteria walls, but is art made from slightly deformed loons under a goalpost really any better? And while it would be cool to hang out with a group of people who actually know the difference between oil paint and watercolors, just thinking about it makes my palms sweat.

Over on the far right corner, there's a lake with some rocks around it—I think it's supposed to be Lake Superior. I look around one last time and the coast is still clear, so

I dig into my bag for my oils. When I check my phone, it's 6:39. I have less than an hour. I hunch into my hoodie, vanishing as much as I can, and get to work.

The next time I check my phone, it's 7:31, and everything's back inside my backpack except the water-skiing Abominable Snowman, who's waving and laughing on the surface of the lake. He's maybe six inches tall, and I kind of put him close to a rock so he'd blend in, but if you get close, it's pretty obvious he doesn't belong. He's completely amazing.

I stretch, trying to pretend I'm just loitering, ho hum, vaguely wandering by, it's early, where's the Mountain Dew, and I turn to see Rory Carlson across the cafeteria, just watching me. How long has she been standing there? If she's seen me defiling Lake Superior, it's not gonna be a good thing. She's not smiling, but she's not frowning.

Our caf is a big open common space with lots of places to enter and exit, so I slide around the tables, heading for a hallway opposite of where Rory is standing. She starts walking toward the mural, and I start walking toward my locker, hoping there's a granola bar in there. I'm hungry. As I go, I don't hear any yelling, but I also don't turn around to see what she's doing. My goal is just to walk fast.

Rory's in the Art Club, and maybe the prettiest girl in my grade. She has no idea who I am, even though I sit behind her every day in Spanish class. And that's exactly perfect. I don't want her to know me. Let the Abominable Snowman stand on his own.

I will admit I spend whole periods of class just staring at the back of her head, which is a perfect oval, not to mention that her hair looks like a waterfall of different kinds of honey, and her shoulders are . . . shapely. I don't even know what to call them other than that. They're totally hot. How can shoulders be hot? But hers are.

The rest of my day is spent in the way of my people: go to class, keep my head down, sketch on stuff, say hi to maybe two guys, pretend I'm not there. At lunch, I casually loiter by the mural to see if anybody did anything to my water-skier. He's still there, smiling in his furry goodness and waving like he's Mr. Minnesota and there's a crowd on the lakeshore. Two girls are looking at him, pointing and laughing. I'm happy.

Now it's Friday night, and Pizza Vendetta is freaking out while I watch. It feels like half my high school is here. Kids are throwing forks and spreading gossip while chowing on the best pizza in the Twin Cities metro area, according to *City Pages*, pizza made by yours truly. Our cute little suburb is good for something.

And, of course, Pizza Vendetta is very segregated, just like high school. Jocks are by the bathrooms, talking game scores and defensive strategies, and the brainy kids are by the jukebox, trying to outdo each other with music trivia and whatever else they talk about. Stoner kids are by the door, so they can go out and get their next hit of whatever as soon as they're done satisfying their munchies, and regular kids who don't really fit anywhere are kind of in the middle, talking about TV shows. The goth emo kids are close to me, by the counter where I'm making their delicious pizza, but they don't care. They're all too busy piercing their lips with a fork to eat much. The Art Club kids don't come here, so it might be a while before I get to hear what they think about my Abominable Water-Skier.

The theater kids—this is where my darling sister, Tallulah, also known as Lou, fits in—are the most boring, annoying people in the world. Their conversations sound like this: "Lou, how are YOU?" "Oh, Brittany, how are YOU?" Air kiss, air kiss. "Have you thought about putting your urine in a jar with a crucifix and then dancing around it?" "No, Brittany, I haven't, have you?" So that conversation's going on while four different kids recite their lines in the next booth and another group's making up a song about how to eat pizza, complete with occasional choreography when someone gets up to refill their soda.

And then there's me.

Back to the green pepper and sausage. The counter I stand behind sticks out into the restaurant like a peninsula, and it's surrounded by shoulder-high glass so everybody can watch the pizza maker design their supper. Pizza Vendetta is on a FUN vendetta, according to our advertising, even though nobody knows what a fun vendetta is, and a vendetta to stop your hunger, after all, so isn't it FUN to watch your pizza get made? Ha. Fun if you like watching someone earn just above minimum wage to make your food. We also design the toppings in Vs—for "vendetta," of course—on top of the cheese, one huge V across the pizza, then smaller Vs all around. If I know the name of the person who's ordering, I also lay out their initials with the toppings, and if I know something about them, I'll make a design with other stuff from their life. Last week, for my English teacher, I made a book out of mushrooms with her initials on it. If someone orders a plain cheese pizza, I'm always tempted to lay down a frowny face made out of toothpicks—why would you come to a place that decorates its pizzas if all you want is plain cheese? But all of this is why I, Frankie Neumann, have won the Cool Pizza Award for three months straight. My picture's on the plaque by the door to prove it.

Seriously. Shoot me. Nobody cares how their pizza toppings are arranged. But my designs make me happy, even

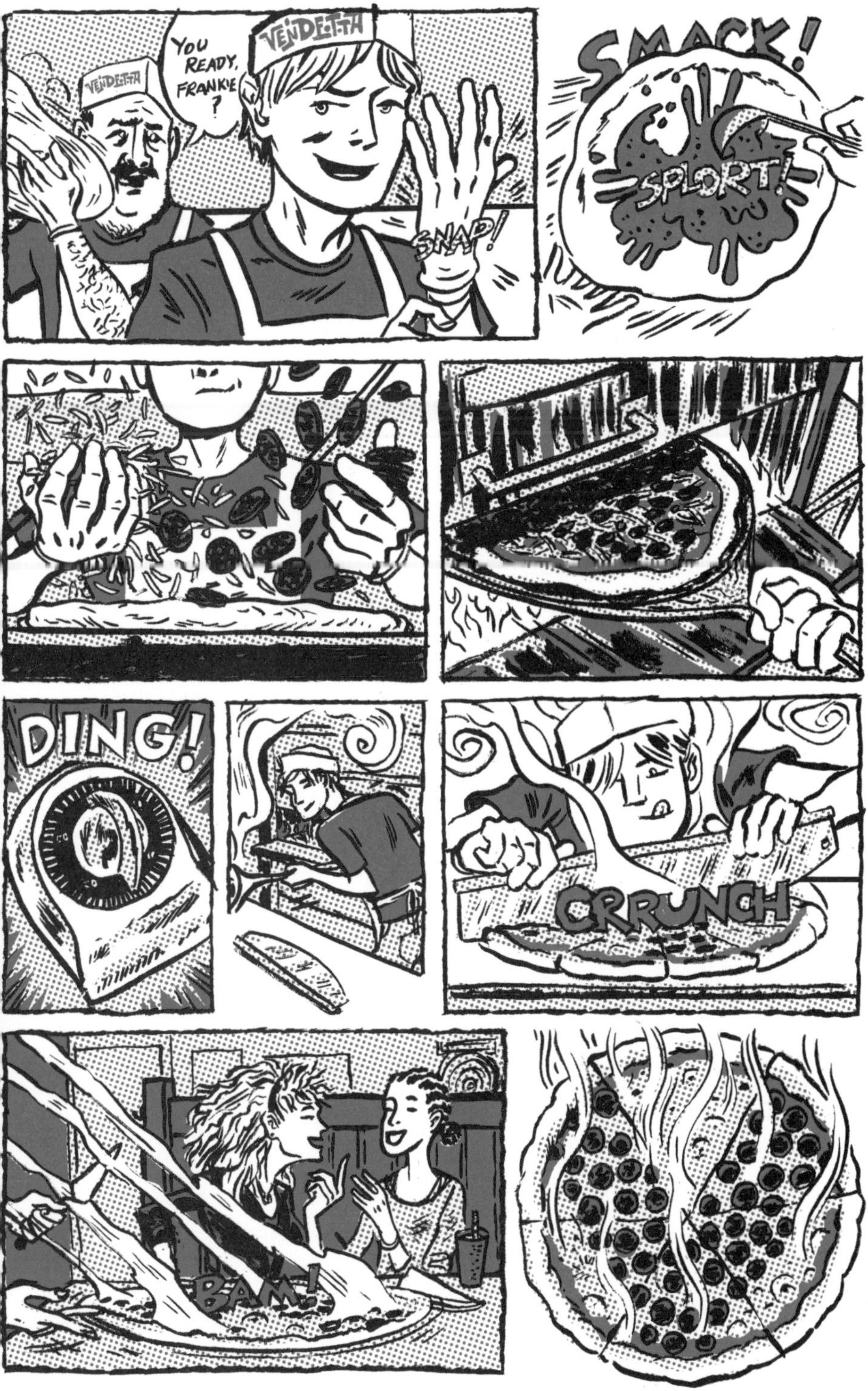
VENDETTA
VENDETTA
YOU READY, FRANKIE?
SNAP!
SMACK!
SPLORT!
DING!
CRRUNCH
BAM!

if nobody else cares, and I watch life go on around me from behind my glass wall. I'm great at observing. And right now I'm observing my nemesis.

Lou is the only person I know who can wear a tulle dance skirt to a pizza place and look completely at home. She's standing by Brittany Serger's booth, talking and laughing and flouncing her skirt like she's onstage, touching her drama mask necklace as if Jennifer Lawrence gave it to her instead of my parents. All the girls are admiring her, like they're talking with a princess from a faraway land, and there are plenty of guys staring like they want to take her home, which totally creeps me out. Girls, too, for that matter. Some people just want to hang out, but there's also a lot of "hey, girl, let's do it" in those stares. Yuck.

Me? I want to push her off a cliff into the ocean.

For a long time, when you're little, you don't know that there's an option for how to feel about your sibling. It's all just "oh yeah, I have to deal with it," and parents don't help because they're always making you live with the stupid stuff that goes down, even if you hate it, which of course you do, and you have to forgive your sibling, especially if they're younger than you. When I was seven and she was five, she stole all my Tinkertoys and threw them into the neighborhood's annual bonfire when we were roasting marshmallows. When I was nine and she was seven, she took my new bike and wrecked it on a hill so badly we couldn't fix it, and my parents had no money to get me another one. When I was eleven and she was nine, she stole my first skateboard and broke it trying to ollie on a curb. It was a cheap board, but still. A thousand paper cuts to my soul, and the face of destruction in my life: That's Lou. Nobody would guess the graceful actress with the lovely face and wonderful voice is actually a soulless demolition machine. After she wrecked my first skateboard, I finally figured out I had the option of not liking her, no matter what my parents said. And it felt so good to hate her, I kept going.

Thayer, the college guy who waits tables on Friday nights, brings over a tray of dishes. "Hey, Pepperoniangelo, will you put these in the kitchen for me? Tables are backing up." He lifts the plates, silverware, and glasses over the partition. I take it without looking at him, because I know he's smirking like an asshole.

"Pepperoniangelo" was the latest incident. A couple weeks ago, it was a slow Thursday night and Lou and my parents were in here, having supper. I was sculpting a version of Michelangelo's *David* with pepperoni and toothpicks, because we'd just talked about it in art history and I didn't have anything else to do, and Lou saw it. From across the room, she yelled, "Hey, Frankie! Don't you think Michelangelo had better things to do than work at a pizza place?" I don't think she knew I was trying for *David*, I think she just picked a sculptor she knew. And the whole room—I mean every single set of eyes in the place—turned to look at me. "Hold it up, Pepperoniangelo!" she yelled. And my parents nodded, and since they were my parents, and I knew I'd get in trouble if I didn't hold it up, I did, even though I would have much preferred to die on the spot. Every single soul in Pizza Vendetta laughed because it didn't look much like anything, and my parents were cackling right along with everyone else. Then Geno, the owner, came out of the back because of the noise and yelled at me, since I was wasting pepperoni. Then he docked my paycheck for the pepperoni and toothpicks I used.

Lou is the Antichrist in a tutu.

When the bell above the door jingles, I look up, because I'm trained like a rat to do it. I need to see how much dough to keep up front based on the number of people who come in. But instead of looking back down at my pizza once I count, I stare. It's Rory Carlson again, making an entrance like a queen, regal and stately. It's obvious she knows people stare at her, because she acknowledges the looks with downcast eyes and a smile. Of course, people wouldn't notice me if I was sitting naked on the counter with my wang covered in pepperoni, holding a big sign that said EAT ME. Though I like it that way. Ninety-eight percent of the time.

I am not paying attention to her. I'm making Vs on the pizza. Pizza Vendetta. Making pizza. Vs. Not looking at her.

Rory walks about twenty feet away from the door and stops by the window, watching as the place begins to flow back into its normal rhythm. Then the bell dings again, and this dude's walking in, and it's like an Old West movie—the new gunfighter enters the Cactus Saloon—and all the grown-ups look at him. The guy is tall and skinny—he'd probably call himself *slender*, because he looks like the kind of guy who'd actually use that word—and he's a cross between David Bowie in the eighties and a refugee from *Ront*. But this gunslinger wears a skirt, with clunky Doc Martens to finish off the outfit. It's obvious by the staring that no adult has ever seen a dude in a skirt. The kids in the place glance up, register the situation, then go back to their various conversations. A little smile keeps creeping onto Rory's face while she watches Pizza Vendetta look at the gunslinger. Maybe she's waiting for a show to start.

I look at Lou because I assume the gunslinger is in her crowd, but given the look on her face, he's not. And she thinks he's cute, too—I can see it. She's biting her lip, like she does when she's thinking, and checking him out like he's a sales rack at Screw, this goth boutique underneath a warehouse in Uptown, the trendiest part of Minneapolis. And of course she's crossed the floor to him in two seconds.

"Hi, I'm Lou. Who are you?" Conversation slowly picks up after the dead silence the gunslinger started, but every table and booth has an eye on them.

The guy looks at her like he's never seen a girl before. "I'm David."

"No way. Really? David? You look just like David Bowie on his Serious Moonlight tour!"

"I get that a lot." And he walks around her and heads toward me.

Burn. Nobody walks around Lou. She stomps back to Brittany Serger and glares at the new gunslinger.

I'm going to stand here and make pizza.

Geno is throwing down dough as fast as he can in the kitchen, and from where he's standing, he can see I'm watching the social situations from my spot at the counter. "Hurry up and move those toppings. We've gotta lotta work to do. Don't be wasteful, Pepperoniangelo." Geno is as old as my grandpa, at least, and he plays the Italian pizza guy stereotype to the max, right down to the white T-shirt, apron, and little white hat. "Be our best guy, OK? Don't slow down. And make some pizzas for slices, too."

"You got it, boss." I fling down the pepperonis as fast as I can and pretend he didn't call me Pepperoniangelo.

David stops at the glass and stares directly at me. "You have a delivery truck."

"How do you know that?" The V under my hands gets finished, and I start two smaller Vs on either side of the big one.

"I've seen it here, and someone else saw you after school."

I step back from the glass partition. "Don't make me call the cops, creeper."

"Get to work, Frankie!" Geno doesn't like it when I talk to people.

"Look, you have a delivery truck, and I am in need of a delivery truck." He raises one eyebrow at me. "Someone I know said you were an OK guy who might be willing to help." He turns to look at Rory, who's still standing by the windows. She nods at him while she smiles/not-smiles. I don't know if this is related to the Abominable Water Skier or not.

"I'm not selling it to you, if that's what you want." I get back to work. Madison Meyer, in booth 3A, is the owner of this pizza, so she gets Ms on top of the V, in green olives, just because she's a regular girl who's not wearing a black tulle skirt with neon green paint streaks.

"We just want to use it. What time do you get off work?"

"I'm not telling you."

"We'll be back at eleven." And he turns around and walks out. The whole place watches him go. All we'd need are those push-open shutter doors that Old West bars have, and the scene would be complete. Then David Bowie gunslinger in a skirt is gone, and the whole saloon gazes after him. Once people start chatting again, I see Rory slip out the door, too.

I don't know if I want to know what they want.

Of course I do.

It's eleven forty-five and I'm in the back parking lot.
David and Rory materialize out of the shadows. Thanks to
the pizza fight that happened at ten thirty, the one that
took forever to clean up, and the one that made us scrub
down six booths after we were closed, I figured they were
long gone. I have no idea what happened to Lou. It's not
my job to watch her, even though my parents think it is.

"We thought you'd never get out here." Rory is smiling
in a way that makes me think of a cartoon cat who's just
caught a mouse.

"Can you unlock this?" David tries to open the door.

"You people are way too forward. I barely know you."
But I unlock the door, because Rory's beautiful and nobody
leads a more boring life than I do. So I'm curious. Intro-
verts don't actually hate hanging out with people, and they
don't have to be alone all the time. Just lots of the time.

David pulls and tugs to get the passenger side door
open, then he and Rory climb in. Rory settles onto a pile
of jackets in the back, shoving them between the seats,
and David perches on top of the passenger seat, like he's
waiting for something wonderful to happen in the magical
delivery truck. He looks like an owl in drag, with his skirt
and his round glasses. His hair even sticks up a little bit in
the back like owl feathers do, though owls don't have the
swoop in the front. He looks like a David Bowie owl.

"Put your seat belt on. Otherwise you'll get thrown around." Riding in a delivery truck is nothing like riding in a car. Things slide, and if you're not ready, you're just a bag of bones that can hit the back wall in two seconds. "And then you need to tell me what you want."

The eighties owl sticks out his hand. "David Carlson."

From the back, I hear, "Rory Carlson. You know who I am." She says it in a voice that's like a Slinky coated in mink.

I turn to look at her. "You might want to hang on to the straps on the side of the truck. Or you'll go flying, too. You guys are brother and sister?"

She smirks. "Thanks for the warning, chief. We're cousins."

David's hand is still hanging in the air, and I reach over and shake it briefly. "Do you go to Henderson?" Our school isn't big, but it isn't small, either. I could have missed him. But I also think a guy like him would stick out. Then again, Henderson High School is just one of the twenty high schools on the west side of "the greater Minneapolis–St. Paul metropolitan area," as the official language goes. Just your average dumb high school in the burbs.

David nods. "I came this year. I'm a freshman."

"How did you know I have delivery truck?"

"Rory saw you after school in it, then I saw the truck behind Pizza Vendetta, and you were working."

I round the corner, out of the parking lot, and David is

thrown into the door. Rory is smart. She grabbed a strap before we started moving.

"Seriously. Your seat belt. And why do you need a delivery truck?"

He's buckling. "It's not for me, actually. It's for my uncle. He's coming home to do some work, and we like to help him out when we can."

"Who's your uncle?"

David doesn't say anything. Neither does Rory. I feel the vibes go between them.

"Who's your uncle?" It sounds like the setup line for a joke.

"You'll see. Take a left." He points.

"I'm parked until you tell me." I turn the engine off, even though we're in the middle of the street. A little hardball can't hurt. Good thing it's late and there's not much traffic.

"I thought you might have a sense of adventure." David sighs and crosses his arms. "You really want to know?"

"Didn't I just say that?" Obviously this owl isn't very smart.

He raises his eyebrows at me. "Uncle Epic."

"THE Uncle Epic?" This isn't possible. "You mean the Uncle Epic who does street art?"

Rory laughs. "What other Uncle Epic is there?"

Uncle Epic is an art legend. Nobody knows who he is because he works anonymously, mostly in the middle of the night, and nobody's ever taken a picture of him. If anyone does know who he is, they've never spilled it. When I was a little kid, he was a tagger, and then he started making garbage sculptures, and then it was art out of crashed cars, and now he has shows and installations all over the world. Insanely cool. People have no idea what he'll do next. Plus everything he does annoys the crap out of the cops and city officials and anybody else in authority. He doesn't do much art in the Twin Cities anymore because people want his work everywhere else—finding out Uncle Epic did a piece in your city is a huge deal—so nobody was even sure he still lived here. And now these two people from Henderson High School are telling me that he's their *actual uncle*?

Cool stuff never happens to me.

Lou loves Uncle Epic, too, but in a pretend-intellectual way, like she could ever actually know anything about art. She says she "admires his sensibility," and she "welcomes his commentary on society, because he's just as smart as Tennessee Williams," who's her favorite playwright. Epic's art, she says, is "just as trenchant as Williams's plays." I heard her say these things to my mom. What does "trenchant" even mean?

I love Uncle Epic in a pure and dedicated fanboy way. I think he's funny and clever, and I admire the shit out of the fact that he's stayed anonymous for so long. That's my kind of art—you make it, you scram, authorities are pissed, and everyone thinks you're awesome. And I will never admit this to anyone, but I have a scrapbook. Clippings from the newspaper, photos from the Web of his stuff around the world, anything and everything. Epic is my ultimate role model. My parents have no idea how serious I am about my art—as serious as Epic is, even if I haven't quite figured out what I want to do or say. They'll make me go to college, but my goal is to be him.

"Prove it to me." This can't be real. "Why doesn't Uncle Epic just rent a truck?"

"He could." Rory's voice is a purr. "But I liked your Abominable Water-Skier. Then I saw you driving home after school and realized he wouldn't have to, if you'd agree to help us. I thought you might be interested, and I told David and Epic about you."

David's rummaging around in his wallet, and comes up with a coin. He hands it to me, and I turn on the light above the driver's seat. The coin says BE EPIC on one side and FOSHAY TOWER on the other.

He's got to be kidding. "This is from the 1994 *Pennies*

from Heaven piece—before we were even born. How the hell did you get this?" Uncle Epic dropped them out of the windows from the top floor of the Foshay Tower, a thirty-two-story building in downtown Minneapolis, one Wednesday in May of 1994. He plinked them over the side of the building off and on for half an hour, and got away from the cops by walking down a set of service stairs nobody'd used since the fifties. People were both mad and happy, because it was unexpected and cool, though it surprised a lot of people when they got hit by money from the sky. There's a coin in the lobby of the Foshay, in a little frame on the wall. The Foshay piece was the first time he risked his anonymity.

David nods. "He dropped about five hundred, but he has a few left at his studio."

"Does he know you have one?" Rory chimes in from the back.

"Yes, don't be dumb." David turns to frown at her. "But he told me if I sold it on eBay, he'd kill me."

I hand the coin back to him. My brain's still trying to catch up with what he's saying.

David points left. "Uncle Epic is that way."

I shift the truck into D and turn left. Boredom is officially over.

Our cute little suburb is west of Minneapolis, and David directs me through a ton of backstreets instead of taking us on the freeway, which makes me really confused. Finally we turn into a driveway in front of a huge brick garage. There are lights on in the windows above the garage, but the garage itself looks dark.

"Wait here." David hops out and disappears around the side of the building. Rory comes up front and slides out the door David left open, giving me a meaningful look before she slams the door. I have no idea what she's thinking.

So I wait, and I almost fall asleep, despite the fact that I can't believe this is happening. I had to get up at five thirty to make sure I'd have time to finish the Abominable Water-Skier, and Fridays are exhausting anyway. The heater is also on, so it's cozy warm in the front seat—even though it's April, it's Minnesota. Heaters are necessary until the end of May. I feel myself slumping out of my seat.

Then I hear David yanking on the passenger door again, and finally he gets it open. "OK! You can drive in, but you have to shut your lights off!" He's almost chirping from delight. Owls don't chirp. He shuts the door, and I move the shifter to D. An enormous garage door is open in front of us, and the inside of the garage is pitch-black. I have no idea how far to go.

I creep the truck forward inch by inch, it seems, until there's a huge THUNK in the front of it and I slam on the brakes. A faint light comes on near the floor at the other end of the garage, and it's just enough to see someone in a hooded bathrobe standing in the middle of the floor, motioning me forward, which sketches me out, because I just hit something. But I let the truck edge up a few more feet. The garage is really, really long, and full of stuff, judging from the shadows, and some of it might be under tarps. But then the place goes dark again. I shut off the truck.

A deep, gravelly voice booms across the space: "GET OUT AND MOVE TO THE FRONT OF YOUR TRUCK." It could be God, it could be Epic, it could be Satan. I could end up pissing myself.

One lone TV lights up about fifteen feet in front of the truck, casting a spooky glow over everything. The hooded dude is walking toward me, so I get out and walk toward the front of the truck, but I trip over something and crash into a pile of something else as I try to escape what I tripped over. All the crashes and stumbles make me look and sound like a serious asshole. As I scramble up, I tangle myself in what are evidently giant empty boxes and it's all I can do not to holler, because I have no idea what's going on. A cardboard edge slices the top of my hand.

Finally I make it to my feet, and the hooded dude is standing right in front of me. I can't see the guy's eyes, just his mouth, because his hood is deep. His body is shapeless under the heavy robe.

I may have underestimated the situation. I hope some-one calls my folks so they can come get my body.

David materializes next to the guy and points. "This is Uncle Epic."

"For real?" I wait for the guy to show his face and say, *No, I'm really Barack Obama. We're just messing with you.*

The guy nods very slowly.

"Prove it."

The God/Epic/Satan voice echoes in the garage. "I did the piece at Target Field with the thirty-five toilets in con-centric circles around the pitcher's mound, and I spelled out BASEBALL = AMERICA'S TIME WASTER in toilet paper in center field, but they picked up all the toilet paper on the field and took down the toilet seats from the flagpoles before the paper came to do the story."

It's him.

Lou told me about the center field thing. Some of her friends were downtown at three a.m. and they saw toilet seats on the flagpoles of Target Field. They went to investi-gate, as anyone would when there were toilet seats on the flagpoles of a baseball stadium, and they saw everything, including the toilets and the TP on the field. Her friends couldn't figure out why the pictures in the paper were dif-ferent than what they saw—just toilets, nothing else.

"Why do you want my truck? Show me your face."

"If I show you my face, you have to swear not to tell anyone who I am." The voice reverberates through me.

"I swear." My insides are shaking.

The hood comes down. And it's Rory.

"You're Uncle Epic? How'd you do that with your voice?" To say I'm disappointed would be the understatement of the year. "And how'd you know about the Target Field thing?"

She grins and turns her head to show me one of those hair-thin mics that goes over your ear and runs on the side of your face. "Vocoder. Our job was to see if you were brave enough to actually get out of your truck. And who do you think helped him find the toilets for Target Field? If we think you're OK, he'll think you're OK, and he'll let you work with us. But I haven't decided yet." She drops her robe and steps away from it, like she's a nude model posing for a painting class, then she turns to David. "Do you think Epic will like Frankie?"

David shrugs. "I don't know. *I* like him." He winks and runs his eyes over me. "Epic will think he's OK, and we need his truck. He should be fine." He flips the hem of his skirt at me.

I have no way to process all the stuff that's just happened. Either I've just stepped into an episode of some mess-with-your-head reality show, or the art gods are smiling on me. I take a deep breath and wait to find out.

VAGABOND

There are cops at my house. Yeah. Whoops.

Here's what I don't know—are the cops here because I've been gone all night? Or because of what I just did with David and Rory? I consider turning around and driving away, but that would just be worse.

Yes, it's six forty-five in the morning, and no, I've never stayed out all night before, especially not at the request of a guy I keep a scrapbook about. No, I will never show him my scrapbook. Yes, it was completely amazing. If there are articles in this weekend's paper—and there will be, because people love and hate Uncle Epic—I will put them in my scrapbook, and will possibly draw stars and smiley faces and exclamation points all over the clippings, even though it's entirely juvenile, and I might write *HELL TO THE FUCKING YES* on them just because I was there and I am still freaking out that my truck carried stuff to make Uncle Epic's art. THE Uncle Epic. The one who's doing new pieces for the next month as a warm-up for his show at the Walker Art Center and who wants to use my truck because his niece liked my Abominable Water-Skier. Yes, THAT Uncle Epic.

All I want to do is sleep, but the police might frown on that before I talk to them, plus my parents' delivery truck is still in the driveway, so they won't leave for work until I explain where I've been. Why are there two delivery trucks in my family? My parents own a cleaning service, and mine used to be their work truck. Now they have a new one, which is deep purple with sparkles and a wand on it, and the words MAGIC WIZARD CLEANING SERVICE on it. Since the old one was painted white, all I had to do was take a roller and paint over the words on the side. My truck looks totally low-rent, but at least it's not purple with sparkles. It just looks like I stole it from FedEx and gave it the world's crappiest paint job to disguise it.

I try and sneak in the back door, taking off my shoes and everything. Nope. They're sitting at the kitchen table: a blond young cop, an older cop with curly gray hair, and my parents, drinking coffee and watching me come in. My dad's in his best pink bathrobe, and my mom is dressed like a Jersey mob boss who just got up—ratty bathrobe, white

ribbed tank top, striped pajama pants. In my house, you can be a boy, a girl, neither, or both—all on the same day. The cops don't seem too fazed by either outfit.

My dad, Brett, is the fill-in Frank-N-Furter at the Hennepin and Broad Dinner Theatre's production of *The Rocky Horror Show*, which runs every Friday and Saturday night at midnight. If you've never seen the movie or the show, Frank is the sweet transvestite from Transsexual, Transylvania, as Frank's first song says. So some nights my dad wears makeup, fishnet stockings and heels, and a bustier. Evidently last night was one of those nights, because he usually wears his pink bathrobe on after-show mornings, when he's still feeling like Frank.

My mom, whose real name is Bridget, is a female Frank Sinatra impersonator, and she works on Friday and Saturday nights at a cabaret show in St. Paul. She met my dad in some theater thing back in college. Even then, Dad was Frank-N-Furter on the weekends, and she said she couldn't get enough of him in his bustier. I don't know which one of them has a lower voice.

You can see why I'm named Frankie.

"So, young man, what's up? Suddenly become a vagabond and forget where you live?" My mom tries to act casual, but she's got her legs crossed and she's not so casually kicking the table leg. Her tense body language isn't matching up with her casual voice. "Why haven't you answered our texts since one thirty this morning?"

The cops take a look at me. The older one writes something down in his notebook. "Is this your son, Mr. Neumann?"

My dad draws his bathrobe around his chest. "Yes, it is. Frankie, where were you?"

"I was . . . helping a friend. With a big project." Maybe that will make a difference. The adrenaline is still flowing from what we did, so I work to keep the shakes out of my voice.

"Come here and let me smell you." My dad beckons me to him, and I walk closer. He stands up, and the cops stand up, too, like they might go after me if he doesn't. He sniffs me. "Breath?" I breathe on him. He sniffs around me again. "You smell clean, which is lucky for you."

"What friend?" My mom sips her coffee again, but the kicking continues.

"Just a girl in my class. You don't know her."

"What's her name?" She looks at my dad. "We need to know her name, don't we?"

The blond cop nods after they sit back down. "A name would be useful." The older one writes something down in his notebook again. Why would a cop care what my friend's name is?

"We weren't doing anything illegal. Just hanging around and looking for location shots for her documentary." It's the first thing I think of. "She had a lot of equipment to carry around, cameras and stuff, so I helped her."

My mom wrinkles her nose. "What's her documentary about? I hope it's something worthwhile."

Seriously, whose parents have a purple sparkly delivery truck, gender-bender performance jobs on the weekends, and stuck-up attitudes about documentaries?

My dad turns to the cops. "Thanks for coming over. I think we can take it from here."

They look him up and down, at his pink bathrobe and his hairy chest. Thank god he doesn't have on his fishnets. The older one flips his notebook closed. "Sure thing, Mr. Neumann." They stand up again and walk out the door without looking back.

My mom yells after them. "Thank you!" She's always polite to authority figures. Then she turns to me. "It doesn't change the fact that you were out all night." When she's wearing pajamas, she's not a particularly menacing figure, but I can tell she means business. She stands up and takes her cereal bowl to the dishwasher. "You need to help us wash the truck before we go to our first job. After that, you can vacuum. And then you can be grounded for two weeks." She shuts the dishwasher door after she puts the bowl and a coffee cup in it. "Does your creative friend have parents we can talk to? Can we call and find out if you were with her?"

"That's just embarrassing. No." I have David's number, but I have no idea what he'd say to them.

She levels a stare at me. "You realize we're cutting you some pretty enormous slack here. You're seventeen, and if you're doing something wrong, it's our heads. We're responsible for you if you happen to be in the wrong place at the wrong time."

"I know. I won't do it again. Thank you." I muster as much humility as I can.

Dad walks toward their room. "Get your truck-washing clothes on. We've only got about an hour before Mom and I have to leave."

"Be right back." I bound up the stairs as fast as my shaky legs will carry me. I'm so tired I could sleep standing up.

While I look for an old pair of jeans and a ratty sweatshirt—it's only fifty degrees out there—I think about what we just did. David and Rory made me help them pack up my truck with ten posters that were at least five feet tall, then ten pieces of plywood to build backs for the posters, plus two-by-fours, hammers, nails, cinder blocks, a bunch of wallpaper paste, and some huge brushes that look like brooms. We also had a couple of staple guns and tape, for good measure. Then we drove over to the capitol in St. Paul. Epic didn't go with us, and David and Rory didn't say where he was. But they said this was a teaser for his show. How an anonymous guy has a show, I don't know. I need to ask.

Obviously Epic has a printing press, or a humongous copy machine, because the posters were all the same—it

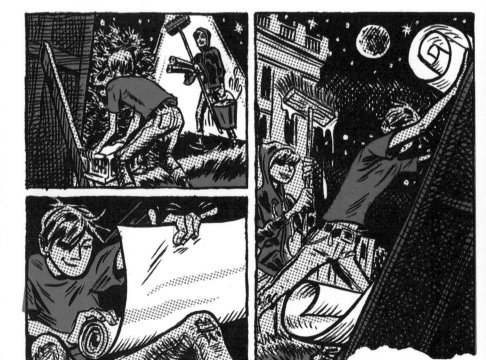

was a photograph of Rory's eye, just one, which kind of creeped me out once there were ten of them lying around, with the words WE'RE WATCHING, GOVERNMENT PAWNS. Rory and I spent two hours pasting up the posters on the boards, then another two and a half hours hammering on the two-by-fours and placing the boards in various locations in the grass. Her eyes kind of overpowered everything, which was cool.

It took forever, but it was phenomenal when it was done. All over one side of the capitol lawn, the posters were tilted up from the ground, so it looked like there

were ten eyes peeling up from the ground and looking at the capitol. It was incredible, and it felt like we were—well, Uncle Epic was—saying something that needed to be said.

Plus, as art goes, it's easily broken down and hauled away. It's not like we spray-painted on the capitol itself. Epic's a little smarter than some artists in that way. According to the law, even Banksy is a vandal—amazing anonymous street art god that he is—when he spray-paints on public buildings. Epic just leaves shit around, which is annoying and qualifies as illegal dumping, but isn't technically much of a crime. This is the first time Epic's been back in the Cities for a while, so he wants the public to think about their homegrown son.

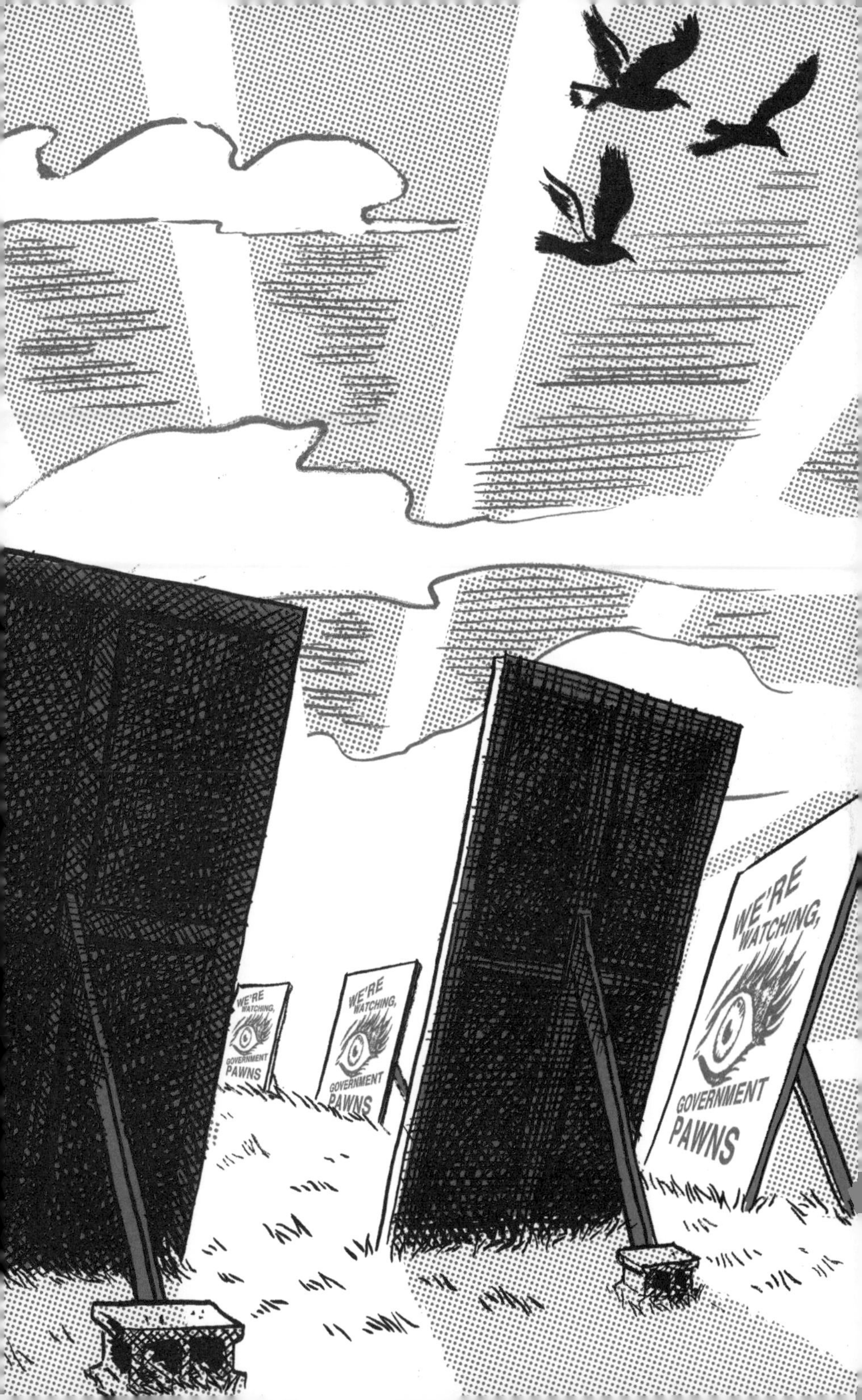
WE'RE WATCHING,
GOVERNMENT PAWNS
WE'RE WATCHING,
GOVERNMENT PAWNS
WE'RE WATCHING,
GOVERNMENT PAWNS

When we finished around five forty-five, there was a thin line of sunrise in the east. But then we saw flashing lights coming at us, which scared the crap out of me, even though Rory and David told me not to sweat it. The truck was loaded, and we looked like delivery people. All we had to do was get in it, casually, casually, and drive away. And that's what we did. Rory and David told me being casual is the key—to always be able to hide your materials, and to be ready to go at a moment's notice. It's a lot harder for cops to arrest people who look like they're just standing around. It's not hard to arrest people with suspicious-looking stuff in their hands. David said they've been helping Epic for the past couple summers, when they're not in school and Epic's doing art in other places, and they learned the act-casual-but-hide-stuff trick when they were in LA with him.

The lights just sped by and didn't stop, thank god. Then I had to take Rory and David back to the garage. When I asked them if I was going to get to meet Epic, they didn't say anything. But when I was helping take stuff back inside the shop, I saw a guy leaning against the back wall of the garage. He had on a hoodie, so I couldn't see his face. But he waved at me. I waved back. I wanted to say something, but I didn't know if I should and I probably would have said the dumbest thing ever. I don't want him to fire me after my first job.

Once I got back in the truck to come home, that's when the adrenaline shakes hit. I kinda, sorta defaced public property—state property, even, a lot of it. I helped Uncle Epic make art. Me. ME. And I stayed out all night *and* I hung out with Rory Carlson for approximately six hours, though it's not like she cares. She wouldn't give me her phone number, but she said I could reach her through David. David didn't look pleased.

By the time I get downstairs again, my dad is wearing his regular cleaning-guy uniform, and he's soaping the truck wheels. He makes me run the power washer, and he tells me to scrub the stars extra well. Like purple glitter stars get really dirty. My mom supervises for a while, but then goes inside to take a shower and change into her work uniform, which is pretty much the same as my dad's. When they do their cleaning stuff, they look like regular people. But it's not like my mom and dad are secret about their theater lives. They invite their employees to their shows all the time.

I'm almost finished vacuuming the back of the truck when my mom appears again. Somebody spilled Ajax powder in there, so now my nose and eyes are coated in this fine white gritty stuff.

When I'm done, she gives me a big hug and wipes off my face with a clean rag. "You scared us, you know. You're only seventeen." She's shorter than me now, and right at the moment she looks more like a mom than a New Jersey mob boss.

"I know. I'm sorry." And I am. A little.

"We'll take away your truck if you do it again." She sighs. "We probably shouldn't let you have it anyway. There's room in there for a bar—or a bed." My parents trust us a lot, which is why Lou and I don't have curfews or take vitamins or go to the dentist, because they figure we'll come home, eat right, and brush our teeth. Sometimes yes, sometimes no.

I sigh back at her. "I'm not going to put a bar OR a bed in there. I put camera supplies in it last night. That's all." Wink wink. Nudge nudge.

"Can you get me a still shot?" She's getting insistent.

"Maybe. I don't know." I could send her a shot of the capitol, without Rory's eyes, but if Epic's art makes the news, she'll put it together.

"You might want to do that." She's stern again. "See you later." She gives me a kiss on the cheek and climbs into the van after my dad, whose been loading up floor wax and that huge buffer thing that looks like you can ride on it. I'd better not tell David and Rory we have one of those, or we'll do floor wax art somewhere just so they can test the ride-on-it theory.

I go inside and flop down on the couch, and I'm almost asleep when something hard hits my foot.

When I open my eyes, she's standing there in her tulle skirt, plaid pajama top above it, looking like I've personally offended her. "Tallulah's always in tulle, you know," she says to her friends, and they say, "Oooooh," like it was some sort of genius artist statement.

She's frowning and giving me her indignant face. "Where were you last night? Mom and Dad were totally worried." Her washed-out blond hair looks like she electrified it.

"They were not." I close my eyes again. "They have too much other stuff to do, like sing Frank Sinatra songs and prance around in a bustier."

"They didn't sleep at all."

I open my eyes again and sit up. "So?"

"So you freaked them out. I got home at one, and no-body was here. Then I got up at three to get a drink, and they were sitting in the kitchen, waiting for you. Then I got up at five because I was hungry, and they were still up. And they were smoking."

First of all, my parents quit smoking about five years ago, which is kind of an uncreative thing to do, nicotine helps the brain and all that. But they're singers, which makes a difference. Gotta preserve the pipes.

"The house doesn't smell like it."

Lou frowns again. "They used almost a whole bottle of Febreze before they called the cops. They were worried, butthead. Don't do that to them again."

"Whatever, brat." I lie back down.

"So where were you? You were out with a girl, weren't you? Or maybe just friends." She won't go away. "But then again, you don't have friends."

"I have friends you don't even know about."

"You were out smoking weed."

"You're thinking of your friends."

She smacks my foot again. "My friends don't smoke weed. At least not much."

"Leave me alone. I'm tired."

"Guess what I did after I left Pizza Vendetta?" She's

staring at me, daring me to ask so she can tell me that her adventure was better than mine.

"You and all your theater girls sat in a circle and brushed each other's hair and recited Shakespeare."

"No." Smack on the foot for emphasis. "Guess again."

"You broke into the Guthrie Theater and performed a soliloquy from *The Glass Menagerie* on the main stage."

"Ha!" She hits me again. "It was illegal, but it wasn't that."

Why does she want me to know this? "Whatever. Get out of here."

"You are a rude, unimaginative jerkwad who has no soul." She crosses her arms.

"You are a fluffy, overly emotive drama queen who bores the crap out of me." I pitch a couch pillow at her.

"Stick it up your ass." Lou hits me one more time and goes into the kitchen. I hear the soundtrack to *Chicago* start up, and she sings along while she makes toast. Then the floor starts shaking, so I know she's dancing, or at least practicing the stage blocking—with emphasis—that she still remembers from when she saw the Broadway show three years ago.

She's relentless. And so freaking *special*. Everyone in this house is *artistic* and *soulful* and *deep* and *special*—everyone but me. And everything is *meaningful*, and people are always *practicing their routine*, which is always *special*. Drama is everywhere, all the time.

Lou can draw, dance, sing, and act. And she's beautiful, with her wavy hair and her classic face and her dancer's body. Lou and my parents treat the whole world as a stage. Me? I'm just an average-as-hell audience member.

I go upstairs to my room but I can still hear the stupid music. So I go up the back stairs to the ballroom.

Our house is one of those big old mansions that were built in the early twentieth century. It's enormous. There are still two junk rooms on the floor with my room and Lou's room, and the main floor has my folks' bedroom, an office for their business, and a living room, which is where we watch DVDs of everybody's performances, yawn, plus the kitchen. Since there's so much space on the other two floors, nobody ever comes all the way up here, so nobody knows about my art. Which is exactly how I like it.

My latest hobby is buying big old couch paintings from thrift stores—not paintings of couches, but horrible paintings that hang above couches—and adding monsters to them. Right now I'm working on a blue-and-purple blob with googly eyes and lots of tentacles who's eating a bunch of peaceful sheep in a very peaceful field.

The monster gets a few more tentacles, plus a few swirly places and contours, and then it seems done, so I lean it against the wall to let it dry. My next monster is a Sasquatch-looking dude, but with a kind face, sitting on the top of a cottage in one of those picturesque villages in England somewhere—at least that's my guess where it is, since there's grass or reeds or something on the roofs instead of shingles. His fur blends in with the grass roof. I'm going to paint some villagers running away while he relaxes and drinks a beer. His name is Sid.

I paint Sid the Sasquatch's legs and think about Rory. She is way too cute, which she knows, and she stomps guys into the ground. I watched her do it with Max Ledermann, an orchestra dude who's also in our Spanish class. She turned him into a pet. He brought her lunch and carried whatever she made him carry, and all she ever gave him in return was a smile. Maybe they were doing it every other night when none of us could see them, but in school it looked like she used him for her lunch slave, and when John Marshall, a choir guy, took the spot at the lunch table that Max Ledermann used to have, I watched Max cry in the corner of the cafeteria, which of course he never lived down.

I'm not letting that happen to me. Maybe we can pretend we don't know each other at school, since I sit behind her in Spanish, so she doesn't have to look at me or anything. I have no idea if doing work for Epic will ever happen again. Maybe that was a once-in-a-lifetime deal. But secretly? I'm hoping we'll be together all day every day and she'll stop her evil ways because she'll know my love is pure and she'll want me for her very own true romantical dude.

Right? Riiiiiiight.

Instead of working some more on Sid's legs, I lie down on the pile of blankets and pillows Mom stashed up here years ago. I don't even put my paints away. I'm such a rebel.

I dream about Rory's eyes all over my ballroom, huge paper eyes, and they're all looking at me. Blinking at me, as if to say, "Me, date you? Think again, dumbass. You're just an audience member."

When I wake up, the sun is low on the wall, which means it's late afternoon. The west sun is the only kind that comes into the window. When I open the stairwell door and wander into the hall, the house is quiet. I go down the next flight of stairs to the main floor. It's definitely time for some food.

Mom, Dad, and Lou are sitting in the living room watching TV. Nobody looks up when I go by, because it's a DVD of *Pippin*, from a long time ago. Maybe the early eighties? It's one of their faves.

I make a sandwich and stop by the living room. They're all singing "Corner of the Sky" at the top of their lungs, and nobody sees or hears me. *Gotta find my corner . . .* yeah, the whole freaking world is your corner.

When I get back up to the attic, I sit on the floor and stare at Donna Russell while I eat my sandwich. Donna's a sculpture. Sort of.

Back in college, my mom used to sew, and she had these

things called dress forms—basically, they're torsos on sticks, made of wire so you can mold them to be different sizes—and they were in the corner of the ballroom when I started coming up here. One form was female and one was male. I say *was* because they're joined together now, mashed into a big blobby body. Donna Russell is kind of unisex, and her torso is a big circle with boobs on one section.

Her arms are broom and mop handles, with a broom for her right hand and a mop for her left, and her legs are made out of old blankets rolled up and tied with ribbons from Lou's dance costumes that got shoved up here. She has wing-tip shoes from my dad's days when he worked in an office. That didn't last long. She also has a vajayjay and a wiener, just because I didn't know which love bits were more appropriate, both made out of old socks. She's got a head I made from some stuff in my dad's shop—wires and bolts and things, with more wire sticking out for hair, kind of like a metal Medusa. All of it is stitched together with blue string.

Donna Russell's face is my favorite. It's a magazine collage. I made eyes, a nose, and a mouth out of ads and pasted them on the front of the metal head. I made her look kind of stern and kind of tender at the same time, like she likes me but she doesn't necessarily approve of what I'm doing. That seems fair.

Lou has never made anything that's like Donna Russell, which is also why I like Donna. And I'm the center of Donna's world, unlike Lou, who's been the center of my parents' world since she showed up when I was two. When they came home from the hospital, they put Lou's car seat in the middle of the kitchen table and told me not to touch what was up there. I climbed up on a chair so I could see what I wasn't supposed to touch, and it was a baby. Then I slipped and knocked myself off the chair, and almost pulled Lou off the table when I fell. I had to go to my room for a long, long time—at least it seemed long to me. When you're that little, everything seems long. But it told me who she was—someone who kicked me out of my parents' lives and promptly set up shop there.

A couple months after that, I remember my mom was changing Lou's diaper, and she yelled for my dad like something was wrong. He dropped everything, including me and the trains we were playing with, and came running. I did, too.

My mom pointed to the crease where Lou's left leg met her body, and I remember her saying, "Look! She's the one! We should have saved it for her!" In the crease of her leg were seven freckles (what baby has freckles?) in the shape of an F. My dad, who thought someone was dying the way my mom had hollered, started to laugh instead, and said,

"Yep, she's the one. She should have been the Frankie in the family."

I know my parents don't remember this, and I have no idea how I do, considering I was so little. But I remember seeing their joy at the F, and then feeling like I'd been fooled. I remember thinking, *If she's the one, I must not belong to them.* It was a brain-popping discovery for a two-year-old.

So, when I was four, I tried to give back my name, and I remember them being confused when I told them it belonged to Lou, not me. She was the Frankie, remember? They said it when they saw her freckles. Of course, they had no idea what I was talking about. I said I wanted to be named Owen, who was the one kid I talked to at my day care—I was so shy, I never talked to anyone else. They said no, I was Frankie. End of story.

I remember being very pissed, but also confused. If they knew Lou was supposed to be their Frankie, shouldn't they be glad I was giving the name back? Kid logic makes no sense, but the problem is, ideas get burned into your brain. It was very clear they loved the real Frankie, who was actually Lou. She belonged to them. They only tolerated the fake Frankie, who was me, thus I didn't belong to them. So why not change my name to Owen?

Life went on, of course, and she was a bratty little sister

while I was your basic introverted kid who didn't think he belonged anywhere. Then she did the worst thing she could—worse than burning my Tinkertoys, or wrecking my skateboard and my bike and the million other little things she did to make my life suck. She stole my work. You don't do that to an artist, not even a kid artist. This wasn't "You're awesome, so I'm going to copy you" stealing. This was outright theft.

When I was twelve and Lou was ten, we both wanted to go to the Split Rock Summer Art Splash, up in Duluth. It's a weeklong camp, and it's got everything—theater, music, painting, drawing, whatever arty-farty thing a kid wants to do. It costs a crap-ton of cash, and double that price when you have two kids who want to go. Lou's best friend at the time was going, and Lou was crying every night, bugging my parents about going with Elizabeth—whose parents have lots of money—and getting on everyone's nerves. My parents were pulling out their hair.

The camp gives away a scholarship to the kid who designs the best poster on the camp theme, and the year we both wanted to go, the theme was "Go bananas for art." And my brain exploded. When I was a little kid, my dad had a bunch of really cool albums, and I was fascinated with his Velvet Underground album that had a banana with a peel-off sticker. In my head, that cover got combined with the Rolling Stones album cover that had a zipper on it, and presto! Zip-up banana bus with happy, art-crazy kids spilling out of it, all with Split Rock Lighthouse looking over us in the background. Frankie wins! It was a done deal.

I made all sorts of sketches before I did a final, and— of course, because this is how it works in my house—Lou saw my idea on my desk and then, line for line, she drew the same poster I did. My parents sent hers to the contest two days before I brought them mine to mail, and when they saw it, they were sure *I'd* copied *her*. No matter what I said, they didn't believe me, and they wouldn't send my poster. Guess who won the scholarship? I still got to go, since my folks suddenly had enough money to send both of us, but Lou got the glory, with *my* zip-up banana bus.

I pinned her down for twenty minutes when she got the letter saying she'd won, trying to get her to swear she copied me. She wouldn't fess up. My parents grounded me for a week for doing it. That summer, her poster with kids and the banana bus was everywhere at camp—they were all so proud of Lou! So much talent, they said—she sings, she acts, she draws, she dances. She's the real deal. She'll go far.

That camp was the worst five days of my life. I was so pissed I couldn't do anything, not even build funky little models out of balsa wood. Everywhere there was evidence of Lou's superiority—she won the contest, she was obviously the better Neumann sibling, she got to hang out with Elizabeth, and all I got was heartbreak. So I quit making art. I came home from that camp and didn't do anything for two years, and when I did start again, I never showed anyone my work.

In my head, I know it's silly to still be pissed, or even annoyed. She was ten, and when you're ten, you do dumb stuff, especially when your best friend's going to camp and you want to go, too. But it hurt, down to my core, so my heart overrides my brain on this one. You don't steal someone else's art. You just don't.

And she never got caught, and she never stopped being awful, and she does shit like calling me Pepperoniangelo, and it just never ends. The true Frankie is loved, because she's just like my parents—outgoing and talented and wonderful. The fake Frankie is tolerated. That's just how it is. Do I belong in this family? Not at all.

I get a text from David: **Thanks for the help. E thinks you're a keeper.** Then a winking emoji. Something I didn't recognize as a knot in my stomach is suddenly unknotted. Maybe there really will be more art with Epic.

I text back: **Glad he likes it.** I don't text a wink.

Donna Russell is at the end of the room, slumped under the big high window. I swallow the last bite of my sandwich, stand up, and go to her. I think of her as the guardian of the ballroom, and I always imagine she could stomp on someone if I needed her to, even though she looks pretty relaxed. Nobody knows Donna Russell is up here, and I like that. She protects me. She's my monster mash-up safe person.

V IS FOR VALIDATION

There is nothing quite so deathly slow as a Monday afternoon in the spring in the suburbs. Nothing. I can hear my longboard, Ramona, calling out to me from my locker: *Fraaaaaaaaankieeeeeee. Get me out of here, Frankie.* And I'm yelling, SHUT UP, I CAN'T HELP IT, IT'S SCHOOL. But she's still calling: *Fraaaaaaaaankieeeeeee. Where are you?* Of course my family thinks it's strange to enjoy being by yourself on a zooming piece of plywood—and dangerous, since a person should wear pads and a helmet and stuff—but I don't care. It's only really dangerous when there are hills involved. Other than that, it's just transportation, though it's also peaceful. Nobody bugs you. You're just whizzing by.

I accidentally made the mistake of calling my longboard Ramona in front of my dad about a month ago. Now his big joke is, "So, you're riding Ramona to school?" Then he falls all over himself, laughing. So clever, Pops.

In debate class, I listened to a couple of the Art Club kids talk about how cool it is that Uncle Epic is back in town, did you see the photos in the paper, and I wanted to shake them and say, "I did that! ME! I made those eyes!" When it's over, it's time for Spanish and time to stare at Rory's head, but when I get there, she's not in front of me anymore. Like a jackass—though a subtle one—I look around to see if I can find her. Then she's sliding into the seat next to mine.

"Mind if I sit here?" She looks at me, all cool and classy, like she used to look at Max Ledermann, and she should have on an evening gown with sequins instead of a skirt and a hoodie and rain boots. Rain boots? People wear rain boots for a fashion statement? Rory smells good, too. Exotic. Like a spice counter in a foreign country would smell, if I'm imagining it right.

"Sit wherever you like." I am too surprised to say anything more than that.

Andie Braswell comes in the door after Rory. She used

to sit next to me, and she glares when she sees Rory in her spot. I shrug, and Andie sits in Rory's spot after giving Rory a pissy look, which Rory ignores.

For the record, the back of Andie's head isn't nearly as nice.

Rory arranges her skirt so it nicely covers her knees, though I'd be happy if she left them bare. "Maybe we should do some planning."

"Planning?"

Her smile is a little secretive. "You know. Projects."

"With your cousin, and your uncle? Those kinds of projects?"

"Well, of course." She looks like she's offering me the grand prize in some sweepstakes. "We've only got a month to get people curious about his Walker show."

"How does an anonymous guy have an art show?"

Her face says that she knows many deep secrets, and this is just one of them. "His assistant Marta makes all the arrangements. Then she places the pieces in the galleries and texts Epic photos of everything. He lets her know if he wants things changed."

"Aren't people pissed that he's not at the opening?"

"Who says he doesn't go to the opening? Nobody knows what he looks like." Then she pretends to flip through her notebook, which I take as a cue to stop asking dumb questions.

"When do we go out next?"

"Didn't I just say we have to plan first?" She gets something wooly out of her bag and puts it on her lap. "Are you free tonight?" She bats her lashes at me, which I thought people only did in movies.

"I have to work at Pizza Vendetta until nine."

"David will be by to help you find the workshop again." But then she looks up front, and composes her face into fake sincerity.

Señor Gonzalez, the Spanish teacher, is giving us the evil eye. "*Hola, estudiantes. Díganme sus nombres.*"

"*Sí, señor.*" We all say it in unison, just like we do every day. And then there's a jumble of sound while we all say our names.

For the rest of the class period, Rory sits next to me and knits. I've never seen her do this before, and I have no idea what she's making, but it's ice blue and screaming orange, in alternating sections, and it's long. That's all I can tell. Señor Gonzalez doesn't even yell at her for not taking notes, which might be the weirdest thing of all.

When the bell rings, she packs up her knitting and her Spanish book and gives me an elegant-lady-leaving-the-party look. "See you after nine, all right? David will show you the way." She waves, then disappears into the crowd, trailing a tail of orange and blue.

I free Ramona from the locker and we kick home. Now

that it's getting to be nice, it's way better to take Ramona to school instead of the truck. That stupid thing takes a space and a half to park, so people bitch at me, plus then I have to take Lou to school. This way she has to get there on her own.

I go up to my room and do my homework, just because I know I should, and I'm at Pizza Vendetta by five, just like I'm supposed to be. Tonight's job is to make sauce and dough. Mix, mix, mix. Knead, knead, knead. Blend, blend, blend. There are pizzas to make, in between things, when the place gets busy—which isn't very busy, since it's Monday—but work gets done, and I get out the back door by nine, just like I'm supposed to. I'm only called Pepperoniangelo twice.

At 9:05, David's standing by the truck, wearing something that looks like cargo shorts but is really a skirt, and he's shifting from foot to foot, like he has to piss or something.

"A cargo skirt?"

He smooths it down. "Technically, it's a utilikilt."

"My bad. Please tell me you have something on underneath your utilikilt, and you're not going traditional Scottish commando." I unlock the door for him to get in.

"That's for you to find out." His grin is big, like he's inviting me to check. "But never mind that right now."

David's eyes flash almost angrily behind his spectacles. "Rory has ideas for a side project. Ideas I think are dumb."

"What are they? Have you done a side project before?"

"No, and you'll just have to wait." He frowns in his seat while he tells me the turns to take. This time I try and remember where I'm going, just in case I ever have to get there without a cousin escort.

When we pull up in the driveway, the big garage door opens and we drive in. Rory's there, motioning us forward like we're parking a ship instead of a delivery truck. Finally she puts her hands up and we stop. The engine isn't even off before she's heading to turn on a TV in the corner of the garage.

David comes around to my side and waits for me. "She's excited."

Rory glides over and squeezes my elbow. "It's amazing. Just wait. It could be almost like a business."

"A business?"

There are ratty old recliners and a couch over there, and I flop into one of the chairs. Rory's got a laptop hooked up to the TV, and YouTube is on the screen.

"Watch this." Her grin is huge. "We want to do something like this, but we'd need more people. And the problem is cops—they're paying attention again, now that Epic's back in town." Of course there was coverage of the capitol eyes in the big Sunday papers, so I casually took out the recycling and stole the sections with the stories and the photos. Into the scrapbook they went, with *FUCK YEAH* written in big letters across the pages.

"Why do the cops care about Epic?"

David laughs. "Because they hate not being able to catch him. It's not like they can charge him with a lot, but it would blow his anonymity, and that would destroy him. Epic would quit making art for sure. Plus, when he was in LA, a bunch of other graffiti artists got involved and spray-painted a whole block's worth of buildings after he left. The city was pissed, even though the public loved it. Then someone spray-painted a bunch of penguins at the zoo and they died from the fumes. So whatever city he's in, the cops are always on hyper-alert, just in case shit goes down, whether Epic does it or it's copycats."

I frown. "Not good. For the penguins or for Epic."

"And none of it was Epic's fault, but the cops don't see it that way." Rory glares, like she's been personally insulted instead of Epic.

"Did any of this hit the Web?" Why don't I know about this?

David shakes his head. "Marta managed to keep it quiet."

"Shut up, you two, and watch this." Rory's impatient.

The video starts, and I realize it's surveillance footage, a security camera in a convenience store, it looks like. Then a kid comes in dressed like he's in the court of Louis XIV, all powdered wig and long coat, but with a mask. He's really broad, so the coat's almost bursting at the seams. Then another guy comes in, dressed in the same kind of costume, and he's just as broad. A couple more seventeenth-century guys bust through the doors, then four girls come with their own white wigs and those dresses that have huge hips on them, then a few more guys and a few more girls. Everyone's got a black silhouette mask on over their eyes, but they also have on white face paint. Some of the people are holding their masks on sticks, like it's a masquerade ball. You hear the clerk ask who they are, and someone shouts, "Flash rob!" Then it's chaos.

Someone's throwing Twinkies, someone else is throwing bags of chips, and someone's pelting someone else with pieces of bubble gum. Everyone's laughing and having a good time, pushing stuff off the shelves and pitching it around, slipping it in their pockets. One girl is laughing and clapping her hands, not throwing things or damaging stuff, just watching and laughing. Then a deep voice says, "You don't want me to hurt you, old man. Move it." Then you hear a SMASH, and you know the cash register has hit the floor.

When the clerk yells, "YOU KIDS GET THE HELL OUT

OF HERE!" they all just laugh. Then a perky voice says, "I've got a gun. You don't want to see me use it." The place goes quiet, and suddenly there's a gun in front of the security camera, held up in a gloved hand as if to record that, yes, there's a gun at this little event. The clerk says, very quietly, "All right." And things explode again.

Food starts whizzing around, including cans, because you can hear them thunking on the floor, and you hear someone scraping money together, probably from the change that's on the floor, since the cash register got knocked over. The craziness continues for probably another twenty seconds. Occasionally a person comes into view of the camera, waving the gun around. It's never the same person twice. At one point the gun is passed to the girl who's been standing off to the side, watching the insanity. She holds it, but like it's a snake that's going to bite her, and she hands it off again to some dude who goes dancing away. Then you hear someone yell, "All right, troupe. We've done our jobs!" And they all trip out the door, laughing and waving. When they wave, you see the white gloves again. They're too smart for fingerprints. One of the big guys is carrying a plastic bag, and you can see money in it. He bows before he leaves. When they're all gone, the store clerk shouts, "GODDAMMIT!" And then the video goes black.

Something's knocking at the back of my brain. Something I can't quite pin down.

"Such well-costumed anarchy. I love it more every time I watch it." Rory laughs like she's seventy-five social levels above everyone in the video. "Maybe they think it's performance art. Think we can pull it off?"

I'm amazed, but not in a good way. "Flash robs are a thing? Scaring clerks and ripping off convenience stores?" Imagine the balls it takes to rob a place, let alone in costume, let alone destroy the place on top of it. I give Rory a look. "I don't think performance art has to be rude or destructive." The whole thing was a real asshole move, if you ask me.

Rory shrugs. "Performance art can be anything. The idea is what matters, not just how you put it out there. And there's a bunch of flash robs on YouTube. This one happened Friday night, at the Kwiky Pik near Golden Valley Boulevard and Highway 12."

It's one of a chain of convenience stores. They're all over the Cities. "How'd you find out about it?"

David answers. "A kid in my algebra class was talking about it."

"How stupid is it to put it on YouTube? That's insane." I feel bad for that poor clerk.

Rory nods. "A senior named Joseph Margo works there,

and he taped it off the security footage with his phone. He'll get fired if anybody finds out."

I can just imagine the fallout if a flash rob happened at Pizza Vendetta and a video went viral. Geno would find out who leaked it and kill that person personally, with his bare hands and a pizza pan.

She points to the TV. "Let's watch it again."

I watch them all start throwing things, and laughing and having a good time. When I focus on the girl clapping and watching, I realize she has on a comedy/tragedy necklace. Simple small gold masks. Her hair is loose around her head, in a big fluff, and she's draped in a huge dress.

When it's over, I want to know for sure. "Play it again."

We watch one more time. There's the necklace. And the way the girl claps her hands—it's very polite, even though it's happy. Very polite and proper. Then I notice how the girl bites her lip on the right side. Like she's thinking.

A word starts to ricochet around my brain: *Pepperoni-angelo. Hey, Pepperoniangelo.* All the staring and laughing.

"So what do you think, Frankie?" Rory's got her slinky voice on. "If we just took a little money, it would be a misdemeanor, wouldn't it? And we wouldn't want a gun. That's too much. Maybe we don't have to take anything. Maybe we could just mess the place up a bit."

The synapses in my head are connecting and reconnecting. *Zip-up banana bus. Happy art kids.*

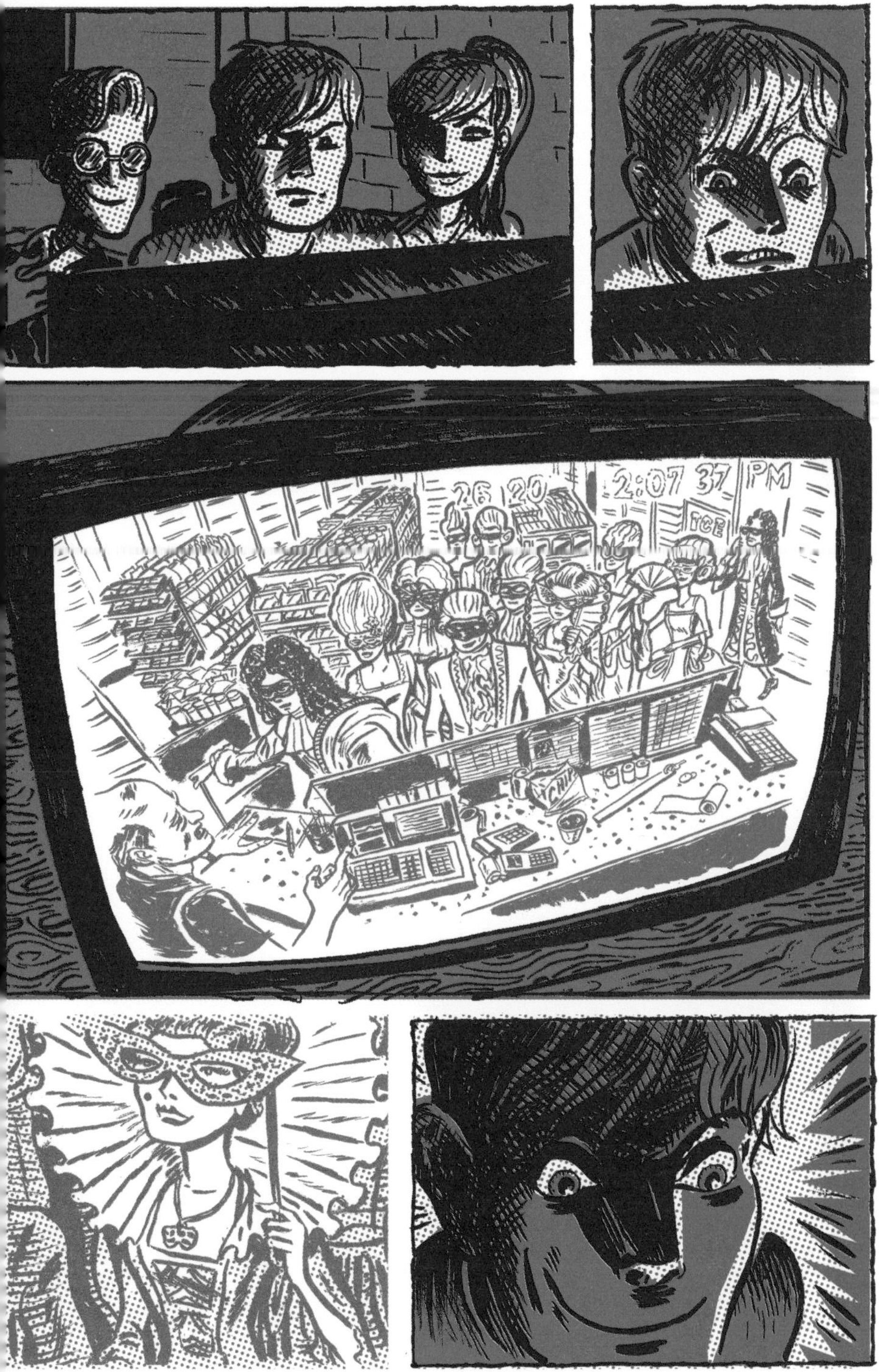
26 20
2:07 37 PM
ICE
CHIP

"Frankie?" David can see that something's going on.

"That's my sister." Momentous connections are happening. *Splintered skateboard deck. Bent bike wheel. The real Frankie is loved. Pepperoniangelo, hey, Pepperoniangelo!*

"We could try the Pick N Go on Riverfront Drive, and . . . who's your sister?" This gets Rory's attention.

"Turn it on again, David."

David laughs. "So your sister's a bit of a felon?"

"She didn't take anything. She's the one who's laughing and clapping."

We watch it one more time. It's definitely Lou.

I can't believe she'd do something that ignorant.

I can't believe what beautiful, enormous, magical, wonderful, intensely flawless blackmail material just fell into my lap.

Do the crime, do the time.

"I WIN!" I jump up from the squishy chair and run around the room. If I could do cartwheels, I would. "Suck it, stupid sister!"

I want to climb the walls and shout it from the roof. This is going to be good. So. So. Good.

Rory and David just look at me. Then Rory shuts off the TV. "So you won't help us pull a flash rob?"

I stop and look at her. "Hell no, I won't help you. I don't do anything more illegal than putting art on public property. I'm here to help Epic, that's it."

David flips Rory off. "I told you he wouldn't help us."

Rory sniffs. "Like I said, I thought this might be a side project."

"Really? Felonies are a side project? What did David just tell me about Epic and the cops? Another flash rob will bring them around for sure, and Epic doesn't need to be connected to that kind of stuff, even accidentally. I'll help you do his pieces, but that's it." Is she really that dumb?

"There's already been a letter to the editor about how people are sorry he's back in town, and how he doesn't deserve his Walker show. The lady wants to help the cops catch him." David goes to a table and picks up a newspaper. "Rory's mom collects his press clippings." He hands it to me.

Sure enough, some woman from Anoka, which is pretty conservative, spent a quarter of a page talking about how Uncle Epic is corrupting America's youth with his "common garbage masquerading as art used to turn kids' minds toward disobeying authority." She wants the cops to go door to door and catch him. She thinks Epic's "blatant defiance for public property laws will convince boys and girls to willfully disobey laws" and says the vandals who cut all the soccer nets out of the soccer goals in Anoka's parks must be part of Epic's "band of hooligans." She is also convinced that the flag that was stolen from the post office must be Epic's work, since "only godless vandals like Uncle Epic would make art that defiles our most cherished American flag." To my knowledge, Epic has never done a flag piece. Maybe he should start. In Anoka.

"Does Epic care about this stuff?"

"He's used to it. What are you going to do about your sister?" Rory's face has a funny look on it. I can't quite read it.

"I don't know yet. You two will be the first ones to find out."

That idea pleases her, and she takes my elbow again. "Well, if flash robs are out, what about guerrilla knitting?"

Her friendly grab feels weird, given that she was just talking about robbing people and I was kind of pissed about it, but I'll go with it. "As long as it doesn't involve guns or jail time, I'm there."

She points to her bag on the floor, which is still leaking its ice-blue-and-violent-orange tail. "I'm part of Yarn Bombers Anonymous, the Twin Cities branch—just me, not Epic or David. We cover weird stuff in knitting."

"That I can handle. But you don't need a delivery truck."

"You never know." She squeezes my arm, and it makes my stomach wobble, which scares me and excites me and makes me realize I have no idea what to do around someone like her. She's looking into my eyes, deep into them, like everything she needs for the rest of her life is in there.

After two seconds I look out the window. Rory starts rambling on, talking about bridges and light poles and street signs. Evidently some people in Pittsburgh just covered a bridge in knitting, and people have done buses, cars, bicycles, trees, and buildings all over the country. I had no idea.

I hear David sigh. Rory ignores him and keeps going. I shoot a look over my shoulder, and he's staring at the floor, like someone's died.

"You don't like knitting, David?"

He doesn't look up.

I don't get home until one, and my mom is in the living room, reading a book about the Rat Pack—Sinatra and his friends. Which must be why she's wearing a fedora.

"Hey, Mom." I try for friendly.

"This late-night thing is getting to be a habit." She looks angrier than she might normally look if she hadn't just called the cops because I was out all night. "I know we don't put many rules on you, but one is too late for a school night."

"I know. I'm sorry." And I am, because my ass will be dragging at six a.m.

"Go." She gestures with her hand. "I'm going, too."

I almost blurt out what I know about Lou, but I don't. That information is best thought about for a while.

She kisses me on the cheek as she goes by, and the kiss

almost knocks the fedora off her head. "You're a good kid, Frankie. I love you."

"Love you, too."

There's a lot of saying "I love you" in this house, but I don't believe it, at least not when it's applied to me. It's easy for them to love the girl with the freckle F, since she's just like them: talented, outgoing, dramatic. I'm the fake Frankie, remember?

I go up to my room, but I can't sleep, so I get my laptop and find the video on YouTube, then watch it over and over again. Knowing who Lou knows, and knowing who'd be dumbass enough to do something like this, by the fifteenth time I've finished it, I think I know at least three guys by their build, and maybe three of the girls by their hair. I think. I hope. Some people are still a mystery, but that's all right. I think I've got enough to go on.

Lou Neumann, the perfect daughter, perfect friend, perfect actress, perfect student, the Chosen Frankie and perfect person, is not actually perfect. I am validated. And I'm going to show the rest of the world just how imperfect she is.

V IS FOR
(NON) VICARIOUS

Wednesday after school. Ramona and I are gliding. Peacing out. Kicking on. Perfecting my plan.

Everybody knows about the flash rob now, thanks to that kid who put it on YouTube, and Lou is jumpy like a cat with fleas. When I saw her Tuesday morning at breakfast, she looked like she hadn't slept at all. But it was also the front-page story of the local section of the Minneapolis *Star Tribune*. Evidently the clerk had a heart attack once the flash rob was over, and he's still in the hospital. He collapsed after the video cut off. The police said whoever's arrested will be facing more than just armed robbery charges, since the guy was hurt.

My parents asked us about it at supper. Lou acted as innocent as the angel my parents think she is, and I wanted to punch her in the face. My parents clean that store, and they know the guy. They're worried about him.

I heard Lou in her room that night, arguing with someone over the phone. There was lots of "Someone's got to get rid of the gun!" and "Is he gonna be all right?" and "Why didn't the costumes get back in the bags?" That kind of stuff.

But by this morning, she looked calm again, even with the dark circles under her eyes, so everything must be under control. Good for Lou and her robbers. Give me a while and I'll turn that around.

I glide around the neighborhood for a while, being careful to skate on all the public properties that have NO SKATEBOARDING ALLOWED signs posted, and then I go home. Lou and my mom are sitting at the table in the kitchen, looking at a slick brochure. Lou keeps begging to go to a very fancy summer drama workshop in Vermont, and my parents keep telling her to get a job. But today it looks like she's making progress.

"If I work for you and Dad, I can earn some money to go. You have to pay a helper anyway, don't you?" Her voice is high and she's excited, like she's been planning her attack for a while.

"When we have big jobs, we do need extra help. That's

true enough." My mom pulls the brochure over and starts browsing. It's the size of a small book. "I suppose you can scrub and mop just as easily as anyone else." She finds what she's looking for and points. "But this is crazy, Tallulah—we can't afford three thousand dollars for one week of classes. It's a month's worth of family expenses."

"I know, Mom, but you know it will be good for me. I'll be able to practice my craft, and it will help me get a scholarship to college, so it really will save you money in the end."

My mom leans back in her chair. "That's a lot of dreaming, Lou."

"But I'm good at dreaming! And what you dream really will come true, right? Just like Disney says. Pleeeeeeease, Mom. Please?"

Mom closes her eyes and takes a deep breath. "Let me talk to your father."

"Oh thank you, thank you!" Lou leaps off her chair and grabs my mom in a huge hug. My mom hugs her back, and I can see she's trying to hold on for just a second longer than Lou wants. Lou goes running off to tell someone about the fact that she might actually get to go to the zillion-dollar theater workshop, and I go to the fridge, get an apple, and scram out of the kitchen. Neither one of them noticed I saw the whole scene.

If I told my parents I wanted to go to a $3,000 art camp, or a skateboarding camp—if there was such a thing—there'd be no way. And if I ever needed confirmation why, I could just point to where I'm standing, which is the hallway to my parents' bedroom. It's plastered in photos of Lou being amazing. Here she is at age four, in the summer production of *Les Misérables* that a local university put on—she was the tiny Cosette, very adorable and charming onstage. There she is, age nine, dancing in a recital. Here's Lou at twelve, as one of the Von Trapp kids in *The Sound of Music*.

Are there any pictures of me? No. She's the one who does things that are camp-worthy.

I grab a pencil from the living room and sketch myself on the wall, longboarding out from the corner of the photo of her performing at last year's talent show at school. I make it light, so the chances of anyone seeing it are pretty much zero, but I even put little motion lines behind the skateboard. Once the sketch is done—I had to erase a couple times, which messed with the paint on the wall, but whatever—I go up and sit with Donna Russell and do my homework. We're to the point in the semester where teachers don't really care what's going to happen. They're counting the days until we get out of school, just like we are.

When I go back downstairs for supper, my dad is home from whatever cleaning job he was doing, and he looks like a normal guy. He and Lou are making plans in the living room about the end-of-the-year talent show, which is run by Lou's drama teacher. My dad and her teacher, Ted Koch, are old friends from college, so Dad's helping Lou and a bunch of her friends do the scene from *Macbeth* with the witches, Act 4, Scene 1, to be precise. They're discussing voice and blocking and all sorts of stuff I don't know or care about. Mom's cooking, and it might be tacos.

I decide to try out my theory about the summer camp.

"Hey, Mom, there's a national traveling skateboard school coming to Wisconsin in July. It's twenty-five hundred dollars. Do you think I could go?"

She's stirring the meat on the stove. "Where in Wisconsin is it?"

"Madison." I'm totally freestyling now.

"You must have Pizza Vendetta money you could put toward it, don't you? We could help, but we can't pay for it all, especially if Lou goes to Vermont. And those ambitions might get her somewhere in college. Skateboarding won't get you into school." She's moved on to grating cheese, and she's not looking at me, which is probably good, because she would see I'm lying about wanting to go to camp and also a little pissed that Lou's talent is more useful than mine, even though I expected her answer.

"Just checking."

Now she's looking up. "What do you mean, 'just checking'?"

"Never mind."

"Frankie?"

But I go back up to hang with Donna Russell for five minutes, who is very stern, but very kind, and very soft and squishy if you lean against her legs.

At supper, Lou is talking about this girl she knows who's gone to the workshop in Vermont and the girl says it's "so super and amazing that a person can't even talk about it." So why are we talking about it? My dad wants to discuss this basement he was cleaning today where he found a rat's nest, and my mom wants to ramble on about this obscure Sinatra song that was just discovered on reel-to-reel tape found in the back room of a radio station in Vegas. I don't want to talk, which is traditional, and they're too busy listening to each other and themselves to notice or care.

At the end of every family dinner, we have to go around and say something we're thankful for—something different every night, we can't repeat for three days. I have no idea how this tradition ever started, but it's really annoying.

Mom starts. "I'm thankful for my two wonderful kids." She beams at Lou, and then at me. I try and smile back.

"I'm thankful we have a truck that sticks out like a sore thumb, because people see it and call me to do work for them." Dad looks proud of himself, like the truck is something special instead of weird and embarrassing. My mom nods and pats his hand. "I'm also thankful for the fact that

Marvin's heart attack wasn't fatal." Marvin's the guy at the Kwiky Pik who endured Lou's flash rob.

"I'm grateful for parents who are awesome and wonderful." Lou smiles as big as she can and blows a kiss to each of them, trying to cover up the fear in her eyes that Marvin's name caused. I try not to gag.

"I'm grateful . . ." And I stop, because I don't know what else to say. Normally I say my longboard, Mountain Dew, and Pop-Tarts, in that order.

"Yes?" Mom is curious. "Grateful for what? Is tonight a Pop-Tarts night?"

I decide on two things: "Grateful I have a job. And grateful for YouTube."

Lou drops her fork, then whacks her head on the edge of the table when she goes down to get it. She glares at me when she comes up. There's more fear in her eyes, too, even though she's trying to look normal. "Why are you grateful for YouTube?"

"Lots of good stuff on there." I smile like the Buddha at her, tranquil and serene.

My dad nods. "Good to have a job." A very dad thing to say, in my opinion.

"Yeah. May I be excused?"

"Put your dishes in the dishwasher." Mom starts to clear the food.

Our house phone rings, which doesn't happen very often. My dad answers.

"Hello? . . . Yes, this is Brett Neumann. . . ." Long pause. "Yes, I saw the article. . . ." Another long pause. "I'll ask." He listens again, then puts his hand over the receiver. "It's the police. You don't know anything about those weird eyes that showed up on the capitol lawn, do you?"

"No." I'm going to throw up any second. "Why are the police calling us about that?"

"They saw a white delivery truck on security camera footage from a store close to the capitol, and they looked up all the registrations for white delivery trucks. One of the cops that was here remembers you saying you were helping a friend. Do you know this Uncle Epic guy?"

"Nope." I hope my face isn't as red as it feels.

"Sorry, Officer. He doesn't know anything. . . . Yes, I will." He hangs up. "You really don't know this guy?"

"Nope." I try very hard to look believable and pray I'm not failing.

"Why would they think Frankie had anything to do with it? Uncle Epic's famous. Frankie's a kid." My mom's washing supper dishes, and Lou's drying, with her eyes glued to me. I am serene. A Zen master.

"Just following all leads, I guess." He picks up the notebook he and Lou have been using to organize their ideas about the *Macbeth* scene and goes back to the living room.

"Going up to my room to study." And I walk super slow, but not too slow, up the stairs, then I close the door, not a slam, then fall on my bed and freak out. Quietly.

Frak frak frak. Did they believe me? It's not like I've been in trouble before, so my folks have no reason to think I'm lying. Nobody can prove anything without a license plate. Rory and David weren't worried that anyone saw us. Right? RIGHT?

If I'm the one to get him arrested and mess up Epic's anonymity, I will throw myself into the Mississippi.

Slowly, slowly, I stop shaking.

Now that I'm calm—calmer—sort of—it's time to plan my Lou vendetta. I grab a sketchbook, but my phone vibrates.

U free? No name attached.

Depends on who u are.

It's Rory.

No way. **How did u get my number?**

David. Duh. U free?

Yeah.

Sneak out.

No need for that. I walk back to the kitchen. "I've got to go to Pizza Vendetta for a while, to help them with inventory."

My mom's at the table, staring into their business laptop, figuring out billing statements. "Don't be late. There's been enough of that."

"Nope." I pick up my keys from the front hall table, and I'm away from the people who will spend $3,000 to send their daughter to camp, but not their son, because her skills are useful.

When I get in my truck, I text Rory: **Where am I going? Pizza Vendetta. Meet you there.**

I drive around back to the parking lot, and she's leaning against the NO PARKING sign by the Dumpster. When I pull up, she hops in and belts into the passenger seat. In my mind's eye I see blinking red and blue lights, and hear a siren. I don't need cop trouble. I don't. But I want to make art with Epic.

I shake my head to clear it. "You learned quick. Last ride too bumpy for you?"

"I don't like bruises." Her smile is bright. "Ready for a new adventure?"

"Now?" So much for not being late. "The cops called my house tonight." I shouldn't do this. I don't need trouble. Yes I do, actually, but no, really, I don't. But I don't make her get out of my truck, either.

"Why?"

"Some security camera had footage of my truck near the capitol, so they looked up registrations."

She looks concerned. "What did your folks say?"

"They believed me when I said I wasn't there. I hope they believed, anyway."

"Then it's all OK. What are there, maybe a thousand white delivery trucks in the Twin Cities? How would they expect to find the right one?" Rory warbles this reassurance like a cheerful bird with all the answers. "What did you say to your sister? Turn here."

I wrench the steering wheel to the left. "Nothing yet."

"Why not?"

"She doesn't need to know I know."

We're at Epic's, somehow. I think I'm beginning to remember the way. Rory hops out of the truck and punches a code into a number panel to make the door go up. I drive in.

David's waiting for us, this time wearing a tulle skirt like Lou's.

"Hello, ballerina."

He shoots me a look. "What's it to you? Offended by my ugly knees?" He sticks his leg out at me. "Just because your boys like to crowd up doesn't mean mine do."

"Fair enough." I watched a kid trip him in the cafeteria today. Not much respect for skirt-wearing guys in high school.

"Ready to strategize?" He rubs his hands together like he's an evil villain. "Epic gave me plans for what he wants next."

"Do you have everything?" Rory walks past David to the table behind him. "Blueprints and a materials list?"

"Yup." David follows Rory, and I follow David.

"Does Epic have a crew wherever he goes? Or is it just you two?" I'm curious. Casual.

Rory's shuffling things on the table, laying them out for us to see. "We help him when he's home, and we told you we travel sometimes. His main crews are in New York and Berlin. He's got warehouses there, too."

"Dang." I feel kind of floaty-headed. Crews in New York, Berlin, and Minneapolis. Me in his crew. No more vicarious living for me. I'm in it.

On the table there's a drawing of Loring Park, and there are Xs at various places on the map. The park is huge, with a pond in it, so there's a lot of space for random art. The Xs aren't labeled.

David points to a huge pile of old TV sets, all sizes of them, in the corner of the garage. "We need at least twenty."

"There aren't twenty Xs." Rory's counting on the map. "What about the sheep?"

"Sheep?" Oh man. "No sheep in my truck."

"There are fifteen Xs, and he wants fifteen sheep/TV combos, then a sculpture with the rest of the TVs and five more sheep." David says this like sheep are easily acquired in the Twin Cities.

"I might know somebody with access to sheep. Let me work on that." Rory winks at David.

"No sheep in my truck. No way." I'm imagining all sorts of gross things.

"Yes, sheep in your truck." David points at me.

"No way in hell."

"Then what are we going to do?" Rory puts her hands on her hips and frowns. Obviously this pout is meant for me.

My Lou vendetta blazes in my head, and ideas suddenly appear to me as if presented by a singing angel choir. "If you're in need of someone to haul sheep, before I agree to do it, I want payment. Live animals in my truck are serious business."

"Like what?" David looks surprised.

Rory smirks. "I told you he wouldn't do it for free."

I shoot Rory a glare but answer David's question. "I want permission to use some of those." I point to the jumble of mannequin parts. "For a piece I'm working on. Just to borrow. Nothing permanent."

David nods to Rory. "Text him and ask." He looks at me. "It's hard to say with Epic, which stuff he's got ideas about. He's been collecting those mannequin parts since we were little."

"Does he have a sewing machine? I could use one of those, too."

Rory nods, texting away. "He doesn't always answer immediately. It could be a few days."

"It could be a few days for his sheep, too." Look at me, trying to be tough. If he walked in the room two seconds from now and showed me his face and told me to get my ass into my truck, I'd say *baa* and grab my keys. Instead I stretch out on the recliner by the TV and try to act nonchalant. Rory is bent over her phone with her hair falling around her face.

There's a pretty girl less than ten feet away from me. I'm in the hideout of one of the greatest street artists in the world. We're planning another piece. I'm asking to borrow some of his stuff.

Cops, parents, whoever, whatever—nobody's making me miss this.

The evening pauses. David stretches out on the couch across from me, and Rory picks up her knitting needles and sits down on the floor next to the recliner. She's close enough that I can smell her again. Flowery, but soothing. An old-fashioned smell, but a little hippieish, with peace signs and Birkenstocks. I'm almost asleep when Rory's voice startles me out of my doze. "He says that's fine, just don't cut the mannequin pieces up. And you can use his big industrial sewing machine."

"Tell him I won't butcher the body parts." I'm not a serial killer. "And you will clean out the inside of my truck if any of those sheep screw it up." Eeew.

David stands up and goes back to the table to consult a list. "Since that's settled, we need some paintbrushes and stencils. And white paint. Help me pick out the best TVs first, though."

So I hop out of the recliner and we pick twenty televisions from a room-sized corner of the garage—there are probably twelve left over when we're done—and we clean them off. Rory's found the stencils, which look like the ones that road crews use for streets, only smaller, and she brings us white paint and brushes.

Epic wants us to paint THINK THIS WAY on fifteen of the televisions, so we do about three, and then I realize it's eleven thirty, and I told my mom I wouldn't be late.

Rory gives me a smile I'm betting she'll give to the guy she gets the sheep from, and draws me a map to get back to Pizza Vendetta, though I think can probably find my way by now. "Just in case you need it." She hands it to me, and she's close enough that I can smell her one last time. Flowery peace sign goodness.

"Come back tomorrow so we can paint more TVs." David waves.

My brain is in knots on the way home, for these reasons:

- Someone is going to put sheep in my truck;
- Rory smells so good;
- I am really late;
- I didn't do my homework;
- These people are kinda sorta maybe a little bit like friends, which makes me nervous;
- I AM ONE DEGREE OF SEPARATION FROM UNCLE EPIC.

Lou is the only one awake when I get home. Unless they're performing, my parents go to bed pretty early— though I kind of expected my mom to stay up. She was up last night. But hauling around huge vacuums takes some energy.

"Where were you?" She's eating peanut butter toast and looking at the booklet for the place in Vermont. "And why do you care so much about YouTube?" She's watching me close again.

"What? I was out. Working."

"Seriously. You're grateful for YouTube? Why?"

"Like I said earlier, lots of interesting stuff on YouTube. I'm sure you know that." I search her eyes for more fear. It's hard to say what she's thinking.

"I know that you weren't out working." Subject redirection. She checks the clock. "Pizza Vendetta closed a long time ago."

"Other places, other work."

"You do not have other work. You don't even have friends."

"I do have friends." In fact, I have a friend who has a piece in the Museum of Modern Art in New York (his Garbage Can Series, which is all about making sculpture from the crap in people's trash cans, gross but it still makes sense), a friend who's one of the best street artists in the world. I have a friend who tells it like it is: Humans are stupid and do stupid but funny shit. I have a friend who tries to find beauty in the ordinary, who thinks ideas are art, too, and who knows art is one of the most powerful forces in the world. I have no idea what he looks like, but he's my friend. I hope. So there, Lou.

Thank god she can't hear what's in my head. "And I know stuff, besides."

"Like what?" Laser beams from her eyes are tearing me to shreds. She's got on a bathrobe that's as bright as Cookie Monster and twice as hairy. Her curls stick out all over her head, like someone whipped them with an egg beater.

"You'll never know. And I have homework to do, if you don't mind." I get a Coke and an apple and start for the stairs.

"You are a half-wit man-child with grand delusions." Lou chomps her toast very loudly in my direction.

"You are a mouth-breathing Miley Cyrus imitator with horrible taste in bathrobes." I show her my ass and point to it. "Kiss this."

"You both need to be in bed." It's my mom, looking very sleepy but also pissed. "It's a school night, and, Frankie, if you haven't done your homework, you'd better get it done now. I'm not impressed."

"Since when have you cared about when we go to bed or if we do our homework?"

Her face tells me that was a low blow. "Since always. Are you saying we can't trust you to do those things? We'll talk more in the morning. And brush your teeth." She stumbles back to bed while Lou and I stare at her.

"You don't know anything." Lou smacks her lips over her last bite of toast, just to bug me.

"Weren't you trying to tell me about it when I got home Saturday morning? You have no idea what I know."

She's speechless. I'm pleased.

I go to my room and do my homework. But before I go to sleep, I sketch out some revenge ideas. With mannequin parts.

V IS FOR VENGEANCE

Thursday after school, and there are cops in the parking lot, talking to people. Nobody from the flash rob, though—at least not that I saw—just random people. How could they tell the robbers were kids? People had on masks. But I guess you might as well check, since kids can be serious shitheads, and it's probably smart to begin with the school closest to the Kwiky Pik—which is ours. It will take them a while if they go student by student. Henderson has a thousand people.

Glad I didn't drive today. A white delivery truck might stick out in a parking lot of regular cars.

Nobody's home when I get there at three thirty. Lou has to walk, of course, since I rode Ramona, so it takes her a while. I think she has drama club and *Macbeth* planning, too. I have to restock my parents' truck when they get home, but they're not home for at least two more hours. There's time for vendetta planning.

The first thing I need is a yearbook, which Lou has, so I grab it out of her room. Then it's time to think about clothes. In the ballroom, there's a closet, and inside that closet is all the fabric my mom used when she sewed, any kind of fabric a person could want. She used to make costumes for a children's theater group, so there's fancy stuff and plain stuff. And tulle. That's what I really want.

I take the yearbook to CopyNow and make ten copies of each flash robber's face, including Lou's, making them bigger and bigger each time. By the time I'm done, I've got a stack of paper a mile high that cost thirty dollars, but I've got lips, noses, and eyes galore, in a bunch of different sizes.

Then I drive over to Epic's garage, which is only about fifteen minutes from CopyNow. I knock on the people-sized door on the side of the building, but nobody answers. When I try the doorknob, it opens. For all I know, Epic's got the door rigged and I'll get slammed on the head by a sandbag, but I go in anyway.

I find three male torsos and three female ones, which is what I need, plus a bunch of arms and legs. Lucky for me there are mannequin stands in the jumble, too.

Before I haul out my last load, I write a note to Epic: *Thank you for allowing me to use your mannequins and stands. I will take good care of them. I will also be over to use your sewing machine later today. You are a god and I am not worthy. Humble thanks again, Frankie Neumann.* Anybody who talks back to the crappy parts of culture the way he does deserves god status.

Because I don't want them to get banged up, I load all my mannequin parts into a net so they don't rattle around in the back of the truck. Netted body parts look almost creepier than a pile of body parts.

When I get home, I lug the net up the stairs to the ball-room, careful not to bang the parts around as I go. Donna Russell is waiting for me, looking surprised that I'm bring-ing her all these scraps of humanity.

Of course there's tulle involved—every mannequin will get a skirt, and underneath the skirt will be tulle. For the fabric of the skirt itself, I try to choose something I know they'd hate. For Carter, he gets roses that look like they'd be more appropriate on someone's grandma's dining room chairs. But I also cut a bunch of footballs out of this ugly brown fabric that looks like it belongs in a barn. I draw the laces on with a marker.

Carter gets footballs because he's the kicker for the Henderson High football team. He's not your regular drama geek. I'm sure he did the flash rob because he wanted to hang out with Sarah Taylor, who's definitely a drama regular. She held the gun more than once.

The footballs get pinned onto an ugly tunic thing I cut out of this circus stripe stuff that looks like it came straight from the seventies, and then I'm ready to go back to Epic's and sew. I stuff it all into a garbage bag, just in case anybody's home downstairs, but nobody is. The house is still quiet, which is a miracle, because it's six and usually everyone's home by now. I make sure Lou's yearbook gets back in its exact spot.

Just as I'm pulling out, my parents are pulling up, Magic Wizards that they are, in their stupid purple truck with stars on it. My mom waves at me and I roll down the window.

"Where are you going? You know you have to restock the truck." No *Hi, how was your day?* or *Gee, Frankie, you're the coolest son ever*, just directions and orders.

"I'm going to Pizza Vendetta for a little bit. Geno needs help with moving the back room around."

"Be home soon." Dad nods. "You're a good guy to help Geno when it's not your day to work."

"Yeah." I wave and try not to gun my engine when I leave the driveway.

When I get back to Epic's, I knock on the door. No answer. But when I open the door, there's a sewing machine set up in the middle of a cleared space, all plugged in with a long extension cord.

Guess it's OK to use it. Except that I have no freaking idea how to sew.

What I do instead could not be considered sewing, it's so ugly, but I manage to close the seams of the shirt, sew the footballs on with one line of stitching for each football, then bind the skirt pieces together and stitch them onto a long piece of elastic. Nobody's ever going to ask me to be on *Project Runway*, but that's OK.

On the front of the shirt, I also tack on a sign that says

HAVE YOU SEEN ME? I DID IT. It's just printed on a white piece of fabric with a black marker. To the bottom of the skirt, I sew another, smaller sign that says ORIGINAL FAKE BY MISS VIXEN. I decided on "Miss Vixen" for a name because it seems Lou-ish, and the letter V is kind of stuck in my consciousness, thanks to Pizza Vendetta and its damn pepperoni fun agenda. But I know if she were choosing aliases for a secret project, she'd adore it. Then I draw a zip-up banana bus, very small, in the corner.

This is the first piece of art I've signed since that damn banana bus poster.

Once I check everything over and make sure I'm done, I shut off the machine and shout, "Thank you, Uncle Epic," into the air.

The lights blink on and off, and I almost jump out of my skin. He's been here watching the whole time. I think back, trying to remember if I farted or did something gross because I thought I was alone.

"You're the best street artist in the world." I can't help myself. The lights blink on and off again.

"I'm your slave for life, except for the sheep thing. I'm not looking forward to that." A laugh comes from somewhere back by the wall, and the lights blink on and off three times.

"Thanks again. You're amazing." I sound like a chucklehead. One last blink. I let myself out the same door I came in.

When I get home, it's seven fifteen. Lou is doing homework at the dining room table, and my mom is making a salad to go with a lasagna that's just out of the oven. Dad and I load the truck up with more bottles of spray cleaner and containers of Ajax, plus enough paper towels to turn all of us into mummies. Lasagna takes forever to cool.

Finally, when supper is over and I've coughed out the fact that I'm thankful for my longboard, I can sneak out to my truck, then visit Donna Russell's lair and see how everything looks on Carter. I get his clothes on, and they actually stay where I put them. I was afraid they'd be too big. I try and give him kind of an Elvis pompadour for his hair, but it sags into a David-like swoop. Yarn doesn't stay where you put it. I also shape a bunch of fabric into a football-looking thing, then cover it all in the brown yarn, so Ghoulie Carter has a football to hold. Then the look is complete. He's draped on the mannequin stand like a rag doll, but a rag doll with attitude. It's completely freaky and very, very cool.

I have no idea if a tulle underskirt will be enough to help people guess who Miss Vixen is, but I hope so.

Around one, the house is quiet. Once I've checked on everybody to make sure they're asleep, I carry Carter down the ballroom stairs. When I get him out the front door, I put him in the passenger seat of the truck and belt him in.

He looks like a drunk. The mannequin stand goes in the back, bungeed to the wall so it doesn't rattle around.

It's taken me a long time to figure out where I want Carter to go, and where I'll put his companions once they're made, but why not be obvious? The Kwiky Pik is the best choice. Carter's mannequin looks like he's being casual, talking to someone invisible on the bench. He's a Big Zombie Ghoulie Man on Campus.

A woman parks at Ghoulie Carter's end of the building while I get him situated, and she gives me a weird look. Hopefully she'll be the only one who sees me. There are no windows over here, and people walking in the front can't see me around the corner. The only thing here is a park bench and a butt-holder for cigarettes. It's shadowy, too— all the lights are in the front of the building. Perfect.

A drunk guy comes around the corner, sits down on the bench and says, "Hey, man, long night, huh?" He nudges Ghoulie Carter and laughs in his face, like he's a real guy, completely ignoring me. The dude's fumes give me a contact high. He smokes a quick butt and leaves, but not until after he's punched Ghoulie Carter in the arm, which almost knocks both of them over.

I make a Twitter profile for Miss Vixen: *Street artist. Careful observer. Dedicated truth-teller.* I follow a bunch of popular people at school, then all of Lou's theater friends,

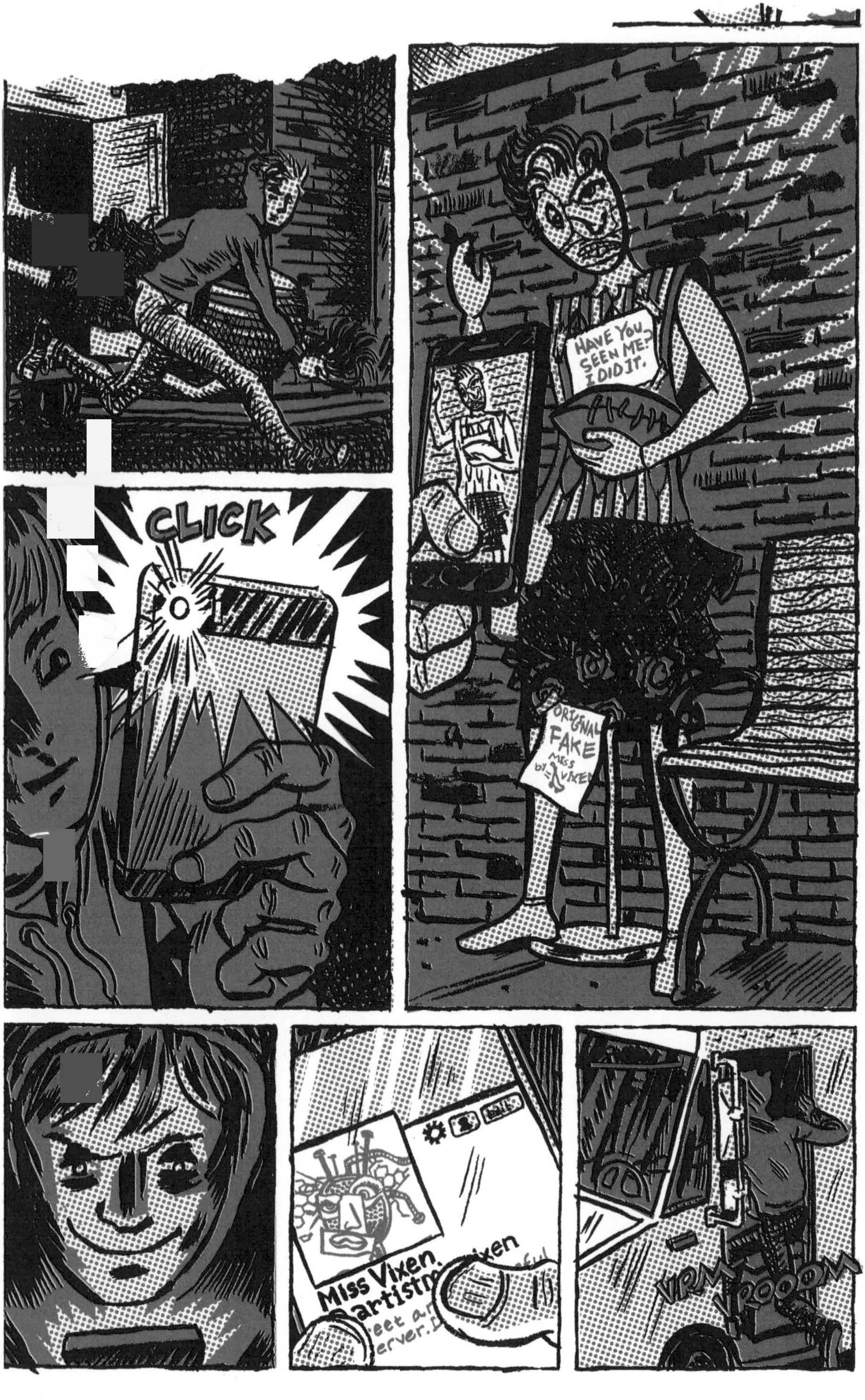
CLICK
HAVE YOU SEEN ME? I DID IT.
ORIGINAL FAKE
MISS VIXEN
Miss Vixen
VRM VROOOM

and then a bunch of random people from a few other schools. You never know how social media will work, so it's good to spread out. A couple people follow back right away—even in the middle of the night.

The Kwiky Pik is two blocks from Henderson High. Enough kids go over and get coffee, muffins, and whatever that word will spread fast.

As long as nobody steals him between now and eight a.m., things are set.

When I get to school in the morning, tired as hell, Ghoulie Carter has already done his job. I hear people buzzing about who they think it is and asking who people think Miss Vixen is, and wow, wasn't that thing cool and ugly. I can't stop smiling. Literally can't stop. In the space of a week, I've gone from a nobody pizza maker to a tiny-bit-famous ghoulie maker. I'm not as epic as Epic, but it's enough for now. No place to go but up.

When Rory sits down next to me in Spanish, she studies my face. "What's wrong with you?"

"Nothing. Why?" I should tell her, but I can't yet. I want to keep it to myself for just a while longer. She'll guess, I'm sure. The mannequin parts will give it away.

She frowns. "Something's different about you. I can't figure it out."

I wave my fingers in front of her face. "Nothing to see here. Move along."

She turns away and focuses on Señor Gonzalez. But there are lots of sideways looks.

I can smell her again. It's grapefruit, I think, and flowers, and something sort of spicy. She always smells different, but it's always phenomenal. I try to smell my pencil instead so I'm not distracted by her. Then she catches me smelling my pencil and rolls her eyes.

At the end of class, she turns to me to say something, then her eyes get big. "I've got it!"

"Got what?"

"You're smiling!"

I'm both embarrassed that I don't smile and annoyed that it took her so long to figure out the emotion on my face. "Am I really that grouchy-looking?"

"Not grouchy, but serious. This is so much nicer!" Her voice tells me she's not kidding. "It's a good look for you." Her smile in return is sweet and slightly do-me-now, all at the same time.

"Um . . . thanks, I guess." Is it bad or good that I'm so serious all the time? Maybe it's just realistic, or maybe I'm a crabby asshole.

Rory's out the door as soon as the bell rings. I don't get a chance to practice my smile on her again.

In the hallway, I hear, "Who do you think Miss Vixen

is?" and "That is one weird-ass face on that creature." Now there's a chance to practice. I can feel the breeze on my teeth, I'm smiling so big.

Then I hear, "Did you hear there was a flash rob at the Best Buy on Golden Valley Boulevard?" That one makes me pause, and I slow down in the hall to eavesdrop. Evidently it was a bunch of people dressed as ninjas. The video's on YouTube again. Lou's group started a trend, it looks like. Or maybe they did it again. Two felonies for Lou. Nice.

After school, I check Twitter, and Miss Vixen has been followed by a hundred people, which isn't much in the real world, but it's fantastic for an imaginary person. A couple people tweeted back pics of Ghoulie Carter—in the first photo he's got shoes, beat-up old brown wing tips, almost exactly like Donna Russell's, down at the bottom of his mannequin stand. Someone wrapped a scarf around his neck, too. In the second photo, he's got a cup of coffee in his hand along with the new shoes and scarf.

There's also a tweet from someone named @reallytruly-epic: **Great creature. Or do you call them creatures?**

@ArtistMissVixen: **I call them ghoulies.**

This can't really be Uncle Epic, can it? It's just someone with "epic" in their Twitter handle. How would he find Miss Vixen?

@reallytrulyepic: **Fantastic work. Body parts went to a worthy cause.**

Oh holy shit. It really is him. I practice my teeth-in-the-breeze smile again.

I glide by the Kwiky Pik on my way home, and Ghoulie Carter's still there, cup of coffee in hand, though it's kind of falling out, since his hand doesn't bend in the way it needs to. The shoes and scarf make him look a little like a *GQ* model, just with a skirt. The football is down by his feet, forgotten in his quest to look fancy.

Friday night again, and I don't have to work, which is rare. Mom's performing, Dad's performing. I'm in my room and there's a knock.

"Yeah?"

Lou sticks her head in the door. "Did you see it?"

"See what?"

"That zombie guy by the Kwiky Pik. Did you see him?"

"Yeah." I'm relaxed. Mellow.

"Who do you think Miss Vixen is?" She's giving me a look like I should know something.

"Who's Miss Vixen?" I am the picture of straight-faced innocence.

"She's the one who made the monster dude. A street artist. She's got a Twitter account and everything." Lou makes it sound like the only thing a person needs to be legit is a Twitter account.

"I have no idea. I'm doing homework here, you know?" I point at the book on my desk, which is a history of street art, but she doesn't know that. I'm on the chapter about Space Invader, and the chapter about Uncle Epic is coming up.

"You're not doing homework on a Friday night, and I think it's Allison Lawson. She's the one who asked me to be a part of it in the first place. I think she's trying to get back at people for—" She clamps her hand over her mouth.

"For what?" I'm interested.

"Forget it." Lou glares. There's a buzz, and she pulls her phone out of her pocket. Her eyes get wide, and she frowns. "Just forget I ever said anything."

She slams the door and disappears. Something isn't right in Lou Land.

Ha.

V is for Virgin Wool

Saturday at Pizza Vendetta, with no pizzas to make. Everybody's got spring fever, so people are having bonfires and making s'mores. By ten thirty, we're done.

Rory and David are painting stuff on my truck when I walk out the back door.

"What the hell are you doing?"

They jump. "Nothing." David has the courtesy to look guilty. "It comes off, don't worry."

"Right." I look at what the side says. Across the entire thing, in huge capital letters, it says SHEEP SHEPHERD.

This is uncool. "Maybe I need to rethink this, and writing on my truck wasn't part of the deal. Mannequin parts or not."

"Help me, Obi-Wan Kenobi. You're my only hope." Rory puts her hand on my shoulder and leans close, but not too close. Of course she smells amazing.

"My parents will flip if they find out I'm hauling sheep in my truck."

Rory rolls her eyes. "First, how will your parents find out? Second, your parents will flip if they find out you're doing anything like what we're doing, so why should sheep make it worse? And technically speaking, all Epic can get is tickets for dumping unless we damage property, and we won't do that. It's not like we're murdering someone. What we're doing is barely illegal."

David hops into the passenger side, followed by Rory. I just stand there. This isn't wise. SHEEP SHEPHERD. Live animals that might pee and poop in my truck. The cops have already called my house. They know Epic's back in town. Seeing my truck could make the cops pay attention, and they might make me tell them stuff, and then Epic's career would be over and it would be my fault. But when the hell will I ever have the chance to do this again? Epic's in books. In the papers. In a museum. Someday I want my art in those places, too. Theoretically, what I'm doing with Epic is my first apprenticeship. I can't blow it now.

After fifteen seconds, Rory opens the door and pops her head out. "You coming? This is going to take a while." She smiles that get-over-here-big-boy smile. "You know it's going to be awesome, and you'll be a part of it." Another smile.

I get in. Of course I do.

We drive west of the Cities, not far out, to a huge farm. The place is dark except for a yard light, but there's a person standing by the road at the beginning of a really long driveway.

"Stop here." Rory rolls down her window and waves out of it.

The person opens the back door and gets in. I realize it's Jess Wistrom, a guy from our Spanish class.

"Hey, Jess!" Rory is bubbly and charming.

"Hi, Rory." He's already under her spell, judging by the look on his face. "Who are these guys? Thought you said it was just you." The disappointment in his voice is hard to miss.

"That's David." She points, and David waves. Tonight he's got on his utilikilt. Maybe there are tools in a few of those pockets. "And you know Frankie. His parents will kill him if his truck's full of sheep poop!" She laughs.

Jess brays like a donkey, which I think is laughing. "I can't promise what the sheep will do. Drive down there."

We follow the long, long lane to a pen at the back of the farm. In it there are probably thirty sheep. Sheep are big. There's no way twenty of them will fit in my truck.

Jess is studying the size of my truck, clearly thinking the same thing I am. "We can probably load up four or five at a time, plus a couple of bales of hay to feed them."

"But that's four trips, at least!" I look at my watch. Eleven o'clock. "And then we have to make each piece. We'll get caught because it will be daylight before it's all done."

David is calm. "Your job is to move sheep. Rory and I are going to set up the TVs, paint the sheep, and match the TVs to the sheep as soon as you bring them to us."

"There's matching involved?" Then I register the other idea. "Paint the sheep?"

"You know what I mean by matching. Get them tethered in front of a TV when they get there. That's all."

"How are you going to paint them?" I'm not going to be responsible for blue and purple sheep.

"Epic wants us to write TELL US WHAT TO DO on each sheep. With water-based paint, of course." Rory looks like what she's just said is totally, completely normal, and that the sheep will have zero issue with it. "So what are we waiting for?" She's clapping her hands. "Time to make sheep sculpture."

The sheep are super calm, which surprises me. I had expected them to be really obnoxious, but Jess puts down some boards to make a ramp and takes them, one at a time, into the back end of the truck. Then he throws in a couple bales of hay, and presto, I have five sheep and their food for the night? weekend? in the back of my formerly clean truck. Hopefully the hay will keep them from getting jostled around too much. But they're pretty packed in.

We buckle up for the ride to the city, and Rory turns to me. "See? This is phenomenal!"

The sheep are reacting to the trip, pawing and baaing and making little round pebbles of poop. Then I hear liquid hitting the bottom of the truck bed, and I cringe.

"You two are going to help me clean this truck. You hear me?"

David is hanging on to a strap in the back, trying to stay out of the sheep piss and looking worried the sheep will eat him. "We hear you. Epic owes us."

We get to Loring Park and there's a white van waiting by the entrance. A shadow in a hoodie waves at us from the curb and points to how we should drive in on a service road that runs through the park. I nod at him, cool as a cucumber, since of course I pass famous street artists all the time. Really I'm sweating rivers.

I follow his finger, and we get the sheep all set up with dog leashes that Rory finds on a picnic table. Then Rory and David stay with Epic to help him paint sheep and lay out TVs. I go back to the farm and Jess is waiting for me. He's a big burly-looking country boy in a gray T-shirt and Wranglers.

"This your farm?" I take the towel he hands me, and we swamp out the worst of things, preparing for another round.

"My grandparents own it. They'll be OK, as long as the sheep come back soon."

"Oh man." It hasn't even occurred to me. "How will we get them back here?"

Jess grins. "Rory figured that one out. She's guessing the cops will call whoever owns them, so I taped my grandpa's phone number on them. Grandpa has a big trailer, so he'll come and get them."

He shows me the underside of a sheep. In blue tape, on the sheep's belly, is a phone number.

"Are you going to tell him you're the one who let them go?"

"No." He shrugs. "Why should I? They'll come back in one piece. Stuff is there for the borrowing. That's why stuff exists."

"But this isn't stuff, it's living animals."

"Same difference, isn't it?" He slaps a sheep on its ass to get it moving.

More sheep shuffle up the ramp—this time there's six of them, because one is a mother-baby pair. As soon as the baby gets in the truck, it starts crying, and it cries all the way to Loring Park. Rory and David have a hard time catching the baby once we get them out into the park, but soon it's tied onto its mom's leash, happily nursing and chewing on the grass by its TV.

I go back two more times to Jess's farm, and soon we have twenty sheep in Loring Park. Fifteen of them are grazing on long dog leashes next to televisions of different sizes. On their sides, in red paint, they say TELL US WHAT TO DO. The fronts of all the TVs say THINK THIS WAY. The sheep do their sheep thing and ignore the TVs. Close to the entrance of Loring Park is a pyramid of televisions with five sheep staked around it. On those TVs, Epic painted LET US LIGHT YOUR WAY.

It's pretty excellent, even if the floor of my truck is completely messed up. That's what I like about art—it's a chance to talk about what bugs you—and I think it's bullshit we have to pay so much attention to screens. And nobody can shut Epic up, just because of how he works. You'll never know what he'll do or where he'll do it, or whether it'll be funny or really important or something in between.

When I was in middle school, he wrapped a bunch of construction equipment in paper and bows and made them look like giant presents. Goofy and interesting, though not world-changing. Then a couple years ago, he

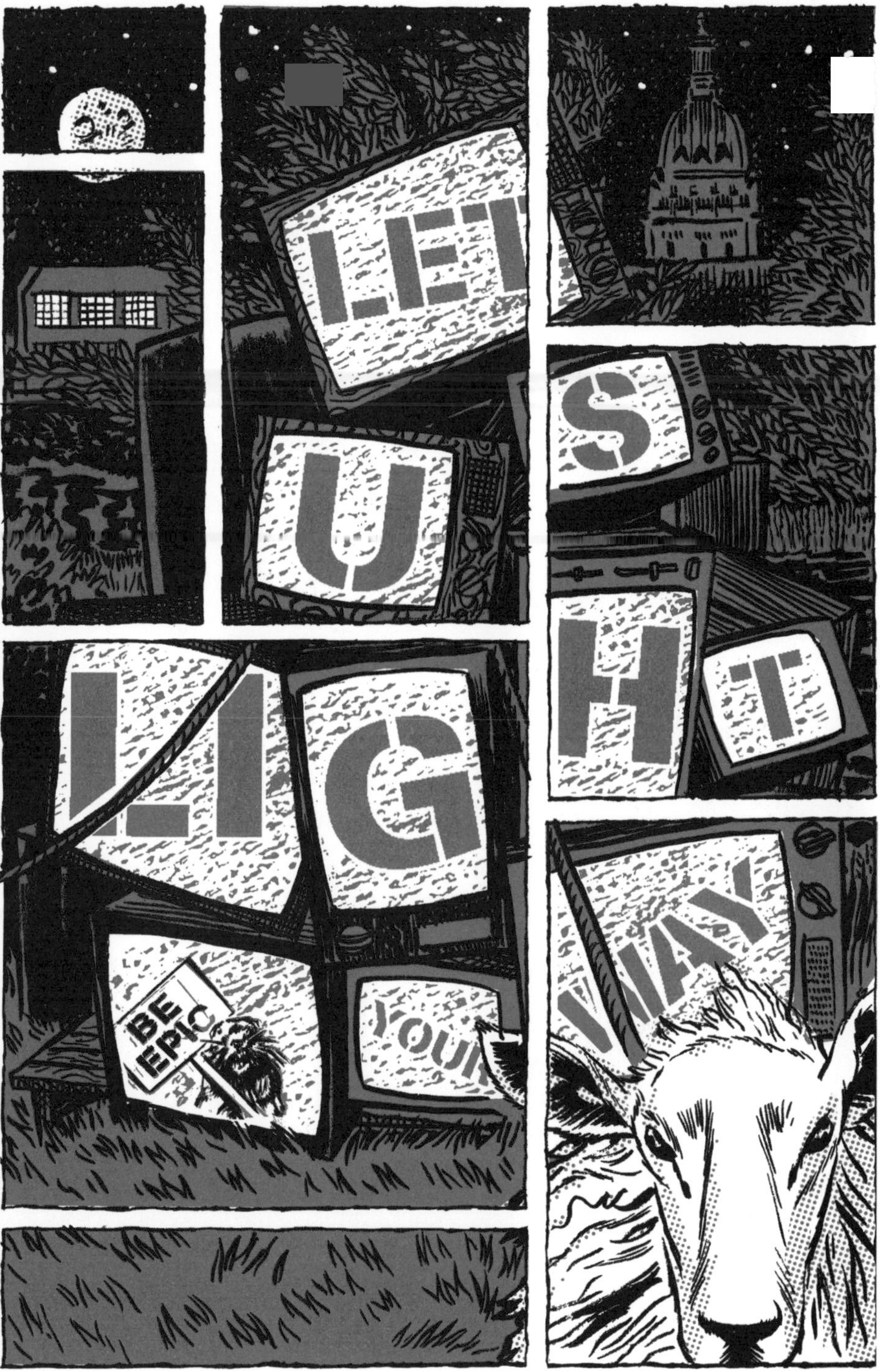
LET
US
LIGHT
YOUR
WAY
BE EPIC

collaborated with a street artist named Breeze to do road signs along the interstate that was close to an Indian reservation in South Dakota. You expected each sign to tell you what town was coming up—they looked like regular direction signs—but instead, they gave you horrible facts about poverty, suicide, and alcoholism, and pointed you toward the reservation. That piece mattered.

Whether the TVs and sheep are world-changing or not, it doesn't matter. Everything's done, and it's four fifteen, so I'm later than late.

I go to the car wash by myself, so I don't have to deliver David and Rory to the garage and make myself even later. Epic sends me two rolls of quarters through David so at least I don't have to pay for it. Hosing out the back of the truck is so gross I can't even tell you. Then I scrub off SHEEP SHEPHERD. When I get home, it's five o'clock, and the entire house is blazing with light, though the ballroom is dark. I'm glad for that.

Dad is in the living room, in his pink bathrobe, no bustier or fishnets, which is good. It's hard to talk to him when he's in costume, because he looks about as far from a dad as a dad can appear. Lou is sitting with him, too. They both seem very concerned.

"What?" I check my phone. Nothing but ten texts from David—pictures of the sheep in their various spots, plus some of the big pyramid. Nobody better ask to see my phone. "Someone die? Nobody texted me. I know I'm late."

"Nobody died." He's not the kind of guy to blow his cool, but he's getting close. I've only seen him blow up once, and that was when someone painted the words FAG HAG on the driveway. My mom laughed, but my dad was insanely angry.

"Then what's wrong?"

"Where've you been?" He's fiddling with a pack of cigarettes, fighting the urge to light one. Lou must be right about the other night.

"Out with friends."

My dad frowns. "You don't have friends."

"WHY DO PEOPLE KEEP SAYING THAT? I do too have friends." Now I'm pissed.

"No, you don't," Lou chimes in, and she sounds very sure of herself. "You don't like other people."

"I like some people, and I was with Rory and David, my FRIENDS. We were by Loring Park." Oh shit. Why did I say Loring Park? Shit. SHIT.

"Cruising?" There's a new look on my dad's face. Loring Park is a premier cruising spot for gay men in the Twin Cities. "You're gay? Why didn't you tell us?"

"What is this, Make Assumptions About Frankie Night? I'm not gay, and we were just hanging out."

"If you were by Loring Park, why did a state patrol officer see you on Highway 212 about two this morning? He said you were speeding but he didn't bother to catch you, because you were only three miles over the limit. When he punched in your license plate number, our phone number came up. As did the fact that they called us last week when they thought you might be involved in putting eyes around the state capitol."

Crap. "We were just goofing off down there, driving around, then we got coffee at Whole Latte Shakin', and then we decided to get out of the city." What a dumbshit. I'm a sucky liar. "You know, and look at the stars."

"Stay in town. Don't speed." My dad is serious and very pissed. "You and your friends can do regular stuff in the city. You can also come home before five in the morning. Do you get it, Frankie?" He turns to Lou. "How about you?" It's crazy to watch him be all hostile in his pink bathrobe.

"Got it, Daddy. But you know I don't stay out that late." She smiles, and I see my dad relax.

"Just so you know." He turns to me. "Frankie? Do you get what I'm saying?" He's daring me to push it, I can tell.

"I get it. Where's Mom?"

"In bed. Where you need to be. No more staying out." He leaves, looking over his shoulder. "I mean it. Go to bed."

Lou looks at me once he's gone. "If you don't have friends, why do you stay out so late?"

"I HAVE FRIENDS. Rory and David. And the rest of it is none of your biz, sister."

"Yes it is. You're getting me in trouble when I'm not even doing anything, just because they're mad at you."

"Like they'd ever do anything to you. They love you."

She preens. "Of course they do. You, on the other hand, are a low-life dickweed of a guy who needs a clue."

"You are a flipped-out asswipe of a girl who needs a hobby." I go to the kitchen, grab some Pop-Tarts, and stomp up the stairs.

Now it's noon on Sunday. Once I make it into the kitchen, Lou assaults me with questions.

"Did you see Epic's new piece in Loring Park? Is that why you were down there?"

"He's got new art?" I am innocent as can be. Must have been stuff on the morning news.

Lou gets her laptop. "Here." Her hands are shaking when she gives it to me, and she won't look at me. She disappears as soon as I take it.

Sure enough, there's Epic's piece, with shots from a helicopter and everything. The sheep look bored as hell, just grazing by their television sets, and Epic was nice enough to give each of them some water with their hay, so the farmer can't say Epic was abusing them.

The news guy is laughing, standing next to a cop, and he makes some comment about how Epic always gets it right. The cop frowns. The news guy sees the frown and asks the cop for a statement. The cop doesn't hesitate: "We just want the public to know that bringing livestock into the city is dangerous and a hazard to others, plain and simple."

News guy: "How can livestock be a hazard? They're just sheep."

Cop: "We take Uncle Epic very seriously. We've alerted police forces around the Twin Cities to keep an eye out for any suspicious art activity. That includes flash robs. And sheep can be a hazard. Uncle Epic is a hazard." And he stomps away while the reporter grins after him.

Epic's probably laughing his ass off.

Lou comes back in the room, looking slightly less jumpy. I hand the laptop back to her. "I love it. Must've happened after we left to look at the stars." I keep my voice light. The flash rob mention must be why she's twitchy.

She rolls her eyes. "TVs and sheep? Epic is smarter than that, isn't he? Or do you think Epic's a she?"

"Good question." I keep my face neutral. "I think Epic can be whoever Epic wants to be. You know why he's epic?"

"No." She studies the computer. The front screen of the video is a still of a sheep chomping grass. "And I don't care. I wonder if Epic and Miss Vixen know each other."

"Here's why Epic is epic: he's unpredictable, funny, and socially aware. You are none of these things."

"Seriously. Do you think Epic and Miss Vixen know each other?" Lou's not giving it up.

"An excellent question." I try to sound serious, but I mostly sound goofy, because they do know each other. Kind of.

Lou hears the laugh in my voice and looks up fast. "You know something." She's digging into me with her eyes.

"Not a thing."

"You said you were by Loring Park and Uncle Epic's piece had to have taken a while to set up, so you had to see something. You swear to me on Ramona that you don't know him?"

"Look, I didn't want to tell Dad, but we were at the Pleasure Palace, buying donkey porn to leave on Principal Mackowski's car." The Pleasure Palace is a sex shop by Loring Park. Lou's mouth drops open. "Speaking of Ramona, I'm glidin'. See you later, pain in the ass."

I rescue Ramona from her place among all the shoes at the back door, and we jet off in the April sunshine. I will not swear falsely on her, but I didn't really lie to Lou, because I actually don't know Epic. All I know is he's a human who lives and/or works in a big garage in Minneapolis, sort of near Lake Calhoun, and we had one conversation involving my voice and a light switch. That's it.

My phone vibrates. I look at it without falling off of Ramona, which took me a while to perfect.

Did you see the piece on KALT? It's David.

Amazing. Is E happy?

David sends about six emoji, which makes me laugh. **The farmer came for his sheep around ten. Big-ass truck. Next time we need to move livestock, we hire him.**

Good. My truck still smells like sheep. If anybody pokes their head in there, I'm big-time busted.

Freaky Guy at Kwiky Pik is your work, isn't he?

Of course he knows it's mine. **Who wants to know?**

Just checking. He's really good. I'm going to say he's mine.

And he would. **Don't you dare. This is how I get back at my soul-stealing harpy of a sister.**

HA!

I glide to the Kwiky Pik, just to check on him. But Ghoulie Carter is gone.

I am dead. My mind zips back to the cop: *police forces . . . Twin Cities . . . suspicious art activity.* Why would cops ever give a shit about a mannequin at a convenience store? They might think it's stupid, but not suspicious.

Whoever took him left his face and his shoes. The face is tacked up to the wall, not far from the bench. His shoes are under the face, where his feet would be, if he had feet, and inside one shoe is a mini-football. Inside his other wing tip is a tall candle in a glass, like the Virgin Mary ones you can get in the Mexican food section at the grocery store, but it's just white with no pictures on it. Tied in the laces of one shoe is a tiny yarn pom-pom in Henderson High School's colors—green and white.

I take a picture and tweet it with Miss Vixen's account: **Bring back the body! Mannequin parts are on loan. But thanks for leaving the face and shoes.** Maybe someone will listen.

Frak. I have to get that body back, or Epic will find an anonymous way to kill me, as he should. I told him I wouldn't hurt his stuff. Losing it is the same thing as hurting it, isn't it? And mannequins can't be cheap, which means I'll be buying replacements if Ghoulie Carter doesn't come back. FRAK.

Sunday night at Pizza Vendetta. Geno is throwing down crust like you can't believe, because we're hopping. Nobody likes to cook on Sunday night. Tons of people are wandering in and out—mostly it's families, but there are a few people on dates, and kids from about six different high schools. I'm just putting Vs on pizza, Vs on pizza, Vs on pizza, and wondering how much a mannequin costs. Gotta Google it. I am dead.

Lou comes in with Brittany Serger and another buddy, Lindy Hayworth. They're laughing and giggling, doing their theater girl things. I see Carter Stone, who's been here for a while with his family, give Lou a death stare. I wonder if he recognized his nose on Ghoulie Carter.

I make pizza and mind my biz.

Pretty soon, Lou comes up to the counter. "So I need a pizza."

"Ask your server. I just make them." The one I'm working on is going to a couple on a date over in the corner. They're looking into each other's eyes like they'll die if they don't locate the bottom of each other's retinas in the next five minutes. They've ordered the Pepperoni Zamboni, which I invented after the Pepperoniangelo fiasco, just to make Geno feel like I hadn't entirely wasted my sculpting experiment. A Zamboni cleans an ice rink, so a Pepperoni Zamboni pizza means the pepperoni goes all over the pizza, like it's ice, and then I build a Zamboni-looking thing out of pepperoni and toothpicks. Usually I make a few for the freezer, but this time there aren't any, so I'm busting my ass and making a Zamboni on the spot, and the stupid-ass thing mostly looks like a bulldozer.

Lou's still standing there when I'm done with the Zamboni.

"I'm trying to work here."

She points. "Brittany wants a pizza, too."

"I said, talk to your waitstaff. Hey, Jen!" Jen's the Sunday night server. She's in college at the U of M and she takes zero flak.

She's at a booth to the right of my counter, and she turns around and gives me the finger, very carefully covered by the side of her order pad so the customers don't see. "Right away, Frankie." Her voice is dripping poison.

Lou gives me a huge grin. "Lindy bet me I couldn't get her to flip you off. I win." And she flounces back to her table, where Brittany and Lindy are laughing.

I could be mad, but I don't have time. Jen finishes at her table and walks close to the counter where I'm trying to position the Pepperoni Zamboni. "You yell at me again and I'll do more than flip you off and win Lou another bet."

"Yes, ma'am." There's nothing else I can say. Too many pizzas backed up and too much to risk if she's mad at me. Waitstaff can make my life hell.

I hear Lou's laugh. I am a peaceful guy, but I want to punch her in the mouth. Miss Vixen will strike again soon.

The pizzas get made, and Geno sighs. "I love this business, but sometimes, not so much." He claps me on the back. "Pepperoniangelo, you're a champ."

"Thanks."

"Now get your ass back to work." Three more orders have shown up from Jen, plus two from Ellen and Sammie, the other two waitstaff tonight. Ellen and Sammie are from Henderson High, too. I heard them getting drinks for customers and talking about Miss Vixen and Ghoulie Carter. Good.

Carter Stone gets up to leave, but he deviates to Lou's booth while his family goes outside. He leans low to her, and I can't see his face, but I can see hers, and it's both horrified and ashamed. He stomps out the door after he leaves their booth, and Lou bursts into tears. Brittany puts her arm around her, and Lindy reaches across the table to them. Lou covers her face in her hands.

My guess is Carter recognized more than just his nose on Ghoulie Carter's face.

Evidently Miss Vixen's first strike was more successful than I thought. I glance over at Lou again. Still crying. Which I should feel bad about, I suppose. Does everyone get more adorable when they cry? Lou's nose gets red right along with her eyes, and she's sobbing on Brittany's shoulder. So sweet. Everyone probably wants to comfort her. Go away, sister. No weeping allowed in my presence.

Then Rory comes in. And she's with a guy I don't know. She looks like she's above it all, like a cat who's gotten plenty of cream, but the guy seems oblivious to the fact that she's not into him or into being at Pizza Vendetta. He's practically drooling on her. They sit with Rory's friend Nina, who's an *artiste*. That's what she calls herself: an *artiste*. She's taken every art class Henderson High has, and she's planning to go to the Minneapolis College of Art and Design, which is a great school, but she'll be outclassed in two seconds. All this information was in her bio in the end of the year exhibit at school—and her work is sexy male alien life forms sneaking through cities and big eyed manga girls with machine guns. Whatever.

The guy looks like all his earthly ambitions have been fulfilled, now that he's sitting with Nina and Rory. Like a dumbass, he puts his arm on the top of the booth, which then looks like he's putting it around Rory, and I see her cuddle up to him the tiniest bit, all the while pretending not to look at me, while I pretend not to look at her. We're our own little comedy of errors, because she knocks over her water about ten minutes later, though not on purpose, and Jen has to clean it up, swearing under her breath, and I forget to put mushrooms on a pizza, so the customers curse out Sammie, then she comes over and swears at me, not under her breath but not loud enough for Geno to hear. What a lovely way to spend a Sunday night. Shouldn't all these people be home getting ready for Monday?

I keep making Vs, and start checking each order very carefully so I don't forget stuff. Out of the corner of my eye, I catch Rory looking at me again. I smile, almost involuntarily, and she smiles back.

What the hell does she want from me? Why are girls like that? Do you ever really know if a girl likes you? Rory's one of those thousand-piece puzzles, and I'm the dumbest puzzle putter-together ever.

Lou and Lindy leave with Brittany once they've eaten their pizza. Lou's tear-stained face is long past cute, and is now just ugly and stressed, plus her makeup is a mess, all of which is perfectly OK with me. Rory and her guy leave not too long after that. She blows me a kiss over his shoulder, and Jen sees. She's bringing me trays of dirty dishes and handing them over the partition. I hate it when she does that.

Jen drops a fork on my hand, on purpose. "She's a bitch. Don't fall for that crap." Her hair, which was up on her head when her shift started, has halfway fallen out of its knot and is now in her face. It's been a long night.

"You don't know if she's a bitch or not."

Jen's threatening to spill her tray of dishes on me. "When I went to clean up her table, she said 'Thanks, service wench,' and she laughed."

That's pretty bitchy, but I'm not going to tell Jen that.

"Maybe she was just in a bad mood." I grab the tray before the dishes fly everywhere.

"If she sits at my table again, I'm sending her to someone else's section." Jen blows me a kiss, just like Rory did, then glares at me and walks off to clear more tables.

Bitchy or not, I tingled a little when Rory did it. Jen's doesn't count.

We clean up, make a few more pizzas, and get out of there by nine forty-five. When I make it to my truck, David is standing there with a longboard in his hand. He's got on an ankle-length black skirt.

"If you're gonna represent for the skirt-wearing dudes of the world, why not be stylish? That's saggy."

He glares. "Everything else was in the wash. What do you care?"

My mind flashes back to him being tripped in the cafeteria. "Where were you earlier? I saw Rory."

"Yeah, she was torturing Ethan. He lives by her, goes to Plymouth Christian." David sighs. "He's stupid to even try."

"She likes them that way, doesn't she? Dumb and easy to manipulate?"

"Exactly. And she'll do the same to you if you're not careful."

"I'm dumb and easy to manipulate?" He didn't really say that, did he?

"I guess that's for you to decide. Rory might like you for more than just your truck, but she might also just want to mess with you." He holds the longboard out to me, like an offering. "Will you teach me?"

I'm pissed. "Right now? It's Sunday. I've got homework." Why should I teach anyone who says things like that? And he's just a kid. A freshman. But in the back of my head, I also know he's wise about Rory—just like he said, she might want to mess with me. But I also might not care.

The skirt-wearing eighties owl sighs. "Do you really want to do homework?"

Good point.

"And I brought you something." I can't tell if he's blushing, since he's standing in a shadow, but it's possible. He hands me a manila envelope with something bumpy inside. I open the flap and slide out the bumpy thing to find a flat canvas covered in little bits that look like beans.

"Seed art. Rory knits, I do this." He sounds a little embarrassed.

It's a sheep, tethered to a TV. The TV says FRANKIE IS EPIC.

My mouth starts running, because I'm so surprised. "Pretty sure this is the goofiest gift anyone's ever given me. Thank you. I'm definitely not as epic as Epic, but maybe someday. I'm going to hang this up in my workroom."

Honestly, it's pretty cool. There might be ten different types of seeds on it, and it's got to be hard to get all the colors and textures in the right places.

"Yeah. Sure." He's moved out of the shadow, and under the parking lot light, I catch a glimpse of the red in his cheeks.

"Thanks again." Do guys flirt in the same way girls do? I am clueless to the ways of human mating behavior. And I've never had a guy flirt with me before. It feels . . . nice, I guess, though I don't know what it's like to flirt with dudes. It might be less complicated than flirting with Rory. Maybe.

We go to my house to get Ramona and drop off the truck. Then we hit the street. David sucks for a long time, then gets the hang, and we glide the neighborhood for another hour, floating in and out of the streetlights, observing the world. I try not to think about Ghoulie Carter's missing body. The neighbors two houses north of me just had a kid, and the husband is up rocking the baby and reading his Kindle. The neighbor across the street and three houses south is having sex with her boyfriend on their deck under a blanket. We see a raccoon in the next-door neighbor's yard, chowing on an apple core. He barely spares us a glance, because his apple is way more interesting than boys floating by.

It's surprisingly OK to have a friend to longboard with, even if that friend might want to be more than friends.

When we get home, my mom and dad are just getting back from Dad's regular Sunday-night rehearsal. They're in the kitchen, drinking a cup of tea at the table. My dad's still got on his bustier and fishnets. My mom is wearing her fedora.

"Mom, Dad, this is David Carlson."

My mom stands up to shake his hand. "Good to meet you." She's not in costume, just the hat, so she looks a little more like a mom when she smiles, a little less like Sinatra in the club.

"Same." He's polite, but his eyes aren't too wide until he really looks at my dad.

"Nice to meet you, David." In his heels, my dad is probably six foot six, and he towers over us. His deep voice doesn't necessarily go with the bustier.

"You too. Um. Sir." He looks at the floor, because he's blushing again.

"I have to take David home. See you in a bit." I grab my keys off the table.

As soon as we're in the truck, David starts talking a mile a minute. "Those are your parents? I've seen both of their shows, and they're amazing! Your dad is the best Frank-N-Furter that place has, way better than the regular guy."

"Um, thanks, I guess. You should tell him. Where do you live?"

"Right down the street from Pizza Vendetta."

"This is a really random time to ask, but do you get beat up a lot?" I'm not sure I want to know. "I saw a guy trip you in the cafeteria the other day."

"You never know what's going to happen." He looks out the side window. "Sometimes I get punched, sometimes it's just a trip. Sometimes it's soup on the head. But Rory always finds them and messes with them."

"How?" This is worth knowing.

"If they're not too young, she'll spread a rumor that she slept with them and that she gave them an STD, or that they have a little dick. That kind of stuff. It's not exactly the same as beating someone up, but mental damage is still something."

"She doesn't care about her own rep, saying that stuff about STDs?"

David rolls his eyes. "Rory's all about going for broke. Haven't you noticed?"

"Remind me never to beat you up."

"I live right there." He points. It's an apartment building I've driven by approximately a million times on my way to work. "Thanks for the ride."

"Seriously, wear a better skirt next time. Represent."

He laughs.

By the time I get home, my parents are in bed and Lou's door is shut, though there's light spilling from the threshold. I hear a sobby sniff, but I just keep walking. Someone else can comfort her. Miss Vixen isn't interested.

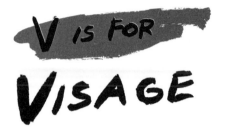

VISAGE

After I finish my homework on Monday night, I tiptoe up to the ballroom. The house is unusually quiet tonight—no show tunes from Lou's room, just my mom crocheting in the living room. My guess is *Macbeth* strikes again, and Dad and Lou are at school rehearsing their scene.

The stairs up to the ballroom creak a lot, and every time I step, I hear a syllable: *Sto. Len. Bo. Dy. Parts. Sto. Len. Bo. Dy. Parts.* There is no way in hell I should make another ghoulie, just because I can't afford to pay Uncle Epic for the mannequins—a good one is about $200, with shipping, and I don't make much at Pizza Vendetta. But there is nothing in the world I want more than to make ghoulies.

When I open the door and see Donna Russell, my heart does a flip-flop of happiness. She's so beautiful. And Ghoulie Carter was awesome, too. If the job of art is to say the things we can't say with our mouths, then Donna Russell and Ghoulie Carter are some version of the statement "Humans and monsters aren't far apart." Or something like that. I don't know. I'm not sure what my paintings say—landscapes are boring without monsters? That must be what I wanted to say with the Abominable Water-Skier—this boring and silly Minnesota mural needs a monster. Maybe I should have added a Nessie instead, but I like my water-skier. He's got a great smile.

Way back in middle school, I made two hundred stickers with an online printing service that said HIPPOS: ADORABLE DEATH MACHINES, complete with a line drawing of two cute hippos standing around with peaceful smiles. I was fascinated with the statistic that hippos kill about three thousand people in Africa every year. It's hard to tell which one's the monster: the hippo, or the human who destroys the hippo's habitat. I plastered them on Dumpsters and utility poles and corners of buildings, then I ditched the rest at Drastic Plastic, this hole-in-the-wall music store in Minneapolis, on the shelf where all the zines and free stuff got left. As a project, it didn't mean much, but it was goofy and kind of funny. And it got me interested in street art. And now I'm in Uncle Epic's crew. And this is still not my life.

What I *really* want to say with my mouth is FUCK YOU, TALLULAH BRIDGET NEUMANN. But I'll say it with ghoulie skirts instead.

Tonight is all about Ghoulie #2, also known as Monster Matt. Matt Havelock is a drama guy more than Carter is, so it makes sense that he was part of the flash rob. But Matt Havelock is also Mr. Science Guy—like a National Science Foundation Scholarship kind of Science Guy. The National Science Foundation came to our school to give him the award, and we had a huge all-school assembly. Matt says he wants to invent another kind of plastic. Robbing a convenience store doesn't sound like the most useful way to celebrate your scholarship, but what do I know?

I dig through the photocopies of faces until I find Matt's largest photo, and I cut it out. Then Sarah Taylor's eyes get stuck on his face, and Brandon Smith's nose goes on top of his. I leave Matt his mouth.

I cut out his mannequin top (blue zigzag fabric from the cushions of our deck chairs), then cut out green test tubes to sew onto his zigzags. With a purple marker, I draw liquid and bubbles in all of them. Maybe one of the test tubes has his new plastic formula in it. The skirt fabric is polka dots, which actually kind of goes well with the zigzags, since the fabrics have similar colors. They might let me on *Project Runway* after all.

When I dig around in the closet for more tulle, I notice there's a huge pile of canvas at the back of the closet, some of it in a camouflage print. It looks like enough to sew three sails for a ship, the pile is so huge. When I move it to check for more tulle, I find—miracle of all miracles—a sewing machine. It's just a tabletop one, not a big one like Epic's, but it could still work.

There's a dining room table up here, our old one, so I clear a space on it for the sewing machine and plug it in. When I press on the foot pedal, the needle whirs into life, and—second miracle of the night—the machine's already threaded. I practice for a little bit on a couple scraps, then I stitch the test tubes onto the shirt pieces and sew up the sides of the shirt when that's done. My seams are a tiny bit less awful than they were on Epic's machine.

The skirt is easy to do: fabric stitched together to make a circle, then gathered onto an elastic band. Ugly as hell, but all done soon enough.

Then I've got another Big Zombie Ghoulie Man on Campus, and it's one forty-five.

When I open the door at the bottom of the stairs, the house is still really quiet. I'm not going to tempt fate by going to see where people are. Monster Matt and I slowly, quietly make our way down out the door and to my truck.

Then I realize I forgot to grab a mannequin stand, so I situate Monster Matt in the passenger seat and race back inside to the ballroom. I must have thumped too hard on the stairs, because when I come back down and out into the hallway, Lou is there.

"What were you doing in the ballroom?" She's rubbing her eyes, like she's been asleep.

"Nothing . . . just . . . thought I heard a noise upstairs. Went up there to smack the raccoon on the head." I wave the mannequin stand around like it was a sword, hoping she won't ask what it is.

"Oh." She yawns. "Don't wake Mom up. She's got a migraine."

"Where's Dad?"

"Sleeping, too. He went to bed when Mom did, like at nine." She walks back to her room. "Shut up and go to bed."

"Yes, boss." I salute her and put the mannequin stand behind my back while I do.

"Not kidding, ignoramus. I need my sleep."

"Of course, Your Majesty."

She shuts her door just a little harder than she needs to, not a slam since everyone's sleeping, but definitely not just a close.

I think of one other thing for Monster Matt, and I find what I'm looking for in our junk drawer. Now he's complete.

• • •

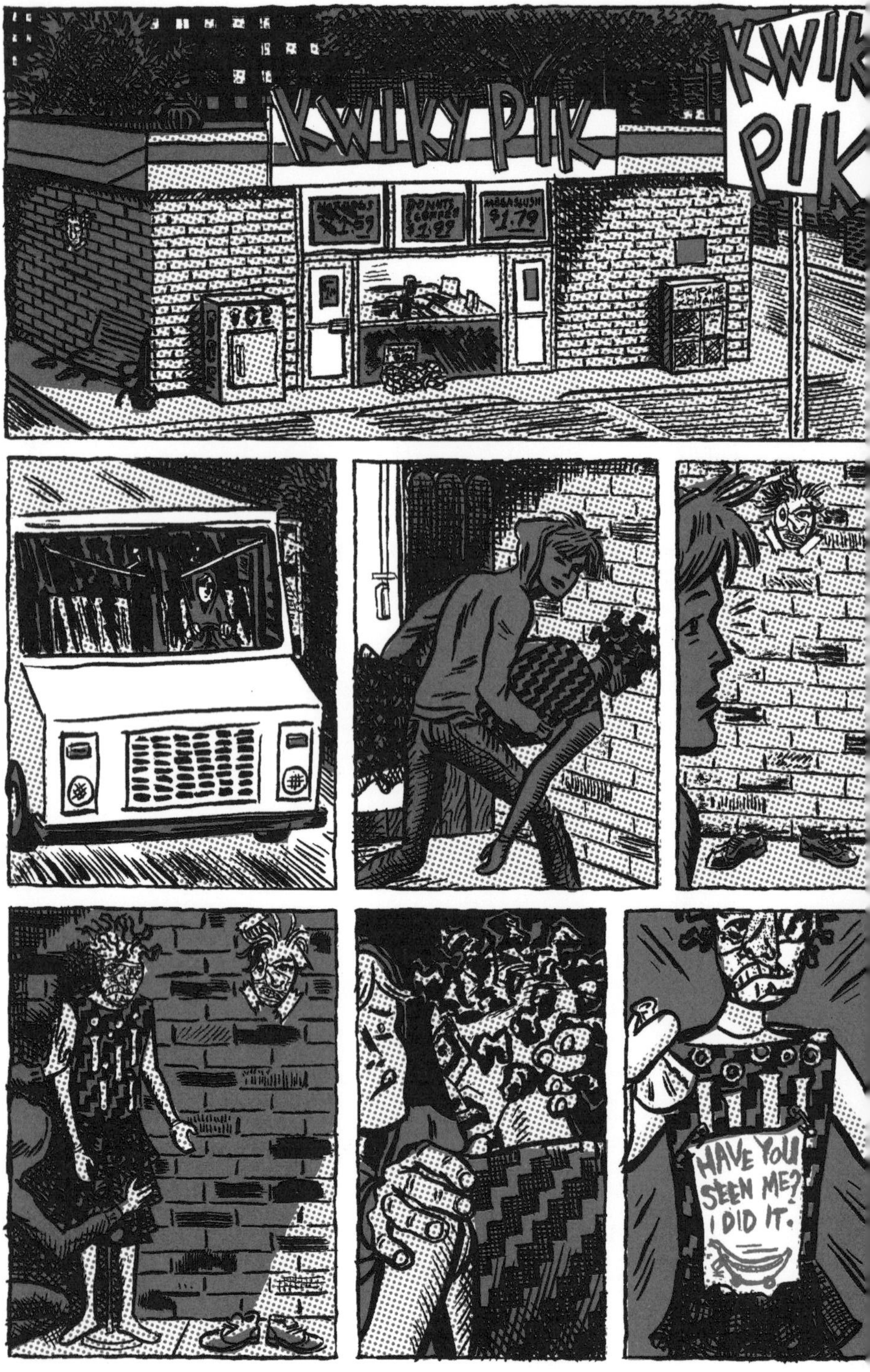
KWIKY PIK
DONUTS & COFFEE $1.99
MEGASLUSH $1.79
HAVE YOU SEEN ME?
I DID IT.

It takes me a few minutes to get him arranged right, but then Monster Matt is settled in, and Miss Vixen goes to work, tweeting pictures of her new creation. Monster Matt looks fantastic, sort of like he's having a conversation with a ghost, since Ghoulie Carter's face is floating. I love their faces. Their visages. They're sort of Picasso meets Miró meets Warhol. Monster Matt doesn't have yarn hair like Ghoulie Carter does, just newspaper strips that kind of look like dreads. The combination of their two faces and one body makes it look like Dr. Frankenstein had a really, really hard night and forgot something at home.

A Kwiky Pik guy comes out to smoke. He's surprised to see me. I wish I had a mask.

"Are you the guy who left the first one?" He lights a smoke, looking like he's not sure if he should run or clobber me on the head with the butt-holder thing.

"Maybe." I straighten Monster Matt's safety glasses, trying to be cool about being caught.

"Are you Uncle Epic?" The guy takes a deep drag.

"Nope." It's an excellent time to lie. "I work for a guy named Mixt UP, from Chicago. He's the one doing these monsters."

"So . . ." He ashes on the parking lot. "Then who's Miss Vixen?" He definitely doesn't believe me.

"Miss Vixen is just a way to throw people off the trail of Mixt UP." I am the crappiest liar ever. "You guys didn't take the body parts from the other monster, did you?"

"Nope. Haven't seen anything lying around the back room, anyway." He takes another deep drag. "Want a job at the shittiest place ever? You can have mine." He stabs out his butt on the wall and throws it into the butt-holder. "Knock yourself out, Mixt UP. Your secret's safe with me." And he goes around the corner again, back to his shitty job.

When I tweet one last pic, I make sure the Miss Vixen signs are right in front, and I add this note: **Truth-telling never looked so ghoulish. I <3 the Kwiky Pik.**

It makes me happy to imagine them standing out here, talking in their monsterish way about what's going to happen in the morning when people see Monster Matt. I hope Epic visits them.

I am crazy tired. It's 2:35.

I want Lou to know what it's like to feel bad. Sad. Misunderstood—*Frankie, this poster can't be yours! Look, Lou signed it and she says it's hers, so it must be hers. Don't be so jealous.* It's her time for unhappiness.

Yes, I really am the world's worst brother. But you do the crime, you do the time. Did they really think the world would ignore a bunch of people dressed like the court of Louis XIV who robbed a store with a gun? I'm just coming after them with art instead of cops.

Four hours of sleep won't be nearly enough. But Monster Matt is pretty incredible, and being tired is worth it when you've finally said what you want to say.

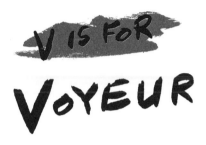

Voyeur

I can't say Tuesdays are my favorite days, but any day a ghoulie goes to the Kwiky Pik is always a good day. It's noon, and there are easily three hundred people in the cafeteria. At least half of them are talking about Carter and Matt—the ghoulies, not the real guys. I've caught a couple people staring outright at Matt, the real guy, and whispering behind their hands. Maybe I should have been more subtle than using test tubes.

In one corner, there are dudes—possible Art Club dudes—studying someone's laptop that seems to have a revolving slide show of all of Uncle Epic's pieces. I sit down kind of close to them, just to hear what they're saying, and it sounds like they're coming up with a plan to lure

Uncle Epic to TCF Bank Stadium—the football stadium at the University of Minnesota, which everybody calls the Bank. They're planning to make a banner on a bedsheet that says UNCLE EPIC, PLEASE BANK HERE. When they're not discussing how to get Epic to make a piece for them, they critique the works on the slide show. They don't like the capitol eyes. Too average, they say. Not epic.

It's hard for me not to lean in and say, *So what have you done that's epic? How hard have you worked on your street art? How many times have you called out your state government?* I get busy digging my lunch out of my bag so I don't say anything.

David sits down across from me. His skirt today is a plaid schoolgirl uniform thing—very pleated.

"Is that a kilt or a schoolgirl skirt?"

"They're kind of interchangeable, not that you'd know." He smooths his hair into its swoop. "I wanted to find you." David leans closer. "Who exactly are the creatures? Is all the gossip right?"

"It's not obvious?" I take a bite of my sandwich. "Footballs and test tubes? Remember who's in the video."

"It's not like I studied it." David looks around. "Obviously you did?"

"Gotta know the players when you're constructing a plot." My ham and cheese sandwich is about as terrible as it gets, but I keep chewing. I never eat school food. Gross.

"True." David rubs his hands together like a mad scientist. "What's your sister think about all this? Where is she?"

"In class somewhere. She eats third lunch." I choke down the rest of my sandwich. The Know-It-All Street Art Boys have now moved on to discussing the piece where Epic spray-painted FASCIST PLAYPEN on a piece of the Berlin Wall. He got in major trouble in the press for that one, since they're all protected memorials now, and it was pretty much the last time he used spray paint.

David's listening to them discuss Epic's work now, too. He looks amused, like he wants to go over and show them his Penny from Heaven and make them wet their pants, but he turns back to me. "So what do you call your monster project?"

"A vendetta." I gather my trash. "A finger-pointing, ghoulie-making, crazy-ass vendetta that may or may not embarrass the shit out of her but I don't care. I get to make art that's fun and wicked cool, and says what I want to say, which is mostly just 'screw you, Lou.'"

"Can I help? Seriously. Those ghoulies are so awesome, and I can make them even better. Please, can I help?" He looks at me like I'm going to conjure a puppy out of thin air.

"But you're . . ." I almost say, *You're way too weird for the rest of the world, just like my family, and I need a different kind of friend,* but I don't. "Aren't vendettas carried out by individuals?"

"No artist works by himself. Come on. All good artists have a crew. Epic has people all around the world. PLEEEEEEASE let me help you." He gets up, comes around to my side of the table, and gets ready to kneel. His hands are clasped in front of him like he's praying to a god. Like I would pray to Epic, if I prayed. This is bizarre.

"Your skirt's too short for you to get down on the floor, and you look like an asshole." I yank him up by his shoulder as I stand up, too. He can't make a scene, because then people will stare at both of us, and I don't need staring. "You can help if you knock it off. There's a few more ghoulies to go, plus a couple of props to make." It's never bad to have a helper.

"Thank you!" David flings his arms around me in a huge hug. The pleats of his skirt fly out from his body.

"Dude. Get off." I move him away as kindly but as quickly as I can. People are, of course, staring at us.

"OK, sorry, yeah. Sorry." He pats his skirt down and checks his hair swoop. "Thanks. When are you doing the next one?"

"Probably this weekend. Strike while the iron's hot, all that. Do you think people are curious?"

"Oh hell yes!" He holds out a fist.

I bump it, then walk toward the trash can with my lunch garbage. "I'll text you."

"Yeah! OK. See ya." David waves the goofiest wave ever seen in this cafeteria and hurries away. I have no idea why this is so exciting for him, but I'm starting to like the idea of having an assistant. Maybe he can sew.

David screeches to a stop before he gets to the edge of the caf and comes rushing back to me. "Did you hear about the other flash robs? At the Best Buy in Golden Valley and over in Wayzata at another Kwiky Pik? The Best Buy was ninjas, and the other Kwiky Pik was hippies." He laughs. "Like hippies ever robbed anything."

I frown. "Does anybody know if it's Lou's theater friends? Or somebody else?"

"No idea. See ya!" He gives me another Muppet wave as he runs off, pleats blooming out as he goes.

The art critic guys are gone, but there's a newspaper where they were, folded to an article about Uncle Epic. I scan it—it's the *Pioneer Press*, and it's about the Loring Park piece. There's a tiny mention of how the police are keeping their eyes open, following up on "any suspicious art activity in the Twin Cities." I imagine some kid drawing on his sidewalk and the cops pulling up: *Hey, son, can we have a look at your art? Are you hiding Uncle Epic in your house?*

It can go in the scrapbook.

• • •

On my way to history, I pass a group of Lou's friends, and they're talking about skirts. Specifically, Ghoulie Carter and Monster Matt's skirts. I love being a voyeur to Miss Vixen's work.

"Did you see the tulle?" Random Girl #1.

"How could you miss it? Was she there that night?" Lou's friend Amanda.

"I don't know for sure. Do you think she'd tell? Do you think she already has?" Random Girl #2. "She's horrible if she actually rats them out."

"She's not a bitch. If she was there, she wouldn't tell." Amanda.

"Maybe it's not her. But who else would it be?" Random Girl #1.

"It could be Shannon Johnson. She's always pissed at Lou for something. And seriously, it *is* a big deal. Someone *should* tell. That clerk guy almost died. I think he's still in the hospital." Lou's friend Betsy, and she's right. Mom said he'll be out in a couple days.

"Why would someone go to the trouble of making those weird monsters?" Random Girl #1. "Too much work just to out some robbers."

"Who knows?" Random Girl #2.

Amanda nods. And they wander away toward their next class.

If Miss Vixen were a real person, I'd shake her hand.

Last class of the day: Spanish. Rory. *La señorita de la bueno* smells. Why haven't we learned the word for *smell* yet?

She's knitting again, something green and blanket-like.

"What is that?" I slide into the chair next to hers.

"Long story. You can find out later, if you want to help me."

"I could probably help you."

"I thought you might." She turns and gives me a smile that makes my heart jumpy. "When do you work next?"

"Um . . ." My brain isn't processing. "Friday."

"Friday night, then. I'll be there after work." She's smiling like she means it. "It'll be great."

"Uh . . . yeah."

We're still close together, and she plants a kiss on my cheek. The sad, barren desert of my heart has been watered.

I have no idea what happens after that. All I know is that I missed telling Señor Gonzalez what the Spanish word for homework is (*la tarea*, duh) and I have extra homework.

When class is over, she packs up her knitting and gives me one more smile. "See you tomorrow."

"Sure thing." I stay far away, and let her leave the room in front of me, to minimize my chances of blushing, stuttering, or doing anything else obscenely dumb.

• • •

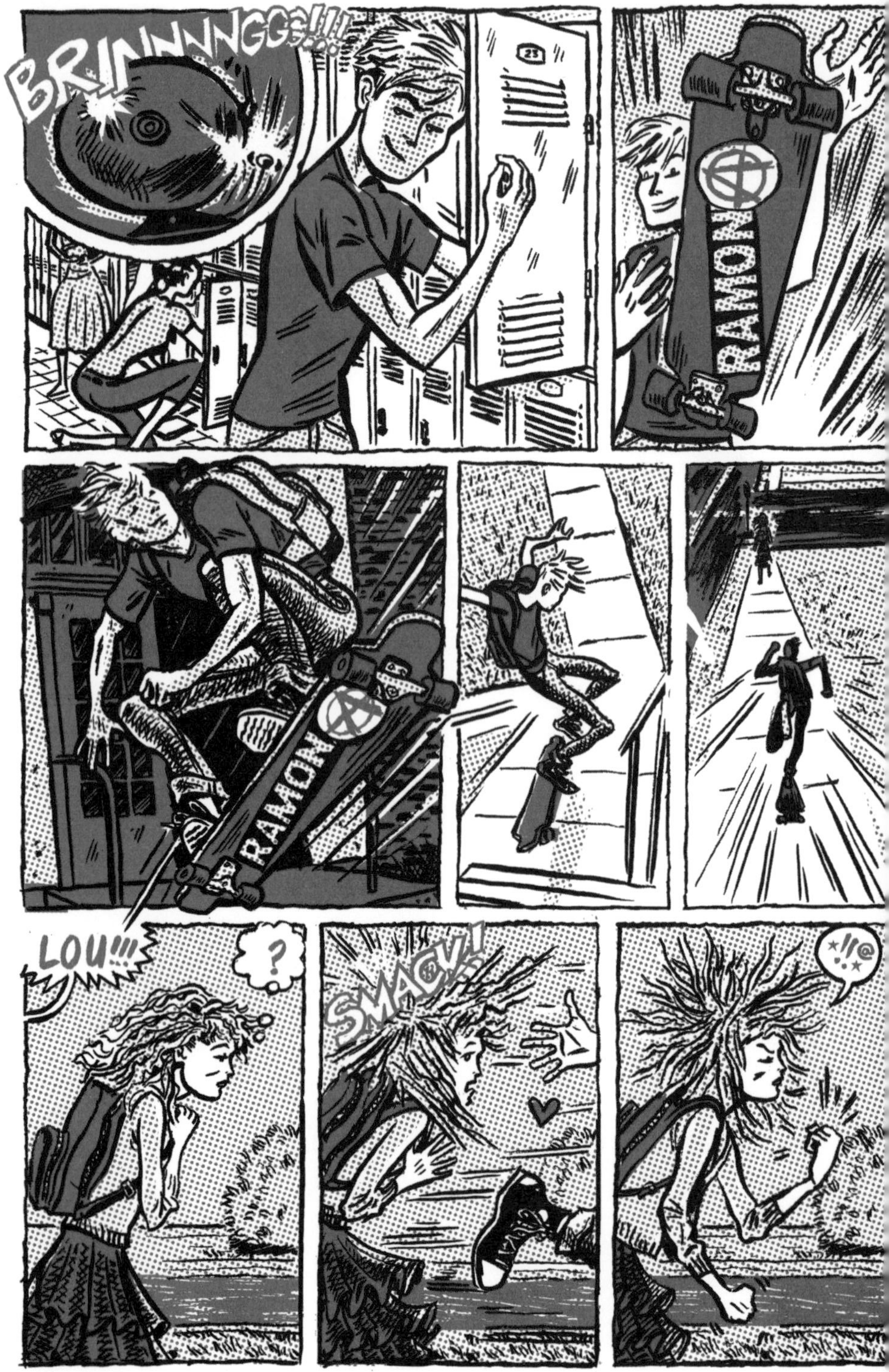
BRIINNNGGG!!!
RAMON
RAMON
LOU!!!
?
SMACK!
★!!@
●●★

"See you at home." I wave as I glide by Lou.

"Frankie, you fartface!" She starts running, trying to catch up. "Wait for me!"

"No room for two on here." And I leave her. When I glance over my shoulder, she's standing at the street corner I just flew through, looking pissed and hurt and sad.

That was mean, not to wait for her. And I feel a tiny bit guilty. But not enough to stop.

After supper and mandatory family bonding time—so gross—I do my extra Spanish homework and all the other stuff that falls out of my backpack. Donna Russell watches over me, calmly making sure I'm safe and loved.

Then I get a call from Geno, asking if I'll come in and make some pepperoni Zambonis, and I say sure. I leave a note on the table, since nobody else seems to be around, and I head to Pizza Vendetta. Dad and Lou are probably being witches.

Zambonis get made. Dough gets made. Geno gets happy. I get hours. Money gets made to replace Uncle Epic's mannequin parts.

When I'm done, I swing by the Kwiky Pik, just to see what's going on. Monster Matt is still there, and someone brought him a glow-stick necklace, which looks pretty kick-ass with the test tubes on his shirt. He's got a pair of shoes, too, but they're silver sparkly drag queen high heels. Someone also brought him a purse.

Miss Vixen goes to work documenting the scene and she tweets her thanks to her fans: **Glow-stick necklace is phenomenal. <3 u, ravers. Shoes are RuPaul amazing, too.** Ghoulie Carter frowns down from his wall, and Monster Matt is poised to take over the Kwiky Pik parking lot with his fabulousness. Somebody lit the candle that's in Ghoulie Carter's wing tip, but I blow it out. Are there flammable chemicals around here? I may want Lou to feel bad, but I sure as frak don't want to blow up the Kwiky Pik.

When I get home, everything is still and dark. It's only ten thirty, but you'd think it was three a.m., given how quiet the place is. My dad is reading in the living room. The pool of radiance from his table lamp is the only light in the house.

"Where were you?" He doesn't look up.

"Didn't you see my note?"

"Yes, but I was just checking." Dad flips through his magazine like he's looking for something specific.

"Checking on what?"

"On whether or not you were being honest. If you weren't, you would have answered me in a different way." He looks up and gives me a very fatherish stare, which fits with what he's got on—jeans and a T-shirt. It's kind of a relief when he looks like other kids' dads.

"I would have?" I have no idea where he's going with this.

"Your behavior's been a little questionable lately, with all the late nights. We just need to be able to trust you again."

"Oh." Great. I brace for a lecture.

He shows the magazine to me. "Do you want to do this? Just us guys? Right after school gets out in June."

He's actually reading a big fat brochure for outdoor adventures and he shows me a kayak trip in the Bound ary Waters, lodges and kayaks and food included. All we bring are hiking boots and bug spray. All four of us used to camp up there when Lou and I were little, and those were crazy trips—tents and battery-powered boom boxes with Broadway show CDs, everybody but me dancing and singing, plus lots of roasting marshmallows—but this is the first time he's wanted to do something that's just us.

"Um . . . why do you ask?"

"I thought it might be fun." I can see in his eyes that he's going to be hurt if I say no, but I have no desire to tramp through the woods and swat the huge-ass mosquitoes.

"Can I think about it? Won't you have to work? Why don't you ask Lou?"

"Your mom can always hold down the fort for a little while, and I can tell the theater I can't be there for a week-end. And I don't want to go with Lou—I want it to be just us. C'mon. You'd have fun, even with your dad." He gives me a bright smile, trying to show me that it's true, we really would have fun.

"Sure. I'll get back to you." And I might.

He calls after me as I leave the room. "We can stop at Betty's in Two Harbors for pie."

"Sure, Dad." I go upstairs.

Lou's door is closed and I hear music from *Wicked* inside her room. That's the show she listens to when she's sad. Or maybe she's amping herself up to be the *Macbeth* witch, I don't know.

The next set of stairs leads to Donna Russell and I pull a couple blankets next to her for a bed, then find a couple more to pile on top of me. I'm not sure why I like sleeping up here, but I do. Donna is my queen. She can watch over me all night and keep me safe from the idea of giant mosquitoes nibbling on me while show tunes play in the pine-scented air.

About three a.m. I realize I have to pee, and I'm really stiff from lying on the floor, so I go downstairs to the bathroom, then to my room. *Wicked* is still drifting from underneath Lou's door. She must be extra sad if it's been on for this long. Or she's asleep.

I don't knock and find out. Something zings through my head, something like a guilt twinge, but I'm too tired to care.

VIP

The most incredible thing happened:
We have a gas leak at school.

That means no school.

That means it's eight forty-five on a Wednesday morning and I don't have anything to do for the next eight hours.

That means it's a Frankie Day.

I took the truck—and Lou—to school because it's raining, and Ramona and rain don't get along. That means I have to bring her home, too. She looks kind of ill, actually, so maybe she needs a day off. My parents, of course, are gone.

Lou disappears into her room and *Wicked* comes back on. Aside from it being her sad music, Lou thinks she and Elphaba share some characteristics, misguided and shunned creatures that they are. It would be cool if Lou's skin was green like Elphaba's. I have to admit that.

Today was supposed to be a college fair, too. Yuck. People at school constantly want to talk about college and all that crap, you're a junior, Frankie, never too early to start finding schools, have you taken the ACT or SAT, have you thought about your FAFSA, blah blah blah, have you thought about sticking it up your ass? Today I'm going to think about art instead, which is way better than thinking about college. Today I am Miss Vixen, VIP of my own life. And my first act as Miss Vixen is to go upstairs and take a nap next to Donna Russell. Naps are never bad.

One thing I don't plan to do: dream about Rory. But she's there, and I can smell her in the dream. She smells like toothpaste and soap, all clean and beautiful, not sexy and spicy like she normally smells. How can a person smell in a dream? I don't know. Sometimes those kinds of dreams lead to those particular urges, and it's uncomfortable when you wake up, so you have to fix that situation.

After lunch, it's monster-painting time. Before I start, Miss Vixen tweets a picture of the corner of the worktable and a tiny bit of Donna Russell at the edge of the photo—just enough to be intriguing. Miss Vixen includes this caption: **Workspace of the gods, guardian angel included. More ghoulies to come, more truth to tell.** But not today.

It doesn't feel like a ghoulie day, whether I'm Miss Vixen or not.

Sid the Sasquatch is in need of some more paint, and I focus on making him look very chill while I also add villagers who are scared out of their minds. When I check my phone after Sid seems more or less done, I realize it's four thirty, and work starts at five fifteen. Drag. But it's been a good day.

I stop in the kitchen to grab a snack to eat on the way to work, and Lou's sitting at the table. Her face is red and blotchy. It looks like someone's slapped her.

"What the hell is wrong with you? You sick?"

"No." Her voice is really small. "Just a bad day."

"How could it be a bad day? We didn't have to go to school."

"Just . . . some dickheads."

Miss Vixen's doing her work, I think. "But nobody's here to bother you."

"Texts."

I see the pools of tears in her eyes. "What are they saying?"

"Just . . . you know. Stupid, mean, untrue stuff."

"So ignore them. Shut your phone off."

"It's not that easy!" She looks like someone's taken away her *Wicked* cast recording.

"As a matter of fact, it is." I take a bite of my apple. I've had one text all day, from David: **We making ghouls today?**

One text more than I normally have, so that's cool. I texted back **No**. I thought about texting Rory, but decided not to. Not after that dream.

She glares at me. "You don't know how my world works. You can't just blow people off."

"Pardon me, Your Highness, for not knowing how the royal kingdom is structured. I thought the queen could do what she wanted."

"Not when she's not the queen anymore!" Lou bursts out of her chair and runs toward the stairs, crying like someone died. Worthy of an Oscar, I swear.

SLAM. Someday she'll slam it off its hinges.

"You'll get your crown back!" I yell after her. "God knows the monarchy will crumble without you." I'm guessing the theater kids will all take her back after a while. Or she could branch out and find friends who don't do stupid things like flash robs.

SLAM. Once more for emphasis.

Just another day in the kingdom of Lou.

Lou had the TV on, and it's the early local news show on KALT. The news lady talks about Epic's upcoming show at the Walker while she shows some footage of the sheep in Loring Park, and she says people are excited to see the show and the preview pieces he's been leaving around the city. Then she slips this in: "However, metro area police forces are concerned that Uncle Epic is behind a string of flash robs—three so far—in various parts of the metro area. Each time, the robbers have been costumed. Though no direct link exists between the robberies and the artist, an all-metro task force has been set up in the hopes of finding Uncle Epic to determine his involvement."

My blood pressure goes from zero to a million within five seconds.

It's a good time to leave the house. If Lou and her idiot theater buddies put Uncle Epic in danger and ruin what I have with him, I will lose my wig.

When I'm on my break, I check Twitter to see if Miss Vixen's hiding place got any retweets or favorites. The picture got retweeted three times—not horrible—and favorited ten times. Miss Vixen also got a few photos in return—one's a table covered in fabric and yarn with the caption **My lair, full of fabric. No guardian angel.** One's a sculpture of an angel made out of fabric plastered onto a wire dress form like Donna's. The caption says **My guardian angel.**

What really blows me out? Miss Vixen has 217 followers. I don't think I know 217 people in real life. Miss Vixen has more friends than I do. And for some reason, that seems appropriate.

One last tweet comes in before my break is done, from someone named @drseussisgod, and it's the wall at the Kwiky Pik. Monster Matt is gone, which makes my stomach sink like a rock. The caption says, **Ghoulies become ghosts. Thanks for the bodies.**

I tweet back: **Stop stealing my shit!**

Nothing in return.

I look at @drseussisgod's photo of the Kwiky Pik again. The glow-stick necklace is draped over one glittery shoe. The glow is gone. Monster Matt's face is next to Ghoulie Carter's, on the wall.

The KALT lady's comments echo in my ear. *Police involvement. Epic. Flash robs.* The worker guy: *Are you Uncle Epic?* The newspaper article: *suspicious art activity.*

Oh my god. What if the cops are watching the ghoulies? They wouldn't care about amateur monster sculptures in a parking lot—would they? What if @drseussisgod is really the police? Cops don't tweet, do they?

I drive by on my way home and take one more picture and tweet it from Miss Vixen: **Plz stop stealing my stuff. Borrowed the mannequin parts cuz truth telling is expensive. Thanks.** The heads on the wall are still cool—even without bodies, the ghoulies are art, I guess.

Before I'm even out of the parking lot, there's a reply from @drseussisgod: **Tough shit.**

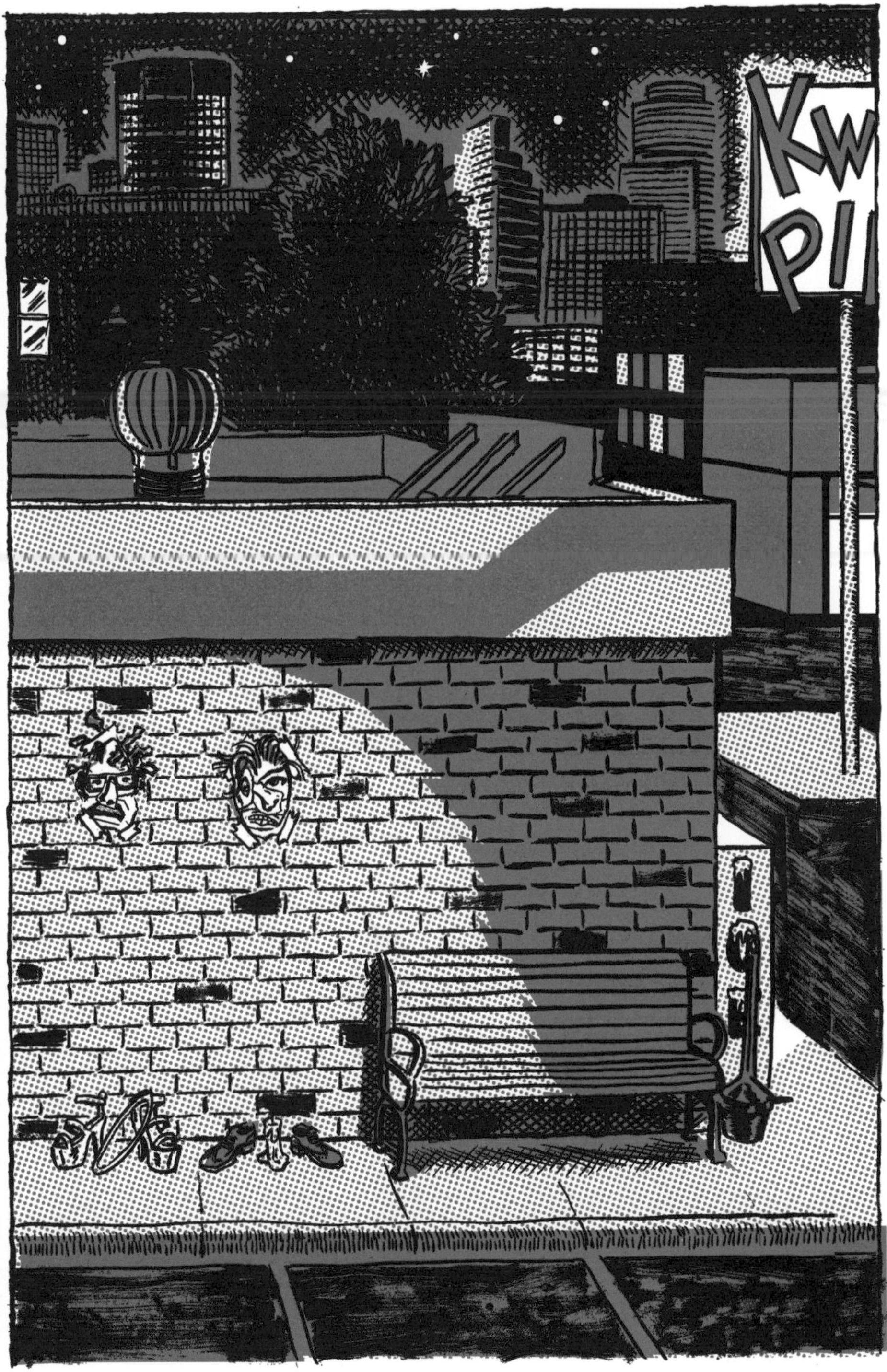
KW
PI

@ArtistMissVixen: **Why do you have to be an asshole? You a cop?**

@drseussisgod: **Not an asshole. Just an artist. Not a cop.**

@ArtistMissVixen: **Artists don't have to be jerks.**

Who does this guy think he is, Kanye West?

Maybe he's not a guy. Who does this chick think she is?

@ArtistMissVixen: **Just bring them back, plz. Costs $ to replace them.**

Nothing after that.

Epic is going to see this photo and never let me do art with him again. Or Lou's stupid asshole flash rob friends will actually get Epic caught before his show, and there won't be any more art. Both of those scenarios are unacceptable.

When I get home, my dad and Lou are in the living room. Lou's curled up in the crook of his arm, sobbing.

My dad looks up when he hears me. "Lou got kicked out of the *Macbeth* scene."

"Why?" This is weird.

"The other two girls in the scene refused to work with her. And Ted couldn't talk them into it. They wouldn't say why."

"Oh." Clear and persuasive evidence that Miss Vixen is getting her job done.

"Be kind, all right?" He gives me his stern face. I must

not be looking properly respectful of the tragedy. "This is important to her."

"Yeah. Um, sure." Lou is still sobbing. I don't even know if she knows I'm in the room.

He goes back to holding and patting her, rocking her like she was six instead of fifteen. It sounds like Lou's heart has shattered into a million tiny pieces.

Do the crime, do the time, right? And if her buddies destroy Epic in the process, then Miss Vixen is even more justified. It is unacceptable—I'll say it again—for Uncle Epic to be brought down by dumbshit high school kids. But one tiny corner of my stomach still feels sick, listening to her sob.

I get them a box of Kleenex, then go up to my room and shut the door. Quieter that way.

VANDAL

Pizza time, pizza time, Friday night is pizza time.
And tonight it's pizza and soap operas, which makes the
time go quick. Geno's behind me, saying, "Work faster,
Pepperoniangelo! Don't be gawking around! We got pies
to make!" And I'm making them. But there's too much to
watch.

Over by where the jocks usually sit, last fall's starting
quarterback for Henderson High School, Sam Ralston, is
discovering he's gonna be a dad in a few months. The girl's
got a serious bump, and he looks like someone smacked
him upside the head with a plate. I don't think she goes

to Henderson High, which may explain why he's so surprised. She isn't letting him off the hook, either.

Good luck, Sam. Hope you do the right thing, and here's your sausage and mushroom thin-crust Pizza Vendetta.

The stoner crowd seems to have a quality-control issue. Evidently somebody's been cutting the good weed from California with crappy Minnesota weed, and customers are complaining. Dewey Decker, who graduated about five years ago, has three different guys yelling at him, though how loud does anyone yell when they're stoned? It's more like a moderately animated conversation. You have to know it's an argument.

Good luck, Dewey. Here's your Monster Meat Pizza Vendetta with extra cheese—one for you and one for your three stoned worker bees—and here's some cinnamon sugar breadsticks for dessert, since the munchies can't be cured with just pizza.

Six brainy kids are having a meltdown because Marshall Geiger just cheated on his SATs. I didn't even know it was possible to cheat on your SATs. Marshall's ranked number one in our class, and even though we're not seniors, it matters a great deal to the brainy posse that SOMEONE FINDS OUT ABOUT THIS, and pronto, dammit, because we don't want a cheater being the top brain in our class, that's just not fair. This crowd is definitely arguing, and they're louder than everyone else. They remind me of a bunch of birds in a tree—squawk, squawk, squawk.

Good luck, smarty-pants kids. Here's your two veggie Pizza Vendettas, since you're all so careful about what you put in those skulls of yours and the preservatives in pepperoni upset your delicate systems.

I'm not even sure how to describe the theater kids. They're so messed up I have three different pizza orders from them. Normally there'd be one. Lou, Allison Lawson, and Brooklyn Smith—one set of flash robbers—are sitting in one booth, heads together, being super quiet. They've got something in front of them, a white piece of paper, and they're whispering. If I squint my eyes, I can almost see the dark cloud that's hanging over their table.

Sarah Taylor, Carter Stone, and Matt Havelock—the other set of flash robbers—are sitting about three booths away, though in the general theater kid vicinity, and each look they send over to Lou's booth is made of shiny daggers.

A third group of theater kids seems oblivious to the split. They're sitting in the middle between the two factions and they're all reciting lines from *Little Shop of Horrors*, which a local college is putting on. They're not paying any attention to anything but themselves.

Good luck, theater kids. Here's a pepperoni with extra cheese for the stressed flash robbers, a Canadian bacon–pineapple for the pissed flash robbers, and hamburger with black olive Pizza Vendetta for the clueless kids in between.

"Frankie! Get your ass back to work!" Geno's pissed, because my hands have stopped moving.

"Sorry. Working!" I go back to throwing down the Vs, and the high school drama goes on without me. Just your invisible neighborhood vandal, grinding his day job.

Closing-time, and everyone's gone. Lucky for me I make it out the door by eleven. Geno is nice and lets me go after I've mopped. He says he'll do dishes.

When I get out back to my truck, it's wrapped in a scarf. The whole freaking truck. But there's nobody around. It's the ice-blue-and-screaming-orange thing that Rory's been knitting in class.

"Rory! What the hell is this?"

No answer.

I walk around the truck, looking for her. "Rory, you need to come take this scarf off my truck. We can't go anywhere unless you take it off. I can't get in the doors."

"Oh, that's true." She steps out from behind one of the Dumpsters. "Duh."

"Yeah, duh." The scarf covers the truck. "How long is this thing?"

"Maybe as long as a football field? I haven't measured it."

"How long does it take to knit a football field of scarf?" This is impressive.

"I've been working on it since Christmas. And now it's, what, late April?" She's rolling the scarf up like a fire hose, and the coil is getting so big it's hard for her to carry. "I had to do it in pieces, then knit the pieces together. Open your truck."

I open the back end, and she heaves it all back there, then goes to where she was hiding by the Dumpster and pulls out five garbage bags. They're white and puffed out, like marshmallows.

"What's all that?"

"More knitting." She flashes her phone at me. "Yarn Bombers Anonymous has a website, and people post stuff through proxy servers so it's really anonymous. We're supposed to do one yarn bomb every three months, minimum, then upload our evidence, but I got an extension because this one is big, and actually more like two jobs. I've been saving up my knitting." She gives me one of those smiles that makes me think I might not be the loser I know I am while she shoves the marshmallows into the back and slams the door. "Let's go fuck with people. Gently, of course. Knitting is pretty, so nobody ever gets too pissed when you mess things up."

I do the gentlemanly thing and open the passenger door for her, and she curtseys before she gets in.

Why have I never heard of these people?

Once I'm in and buckled, I turn to her. "Where to, pretty destroyer?" Gag. Stupid thing to say.

"Our first stop is a bank." She's not even paying attention, because she's consulting a list she's produced from a jacket pocket. "The one over on Marquette Street."

When we get there, I park in the lot of the grocery store that's next door, which is hopefully outside the range of the security cameras I'm sure are all over the outside of that building. Rory pulls on a ski mask that's got a face sewn on it—eyelashes above the eye holes, a big red set of felt lips around the mouth hole, a butterfly on its cheek.

"Did you make that?"

"Yup. I'm the Butterfly Bandit—that's my YBA name. Do you like me?"

"I do."

"Stay here and wait. It won't take long. I have zip ties."

She pulls a handful of them out of her pocket and points them at me like they're a gun. "No sewing necessary."

She hops out of the back, white marshmallow bag of knitting over her shoulder, and she's running across the parking lot to the bank. I watch out the front window.

The first thing she does is wrap the outside of the ATM in a big green blanket, and she zip-ties it all together so the blanket won't come off the machine. On top of the blanket she lays out something that looks like a snake and she moves it into a shape. Then she zip-ties the snake into place, snaps photos, and runs back to my truck.

Rory pulls off her mask, and her face is flushed. She's breathing hard. "Such a rush! God, I could do this all day."

Of course she smells good—a little bit sweaty, a little bit clean, a little like fresh air. I need to think about something besides how gorgeous she is, like her brains, or the fact that she's making cool art, but god. It's hard. Ha ha, that's a pun. I roll the window down. "What the hell is the thing on top of the green blanket? The snake swirly thing?" I make myself sound normal, instead of like a worshipper gushing over a goddess.

"It spells out 'greedy' in cursive." She puts the mask on the dash of the truck and shakes out her hair. "It's easier to knit a chain of stitches and then shape it into the word instead of knitting individual letters."

"Now where?" I can't watch her anymore, because I don't have anything to put in my lap to cover up what's going on down there. Clever, socially conscious public art makes me hard.

"The bank on Jackson Street. We have four more ATMs to do, then a mission with the blue-and-orange scarf."

"Guerilla knitting, take two." I gun the truck and we go. "Good stuff. You think of it yourself?"

"Of course." She smiles. "Though I might have run it by Epic."

Rory does four more ATMs, and I wait in four more parking lots next to the banks. I have no idea if she's caught on any surveillance cameras, but I'm guessing yes. I hope their reach isn't far enough to catch the truck, too. Finally we're done, and she's panting in the passenger seat beside me, shaking out her hair one last time. There goes my art boner again.

"Ready for the finale?" She leans over from the passenger seat toward me.

"Absolutely ready." I lean back, but I can still smell her.

"Why are you doing that?" Her face looks like it's lit from inside, like she's a jack-o'-lantern. "I'm coming close to you for a reason."

If all the knowledge I have in the world was in this truck, the knowledge of what to do when a girl wants to kiss you, especially a girl like Rory, would be in a truck parked three blocks away. And I'm still not sure I want to be her latest chump, even though she's hot and smart and smells good.

I turn away, like a moron, and start the engine. "Where to now?"

She leans back and sighs, maybe pissed and maybe not. "Betty Crocker."

"Seriously?"

"Absolutely." She checks her phone. "It's one forty-five, and this one will take a bit longer. And I need your help."

Frak. How did it get to be that late? I close my eyes and make a wish that nobody hears me come in, then take a deep breath. The art world needs me. Rory needs me.

"I don't have a mask."

"Yes you do." She throws me one that she fishes out of a deflated marshmallow trash bag, and it lands in my lap, which is good. Extra coverage right about now in that spot is excellent, in fact. She continues her upload, giving me the side eye once in a while.

We get on the road to Betty.

General Mills is the largest employer we have around here, and who's one of the most famous faces of the General Mills brands? Betty Crocker, of course. A ten-foot-tall bronze statue of Betty Crocker stands outside their headquarters. She's all sixties housewife, in a cute dress and apron, and she's stirring a bowl of something. Many different things have appeared in that bowl in the last few years. My favorite was a sign that said POT BROWNIES WOULD BE HOT SELLERS. MAKE ME A MIX, BETTY. But obviously the big guns disagreed, because I've never seen a box in the grocery stores. Stupid them.

Rory's surveying the scene. "Do you think there are surveillance cams on Betty?" She looks on the light poles.

"Of course." Which makes me wonder what people see on those tapes, if people are always throwing stuff in the bowl.

She reaches in her purse and comes up with a pair of scissors. "Come in the back and help me put stuff together. Do you have a light in here?"

"Flashlight." I dig it out of the glove box and take it back to her.

"Nothing bigger?" She's unrolling the fire hose of ice blue and screaming orange.

"Nope." I watch her with the scissors. Rory is chopping the scarf into sections, some of which are about ten feet long, and some of which are maybe a foot long.

"Here." She throws me a bunch of zip ties, then hands me some of the short sections. "Make these into a puff."

"A what?"

Rory moves her hands like she's sculpting the air. "A

puff. *Like a cheerleader's pom-pom. Like a shower puff for soap.*"

"Don't be surprised if it ends up looking like something else."

She sighs without looking up. "I think you can figure it out."

She's concentrating, surveying her work, deciding where to cut things. The parking lot lights are seeping in through the window and onto her hair, which is long and dark on her shapely shoulders. The light on her hair flickers when she moves, almost like it's Christmas tinsel. She's all in black tonight, and she looks like a cross between a ninja and a ballet dancer.

Why didn't I let her kiss me? Max Ledermann mopes through my head.

Rory starts zip-tying the longer strips of knitting together. Once she's got a blanket-ish thing, she threads a white cotton rope through the top of her creation. I'm still fiddling with the little sections. It takes a while, but eventually I get a few blue-and-orange puffballs. They look pretty cool, and they're round. Round-ish.

"Ready to go?" Her piece is draped over her arm, and she's poised to jump out the back door.

"Hold on, Butterfly. We're gonna move the truck, just in case." I drive it to the farthest corner of the lot, where there are probably still cameras, but maybe not ones that can see close up. Then I throw Rory her mask, which is lying on the passenger seat. "You need this." I pull mine over my head, and immediately I'm a badass. Or so I think. Rory laughs.

"What?"

She points. "Look at yourself in the mirror."

I do, and I see a kind of crooked butterfly wing by one eye, and sort of a curlicue thing by the other eyehole, then some sort of pink lip above the mouth hole. "This was your practice mask, I take it?"

"Sure was. And you look completely silly. But let's go, accomplice."

She opens the door and starts running. I slam the door and follow, carrying the puff. The parking lot is actually pretty huge, and I feel exposed and scared, like any second a helicopter will turn a spotlight on us. Not my favorite set of emotions.

Betty's really tall, not including her platform, and I don't know if Rory forgot this, or what, but she looks concerned. She studies for a minute.

"Boost me up." She flings part of the knitting over her shoulder and points to where Betty's standing on her broad platform. "I need to reach her shoulders."

"You can't do that. She's too tall." But I boost Rory up to Betty's feet.

"Watch me." Rory jumps and scales
up Betty's skirt and gets the rope around Betty's
shoulders with one arm. She does more tricky maneuvering
while clinging on like a leaf, then suddenly Betty is wearing
a flowing knitted cape, like a bronze Wonder Woman.

She holds one hand out to me. "Toss me the puff."

I do, and she catches it, amazingly, then pitches it inside
Betty's bowl, which is shallow enough that the puff sticks
out the top, like she's holding some sort of alien stew.

"Give me your hands."

I hold my arms up to grab her, and I don't know if she
does it on purpose, but she comes down hard, and she slams
against me. I grab her tight. And then, well, we're hugging.

"Thanks." Rory pulls away, and her smile tells me that the extra-hard leap wasn't on purpose, but it also wasn't such a bad thing.

Betty now looks like a crusader for truth, justice, and baked goods made from ingredients the color of Kool-Aid. If Rory's ATMs had a social message, this one doesn't. It's just a yarn bomb. But it's still cool as hell.

I look from Betty to Rory. "Happy with your work?"

"It's fantastic." She's grinning like she just ate a pot brownie, and she clicks a few photos with her phone.

Then the headlights hit us, and we freeze. I have no idea if we should put our hands up or not, so I don't, just so I'm not a cliché. Rory does, but she's laughing.

A security guard parks about fifteen feet away from us and gets out. He's short, squatty, and maybe five years older than we are. "What's the purpose?" He points at Betty, and then at Rory. "Why did you do that to her?" He looks confused, amused, and pissed. We still have our masks on, which is a really good thing.

"Art has lots of purposes." Rory doesn't back down. "Why not make it funny?"

"Oh." He gazes at the statue like it's going to reveal the mysteries of the universe. "Deep. Are you guys Uncle Epic?"

I burst out laughing. "Oh my god, I wish. Please don't tell the cops we were here."

Rory just gives him a look. "Wouldn't you like to know? And the guerilla-knitting assault is now over." I clap, and the security guard does, too, even though you can see he doesn't know why he's doing it. She addresses the guard. "You won't be taking this down, will you?"

"Nah. It's pretty damn hilarious." And he gets back in his car and drives out of the parking lot, off to watch over some other part of General Mills besides Superhero Betty.

Rory turns back to me. "Take me to Pizza Vendetta."

"Why there?" It's 3:12 a.m.

"Because that's where my car is." She strips off her mask and shakes her hair again. Why can't she be ugly, dumb, and talentless?

We walk back to the truck and head to our cute little suburb. It takes us a while, and Rory falls asleep on the way. I watch her breathe when we pass under the freeway lights. She should be in magazines, or museums, or anywhere but inside my truck, because I am just a boring introvert artist and she is a goddess of knitting and the night.

When I turn into the lot, she shifts around.

"Wake up, Sleeping Beauty."

"Where are we?" She sits up. "Oh."

I park next to the only car left in the lot. "Do you want all your garbage bags?"

She yawns. "You can keep them to remember me by."

"Bus your own table." I hand them to her. "That's why there's a Dumpster."

"Good night." She leans in, and this time I don't lean away. It's barely a kiss, but her lips linger on mine and I feel like I'm drowning in a sea of yarn, which is soft and warm and smells like Rory.

She's gonna treat me like all those other guys. I know that in my heart. It's just her way. But I don't care.

Both my parents are waiting up for me. It's 4:10 a.m. The nuclear explosion starts when I walk in the door.

"Where the hell have you been? Why haven't you answered your phone? You can't do this anymore. We were worried sick!" My mother's screeching like a crazy woman, which is an odd combination with her Frank Sinatra suit. Why hasn't she changed?

"Answer her, Frankie." My dad is still in his bustier and fishnets, which I also don't understand. That stuff has to be uncomfortable.

I look at my phone. "There's nothing here." I show them. "Who were you calling?"

My mother looks at her phone. "Oh. Shit." She holds it out to me to show me she's been calling Lou instead.

"So why not get pissed at her? Why hasn't she been calling you back?"

"Because she's upstairs asleep! She came home crying at eleven. Where have you been? You can't do this, Frankie." My mom is shaking, she's so mad. My heart stutters a bit. Nobody wants to make their mom shake like that.

"We thought you'd been hurt or something. The cops will be here any second." Dad's trying to calm my mother down, with his arm around her.

"I'm fine. I was out with a friend. Rory."

"Were you doing illegal stuff?" My dad looks pretty convinced I was.

I think for a second, just to be sure. "No."

My mom pulls away from my dad. "If you get arrested, Frankie, it's all over for you. Keep that in mind the next time you decide to stay out all night. Your truck privileges are hereby limited. Work and maybe school. No going out. And only work and school because we're not always around to drive you, and sometimes you have to drive your sister. Otherwise I'd take it entirely." She glares at us both, even though my dad doesn't deserve it, and storms toward their bedroom, slamming her hand down on the light switch. The room goes dark except for the streetlights outside.

"You have to consider other people, Frankie." My dad's shaking his head, though I don't know if it's at me or at my mom. "We need to know where you are. You're going to have a curfew from now on."

"Pardon me?" He didn't really just say that.

"The city's too big, too much can happen, your truck is big enough to get you in a lot of trouble, and you're too young to be out so late. We'll talk in the morning. Your mom and I are tired. Have some consideration for us."

He gives me a look like I've just snapped the heels off his favorite pair of stilettos, then he glances at the window when car lights sweep into the living room. "That's the cops. Go talk to them. It's your fault they're here." He heads toward his bedroom.

A curfew? Limited truck privileges?

I can't think it through right now. I put on my I'm-sorry face and go outside.

Two officers are just getting out of their car that's now parked in our driveway, next to my truck and behind my parents' purple one. One man and one woman. They look like it's been a long night already, and they're not ready for a smart-ass high school kid.

I am as contrite as possible. "Good morning, Officers. My parents called you because they thought I'd been hurt or killed, but as you can see, I'm home now, so everything's fine." I have no idea what to say that's convincing.

The man nods his head. "Could you please go get one of your parents, son? We need to confirm what you're telling us. And we need to talk about this truck." He cocks his thumb at mine, not my parents'. My throat starts to close up.

"Just a minute, sir." I almost strangle on the words, and I'm trying not to sweat, but my armpits are suddenly soaked. I go in and knock on my parents' door. "Dad, could you come out here?"

He emerges in his boxers, pulling his pink bathrobe over him. "What's the trouble?"

"I don't know. The cops want you to say I'm telling the truth."

He frowns but he follows me outside.

The female officer starts talking. "Sir, are you Mr. Neumann? Did your wife, Bridget, call the police at approximately 4:01 this morning?" The other officer is reading from a sheet of paper, checking details.

"Yes, I'm Brett Neumann. This is my son. He's home safe now." He puts his hand on my shoulder, which feels heavy. Like it means business. Like I should tell the truth. And I'm not sure I'm going to be able to do that.

"Thank you for the confirmation. Is this your truck?" The male officer points.

"Yes, it is." The hand on my shoulder clamps down. I try not to squirm.

"We had a report of a truck like that at Uncle Epic's sheep installation. Were you in Loring Park the night Uncle Epic made his mess?" The female officer is looking directly at me.

My dad's giving me the death stare, too, and I blink, making my face look innocent. "Remember? We were in the country, looking at the stars. You got called. I told you I was at Whole Latte Shakin' beforehand, which is close to Loring Park, but I didn't tell you we were at Pleasure Palace buying gross porn to leave on the principal's car, and Pleasure Palace is close to Loring Park, too, so we were there, but we weren't there when Epic was making his piece." I end up talking faster and faster as that sentence goes on, which could totally mess me up.

"Sorry, Officer." My dad takes his hand off my shoulder, and it's such sweet relief. "He wasn't there."

"Thank you, sir. Get some sleep." The female officer sounds like she doesn't believe me, but she turns and gets back in the car. The male one raises a hand in acknowledgment as he gets in the driver's side, and Dad raises a hand in return. Then he grabs my elbow and shoves me inside, but not so hard the cops will notice.

Once we're inside, he stops and turns to me. "You'd better not be doing something stupid. And stay out of Pleasure Palace. I don't know how you got in there anyway. You have to be eighteen to go into a porn shop."

"I didn't actually go in. Tanner Castle did, and he's eighteen." I'm so glad it's dim and he can't see the red on my cheeks, and I hope he doesn't look to see if there's a dude named Tanner Castle at Henderson, because there isn't. "I'm clean. I'm not being stupid."

For the record, making art is not stupid. Uncle Epic is not stupid.

"I was seventeen once, remember. I know the special brand of dumbass a seventeen-year-old boy is." In his pink bathrobe, this statement seems pretty unbelievable.

"Yes, sir."

"Go to bed." He turns away from me and heads toward his room.

I go to the kitchen and make myself a peanut butter

sandwich. Ramona is in the corner, by the back door, and I hear her whisper, very faintly: *Fraaaaaaaaaankieeeeeeeee. It's gonna be just you and me, baby, if you don't watch it.*

I take my sandwich and my memory of Rory's kiss to my room, and I don't wake up until midafternoon. My parents are watching a DVD of *The Book of Mormon*, which has to be bootlegged from somewhere, since there's no official record-ing of the show. It's a musical I actually like, but it's hard not to like a show made by the writers of *South Park* that includes a character named General Butt-Fucking Naked.

I try and sneak by the living room when I'm getting a sandwich, but I don't make it.

"Frankie, come in here." My mom pats the couch next to her, the look on her face not really giving me a chance to refuse. I go and sit.

She looks directly into my eyes. "Nobody was kidding about limited truck privileges."

I try not to blink. "I didn't think you were."

"What's so interesting that you stay out so late?"

"Friends." I blurt it out before I even think. "I like being out with my friends." God, how dumb does that sound? But I guess it's the truth. Probably the most truth I've told them since the night we did the eyes at the capitol.

This isn't the answer she's expecting. It's all over her face. She feels sorry for me. But she pulls it together enough to get the stern mom look back. "I can understand that, but you have to be more responsible. Curfew is ten on weeknights, one on weekends. And truck limitations are what I told you last night: only school and work. So I hope your friends have cars."

David's definitely too young to drive, but Rory isn't. "I have to go to work. Anything else?"

"No." Her face softens. "We love you, Frankie. We're not asking because we're awful, and Dad and I want you to hang out with friends. We really do. But we want you to be safe, too, and you don't even know what kinds of threats are out there."

"OK." I can't bear the look on her face, or the tears in her eyes. "Gotta go."

My dad hasn't said a word the whole time, just nodded along with what Mom said. He looks almost as sad as she does. When he holds his fist out for a bump, I do it as I go past, even though it's the dorkiest thing ever.

They could be worse parents. But they could also be better. Or I could be a better son.

The most interesting thing: Lou is nowhere to be seen. Not before I leave for work. Not after I get home around eleven thirty. Very faintly, when I go by on my way up to see Donna Russell, I hear *Wicked* from under her door.

My hand comes up to knock, but I pull it back down and walk on.

V IS FOR VIRTUOSO

Sunday mornings are really quiet around here, and I have been known to make muffins on Sundays because I'm bored and because they're tasty. Today the house smells like apple pie, because the muffin mix was apple strudel. It's ten a.m. and nobody's up but me.

When the muffins are done, I put two warm ones on a plate, smother them in butter, and sit down to read the paper. Sunday papers are interesting, and this one doesn't disappoint. Two full pages of the Opinion section are devoted to Uncle Epic. One page talks about how great Epic is and how we're so lucky to have him as a Minnesota son. His pieces are socially relevant, sometimes funny, and always useful to provide a snapshot of the current cultural mood. On and on. There's an editorial from the paper, plus letters to the editor, plus an old column from the *New York Times* back when he spent a month in New York making pieces about the Iraq and Afghanistan wars in 2009. It's a whole page of Epic love. The opposite page is Epic hate, with more letters to the editor (Epic's an idiot, a fool, and a worthless has-been), another editorial from the paper, this one negative (Epic's pieces are a waste of space, they have nothing socially relevant to say, and he's a vandal), from a different set of editors, and a letter from a police chief with a box around it. The letter talks about a fourth flash rob, this time at a Walgreens in downtown Minneapolis, and it asks Epic to stop being a felon. The police chief says Epic's move into robbery is "unfortunate, and highly prosecutable." The chief also says he's spoken to the Walker's director in the hopes of convincing them not to have Epic's show. A criminal like Epic doesn't deserve a show in one of the premier art museums in the country.

The anger races through my body, so I'm instantly hot and sweaty. I read both pages again, word by word, starting with the good page, but the hatefest page makes it hard to breathe, and I just get hotter and sweatier. They're so wrong about him. It takes serious guts—and brains—to do what he does, and he's just as relevant now as he was. I try and eat a muffin, to take my mind off it, but it's hard to choke it down. Yeah, people are entitled to their opinions, but what a bunch of assholes. And the police are just idiots. Epic's been a street artist for more than twenty years. Don't they think the felony bug would have hit before now? And why would he come to town and talk people into robbing places when he's getting ready for a big show? Especially dressed as mimes, like the ones in Walgreens. Did they have to carry signs so people knew it was a flash rob? Flash robbers are idiots, and so are the police. IDIOTS.

I move the Opinion section off the stack of newspaper pages. The City Living section is right underneath. And there they are, photos of yarn-covered ATMs complete with a couple paragraphs wondering why someone would do such a weird thing, and speculating on the presence of a Yarn Bombers Anonymous chapter here in the Twin Cities. The piece also tries to connect Epic to YBA, but the police say there's no connection between them. They've investigated. Yarn bombing is just random nonsense, according to the police chief in Edina.

Despite the anger, my grin is wall to wall.

One of the ATMs is photographed so you can see the word "greedy" spelled out on the front of it. Then there's a photo of a bank manager cutting the green blanket off one, and my stomach gives a funny lurch to think of all of

Rory's work being wrecked like that. Maybe she's used to it being destroyed. Then there's a photo of Betty Crocker, and she's in color, so the entire newspaper-reading audience can see her superhero scarf and her bowl full of alien puff. The puff looks good, if I do say so myself. Betty looks like she's going to take on the world, one ice blue–screaming orange cake mix at a time. But if any other teenager from Rory's classes at Henderson High sees the paper, her anonymity's blown.

Rory won't care. It's awesome coverage. Yarn Bombers Anonymous will probably promote her to Head Bomber or something. When you think about it, yarn bombing is really kind of cool, because it's all contradictory— something is just itself, but then it becomes beautiful, too, or at least softer, when you cover it in pretty yarn. If you wrap a tank in knitting—which someone did, Rory told me about it, in pink blanket-ish things, with a pink fuzzball hanging down from the barrel of the gun—then the tank becomes a little bit gentle and pretty. Nice contradiction, I have to say. And simple, in a complex way.

Speaking of soft, pretty, gentle, lovely, contradictory little things, Rory's kiss was also simple, but in a good way, and better than warm muffins, or even Pop-Tarts. It's almost embarrassing it was so short, but for someone like me, it's better to start small. I eat my other muffin and think about it. My mind flashes on Max Ledermann, and him crying in the cafeteria, but I blank him out.

By eleven thirty, I'm still alone, which doesn't make sense. Usually someone's up by now. Then I get the bright idea to go look outside, and duh, the truck is gone. They're not even here. Which is really weird, but OK.

I bang on Lou's door, just for fun. No answer.

"Hey, crusty ass, I might give you a muffin." Bang bang bang.

No answer. So I open the door. Her window is open, and the curtains are fluttering in the breeze.

Alien abduction? Snuck out and never came back in? Just an open window?

What if someone took her? No way.

My phone buzzes.

When are we making monsters? Today, right? What time? David. We're making girl ghouls this time. It's been almost a week since Monster Matt went to the Kwiky Pik. That's too long.

Something sharp shoots through me. It's almost pain and almost guilt, but not quite. If I make more ghoulies, Lou's gonna feel it even harder, and that makes me evil for continuing to hurt her. Even though the ghoulies started out as years of rage for stupid shit, big and small, now they're just my art, and art shouldn't hurt people. But at the same time, I don't want to quit making them, because making art is fun. Plus, Lou made her own decisions about being at the flash rob. I just found out about it. I'm not responsible for her stupidity.

My mind hops around: flash robs. Epic. The cops. The cops could know about the ghoulies, so maybe I should stop. Quit before *I* hurt Epic.

Hurting Epic plays tug-of-war with the idea that the cops aren't going to notice some stupid-ass ghoulies at a place that's already been robbed. Robbers wouldn't go back to the first Kwiky Pik when there are flash robs happening all over the city.

Three more ghoulies. That's a nice number. Three more and I'll quit, I swear. I'll be as stealthy as possible, and when I'm done, I'm done forever. And I'll try not to be angry at Lou anymore.

I text David: **Come over around two.**

I need to start thinking about what to put on these ghouls' clothes, because I don't know Sarah Taylor or Brooklyn Smith enough to know what they're into. Matt and Carter were obvious, because football and scholarships are public. Sarah and Brooklyn aren't like that.

Then I realize I'm standing in front of a potential research gold mine—Lou's room. Not that I should snoop, but it's research.

And, of course, the answers are there: Girls are obsessed

with documenting every single dopey thing they do. From Lou's picture boards, it looks like Sarah is a polka-dot kind of girl who likes mop dogs and purse dogs as well as *The Lion King*, because there's a picture of her and Lou at a Broadway touring production a few years ago when it was in St. Paul. She's got lions on her shirt and her skirt, and she's carrying a lion purse. Where the hell does a person get a lion purse? I can work with lions.

Brooklyn is a little more difficult—only one photo of her on Lou's photo boards, so I resort to a yearbook Lou has on her shelf. Brooklyn was in *Phantom of the Opera*. Easy enough.

I put the yearbook back and take one more look around Lou's room. On the floor by the window is a white piece of paper. It's wrinkled and crinkly and it has letters from a magazine pasted on it. All it says is SHUT UP, MISS VIXEN. WE KNOW WHERE YOU LIVE.

It's just someone bullshitting around. Right? Three more ghouls. That's it.

I am not the world's worst brother. I am not. I just want someone to see my work, and maybe even like it, for once in my dumbass life.

But I do something I never do: I text Lou. **You all right? Where are you?**

She'll never answer me—she never does. But the guilt twinge in my gut settles down, just a little.

Then I spend the next two hours trying to design a gun, which is probably the most important member of the flash rob. Small thing, big destruction, even though nobody fired it. Marvin, the Kwiky Pik manager, did get out of the hospital, but he's still in cardiac rehab every day. Mom and Dad said his son is running the store now.

Eventually I get my dad's band saw running and I cut a really crude gun out of a piece of scrap lumber without slicing off a thumb. Then I go up to Donna Russell's domain and find a can of gold spray paint from some long-ago stage project and paint my gun behind the garage. It looks like crap, but it gets the point across. And it's glam enough that the girl ghoulies will look good with it.

I have a couple more muffins and a turkey sandwich for protein, and text my dad, just out of curiosity: **Where is everyone?** Then I hear the doorbell.

David's standing there, carrying two tote bags from Mood, the store where all the *Project Runway* people get their fabric. I only know this because Lou wants to go to New York just to go to Mood—after she's seen at least three Broadway shows, of course. He's wearing a long skirt, the crinkly kind, very airy and bohemian. There are curlicues and flowers all over it.

"Seriously, Mood tote bags? You've been to New York?"

David comes inside and kisses me on the cheek as he goes by. "Remember I told you we went to LA with Epic? There's a Mood there, too." He dumps each bag in the middle of the living room floor, and so much crazy stuff flies out—yarn, felt, scissors, googly eyes, glue.

I focus on the crafty crap instead of the kiss, which freaked me out a little, though I try not to show it, and use my best stern voice on him. "This is sculpture, goddamn it, not Sunday school Popsicle stick projects."

He's got to know this isn't a romantic thing. Doesn't he?

"I have Popsicle sticks, too!" He uncovers a few from the pile of supplies and tries to look serious, but I can tell he's teasing. "Best art ingredient ever."

I shake my head, trying not to laugh. "Pick that crap up. You should be ashamed."

Once David's got all his craftiness re-contained, I take him up to meet Donna Russell. Now he's the one with googly eyes.

"Oh my god, those paintings are the best!" He's moving from canvas to canvas, staring at all the monsters in their natural habitats of peaceful countrysides. "Where did you get the idea to do this?"

"Out of my head. Where else do people get ideas?"

He nods. "I bet you could sell these. You should open an online store."

"Who's got time to make an online store?"

David goes over to Donna Russell and looks her up and down, like he's going to miss something crucial. "It didn't take me long when I did it."

"What do you sell?" This is news to me.

"Skirts for guys." He's still looking at Donna Russell. "Why do you think I offered to help you make your monster people? Your clothes need some serious assistance."

"You make all your own skirts?"

He glares. "Yes. Even the saggy black one."

I send him to the big pile of fabric to find something for each girl's skirt and shirt, and I start drawing *Phantom* masks on a big piece of cream-colored canvas that looks like you could make a parachute out of it.

The lions for Sarah are a little more complicated. There's some tawny brown fabric, so I cut out some circles that have kind of wavy edges. Then I draw lion faces on them, so the wavy edges end up looking like the lion's mane, and I add more curls at the edge of the circle, for mane fluff. They end up looking like crazed kittens with misplaced fur, but they'll do.

David has found a polka-dot print for Sarah's top and he claimed a zebra print for Brooklyn's top. Sarah's skirt is kind of a green stripe, like the awning over a store, and

Brooklyn's skirt looks a lot like the upholstery in my parents' truck—boring dark blue with stars on it. He's already got the skirts and shirts put together, and you can tell it's not some jackass like me who sewed them—it's someone with sewing knowledge.

I bring him the cutouts of the *Phantom* masks and the lion heads. "The masks go with the zebra and blue stars, and the lion heads are for the polka dots and awning."

"Easy enough." He looks them over. "Do you care how I put them on?"

"Why would I care?"

"Good." He pushes back from the sewing machine. "I'm going to sew them on by hand."

"That'll take forever!"

He laughs. "Shows what you know. Just give them here and be amazed. I'll be done before you get their bodies and faces set up."

"No you won't."

"Watch me." He points at me. "Grab my sewing box for me."

"Where is it?"

"Bottom of the Mood bag." David points to which one, and I retrieve his sewing box, which is pink and multi-layered, kind of like a fishing tackle box.

While he sews, I get out my photocopies and pick out face parts for Sarah and Brooklyn, mixing various robbers' features, though I leave Sarah her eyes and Brooklyn her mouth. Pretty soon they look like the other ghoulies' faces—messed up but cool.

Their hair takes a bit of thinking, but it comes to me. I go down to the kitchen and dig under the sink, then bring back two round plastic dish scrubbers. When I unwind them—one blue scrubby, one green one—I have long wavy plastic curls. With some tape in strategic places, the plastic ends up being pretty decent girl hair.

David's got all the *Phantom* masks on Brooklyn's clothes by the time both faces have their hair attached and he's working on Sarah's lions.

"You really are fast." I examine what he's done. The stitches are tight and very neat. "You should do this for a living."

"I just might someday." He's bent over a lion. "Almost finished here."

I get the bodies assembled for both Sarah and Brooklyn, then get the clothes onto the bodies and the faces on the torsos. Then it hits me.

"You realize the skirts are all wrong." I give him a look.

"Why?" He's bent over the last lion to sew on Sarah's shirt. Her ghoulie's still topless.

"There's no tulle anywhere. And the tulle is the point." One of those almost-pains shoots through my chest when I say it, but I don't take it back.

David ties his knot and bites the thread off. "Got you covered, Miss Vixen." He slides his needle into the sleeve of his shirt, on the cuff so he doesn't lose it. "I've got something better than that patch-ass stuff you were doing with the other two skirts." He grins. "Your monsters are gonna be high-end instead of thrift. Take their skirts back off."

"I like my monsters' thrift store."

"Yeah, but you'll like them better high-end. I promise." He points. "Skirts off."

"Yes, sir." I lay them down and yank off their skirts, which feels creepy, like I'm doing something improper.

David produces two very nice underskirts of tulle, looking one thousand percent better than the ones I made for Carter and Matt and looking very suspiciously like Lou's skirts that she wears on a regular day—or used to wear. In the ten days since Ghoulie Carter went to the Kwiky Pik, Lou's been wearing lots of leggings and long sweatshirts.

"Give me your phone." He gestures. "Miss Vixen should tweet this."

"A teaser for the next installation?" I like this idea. I hand him my phone.

"Exactly." He snaps a couple shots, then tweets them out as Miss Vixen: **New tulle skirts to go with new ghoulies?**

Wait and find out! He hands the phone back.

The tulle slips go on over the wheels, then the regular skirts, and then I stand the mannequins up and yank their skirts to their pretend hips. The Lou suggestion is even harder to miss, with the tulle, and it's very clear that, along with kissing, I know nothing about sewing. Ghoulie Carter and Monster Matt's clothes prove it without a doubt.

"That looks so freaking cool I can't believe it. You are a serious virtuoso."

David sniffs. "Thrift store to high-end. Even though the canvas does nothing for anybody. Why can't you make the skirts out of something that will fluff out and be beautiful?"

"Did you seriously just say that? This is art, not fashion."

He glares. "But you're wasting the effect of the tulle."

"Oh no we're not. Trust me on that one." I swallow the guilt, and it goes down like clumpy peanut butter.

"What are you going to do if someone steals the mannequins again?" He's obviously noticed the faces and the accessories are all that's left of the ghoulies at Kwiky Pik. "Epic's not going to be happy if you don't replace them."

"I'm saving Pizza Vendetta money. Hopefully nobody will mess with them." I cross my fingers and say a quick prayer that I'm right.

I make the signs that say HAVE YOU SEEN ME? and ORIGINAL FAKE BY MISS VIXEN. David watches while I draw the zip-up banana bus, very tiny in the corner, then pin the signs to the skirts. "You really hate your sister, don't you, Pepperoniangelo?" I told him about that night.

"I wouldn't say hate. I would say severely want to get back at her."

It's five forty-five, and I realize my dad never texted me back. Nobody's texted me today, including Rory. I didn't text her yesterday—I didn't know if I should. Maybe the kiss was spur of the moment. Maybe it didn't mean anything. I could be reading too much into it. Maybe it was just an instant between two people who'd spent so much time together. But maybe Rory wanted me to text and I didn't do it, so now I've blown my chances for more.

How the hell does anyone know what to do? I'm going to have to retire from girlfriends before I've even started.

"So what now?"

David's question snaps me back to reality. "Now we wait. You can stay for supper if you want."

He blushes. "Here? With you and Frank-N-Furter?"

"Who else is going to be here? Santa Claus and Heidi Klum?"

"Fine, whatever, yes, I'll stay." He's embarrassed, I can tell, and he starts gathering up scraps of materials. "Thanks for letting me help you."

"Are you kidding? I owe you. They look insanely good. Did you bring your longboard?"

"How do you think I got here?" He throws all the scraps in the garbage. "I can't drive yet, fool."

"Where's your board?" He wasn't carrying it when he came in.

"Downstairs on your front porch."

"We'll come back up later. Right now we need to sneak out of here before my family starts looking for me."

"Why?" David looks confused.

"They don't even remember this room is up here, and I don't want people messing with my stuff." I put my finger to my lips. "Hush on the stairs."

We sneak down to the hallway, and I check before we come out. Deserted. Then we slide into my room and close the door. Two seconds go by, literally, before I hear my mom.

"Frankie, where are you? We're here."

I holler back, "Yeah, Mom. Be right down."

"You knew she'd yell for you?" David's impressed.

"Supper's always at six." I shrug.

"You're pretty lucky." He looks sad. "My mom and I never get to eat together."

"Sounds like heaven to me." I give him a shove out of my room, but not before I can see that he's looking around and taking everything in. "Nothing good to look at in here."

"Nothing except those collages." He points to a bunch of mash-ups I made from a *GQ* I stole from the library, a *Cosmo* Lou had lying around, and an *National Geographic* kids' mag someone left at Pizza Vendetta. It's all headlines like "Please Your Man" pasted over a picture of a man and woman throwing a Frisbee around with skirts on their heads while they're riding llamas. Totally dumb.

"You can stare later. Right now it's family time, hallelujah, kill me now." I shut the door and we go downstairs.

Lou, my mom, and my dad are in the kitchen, sweaty and dirty and gross. They look like they've been crawling through sewer pipes. Everybody's dressed in work clothes, and there are two Pizza Vendetta boxes on the counter.

"Where were you guys today? I texted you, Dad."

He looks surprised, and he checks his phone. "Yup, you did. Sorry. We were in the basement of Global Heating and Cooling—nobody's been down there since the seventies, I think. Pure grossness."

My mom snorts. "More like the fifties. I haven't seen dust bunnies that big since we cleaned the basement of the post office, which was last touched in 1957."

"So gross." Lou wipes her face with a towel. "But it's camp money."

"Why didn't I get the chance to make camp money?"

My dad raises his eyebrows at me. "You want to go to that drama camp too?"

"No, but . . ."

"When you have final plans for the skateboard camp, then we can help you make some money." Mom's getting plates out of the cupboard. "Hello, David. Welcome." You can see she's happy to have proof I really do have a friend.

"Can I help you with that?" David is nothing but charming. He rushes over to her and takes the plates out of her hands.

"Thank you." She gives him a big smile.

Lou's giving him a bigger smile. "I have a skirt almost like that, and I met you at Pizza Vendetta one night, when you were there to talk to Frankie."

I immediately derail that conversation by opening the boxes. "What kind of pizza did you bring? Did Geno make them for you?" If he did, then they'll be good. If anybody else is working, they could be sketchy.

"Geno made them. Pepperoni and veggie." My dad puts them on the table with a bunch of paper towels. "Dig in, people."

David and I shovel down some pizza and drink Cokes with the fam, try a little small talk. Lou makes googly eyes at David, complete with flirty smiles and comments like, "Are we in any of the same classes?" since they're both freshmen. My parents are lovey-dovey, like usual. When we say what we're grateful for, David says he's thankful for friends like me. It's a good thing I went before he did, because I'd have no idea what to say after that.

It's obvious he's happy to get away when it's over. "Your sister is relentless." He pats his hair swoop to settle himself down. "But your dad's super cool. So's your mom." David grins. "Who knew I'd get to have pizza with the best Frank-N-Furter in town?"

"Lou's convinced you should fall under her charming spell, so she's working extra hard to lure you into her web. That's why she was such a freak."

David's examining the collages on the wall again. "So what do we do with your creatures upstairs?"

"We wait until everyone's asleep and we put them in my truck and take them to the Kwiky Pik." I check the clock. Seven fifteen. Still a bit of light. "Let's go longboard."

We don't get home until after dark. The house is quiet, even though it's only eight thirty. Lou's in the living room, watching the movie version of the musical *Chicago*.

"Mom and Dad in bed already?" I stand in front of the TV so she can't see. David stays out of the way behind the couch.

She moves her head. "Yes. And they told me to remind you that curfew's at ten tonight, but that you can take David home with your truck. Get out of the way, jerkass."

She hasn't been out with her friends at all this weekend. Strange. And she's not holding her phone, which has been her constant friend for as long as she's had it. She looks truly alone, huddled on the couch in a blanket.

I may feel bad. I may not. I don't know.

"You should go to bed, too. You need a lot of beauty sleep, you know. Otherwise nobody will be able to look at you tomorrow." I groove around in front of the TV, to block as much view as possible.

"Take your asshole comments elsewhere." She flips me the bird.

I smile the evilest grin I can manage. "Big day, Monday. Monday always is." David gives me a thumbs-up and a wide grin. Lou can't see him because he's behind her.

She jumps up and stomps out. "You're a jacked-up fartbox who likes to think he's important." David moves closer to the door, just to stay out of her way.

"You're a frilly Medusa who thinks the world revolves around her." I shout it down the hallway at her back.

"You're just so BASIC, Frankie. You know NOTHING!" SLAM goes Lou's door.

David's watching with interest. "You do this all the time?"

I shut the TV off. "I like trying to knock the queen bee off her throne."

We go up to visit the ghoulies and Donna Russell.

"You know Epic's got some big plans going." David stretches out on the floor, his long skirt flowing everywhere. "He's aiming for Nicollet Mall."

"Never happen." It's a pedestrian mall in downtown Minneapolis. Lots of upscale shops, plus some big department stores. Some restaurants and office buildings. A library. No cars, only pedestrians. Lots of security cameras, lots of people watching, even at three a.m. "With the police interest, he'll never pull it off, whatever it is. The cops will grab him for sure. Did you read the paper today?"

"No." He looks relaxed. "Why would anybody read the paper?"

"To find pictures of Rory's yarn bomb, and a two-page editorial spread about Epic? Including something about cancelling his Walker show?"

"Show me." He doesn't look relaxed anymore.

I go out to the recycling, retrieve the paper, and bring it back. The whole house is dark and quiet. "See for yourself."

He reads. "Nothing new here." I'm quiet while he finishes and hands the paper back to me. "Too bad that police chief will never come close to finding Epic. And Marta will handle the Walker. She's good at PR. Epic wants you to come over this week to talk transportation, by the way. Plus he needs more hands. This one takes a lot of work."

"Do you know what it is?"

David grins. "I have an idea. It involves naughty bits."

"Whose naughty bits?" I'm not sure I even want to know.

"Not yours or mine. And printing money."

I'm confused. "On somebody's naughty bits?"

David rolls his eyes. "On paper. He's going to print hundred-dollar bills that have Andy Warhol on them."

"Why Warhol?"

"Why not?" David looks around. "Let's make something while we wait. What else do you have to do in here?"

I spin around, my arms wide. "Take your pick." Then I look at my phone—9:55. "Just be quiet. I'll be gone about fifteen minutes."

My parents' alarm is buzzing faintly—I can hear it—when I slide into my room and close the door. About three minutes later, there's a knock. "Frankie?" It's my mom.

"Come on in."

She sticks her head in. "Just making sure you're here for curfew."

"Right here." I'm casual, reading a book on my bed,

looking like I'm not ready to break the brand-new rule she's just laid down two days ago.

"Good night, honey. Love you." She retreats.

I give it about ten more minutes, then scram back up to Donna Russell and David. He's reading an old *Rolling Stone* my dad has up here—there must be about a thousand of them.

I get out my paints. "You want a painting to work on?" I point to the corner where all the couch paintings are. "Take your pick." I choose one that has big sea cliffs and a long expanse of beach. This will be perfect for a sea monster, though I'm thinking something more like an octopus with fifty-foot-long tentacles rather than a Nessie. Though maybe Nessie could be offshore and the octopus could just be walking on the beach, scaring people.

"Could I?" David's face lights up. "I want to do the one with the big open field. There's gotta be something good that could land in the middle of it."

"Knock yourself out." I put the paints in between us on the floor, and we paint. And paint. And paint. For a long time, we're just two

people painting, sitting on the floor, making funky monsters that invade very calm spaces.

I've never had a real friend to paint with before, which makes me consider whether or not I've ever had a friend before. In third grade, there was a kid who lived down the block, Marcus, and we used to ride our bikes together. But when he moved in fifth grade, that was pretty much that. In middle school, I was just too awkward to have a friend. Plus I was pissed all the time, most specifically at Lou. Now I don't fit into anyone's cliques, and people just think I'm a weirdo loner, which I am, so nobody makes the effort and I don't either. David and Rory wouldn't be around if they hadn't needed transportation. I'm sure things will fade when Epic leaves town. Though maybe not, if David was thankful for me at supper. But why wouldn't they forget about me? They won't need me anymore, once Epic's gone.

It's pretty sad and ugly, to say it like that. But truth is best. Lies just make the truth hurt worse.

"Doesn't your mom care where you are?" I say it just to break the silence.

"No. She usually figures I'm with Epic. All she does is work, eat, and sleep."

"But today is Sunday. Won't she be home today?"

"I saw her this morning. And she'll be asleep by the time I get home. I left her a note. We're not all that close, like your family." He squints at the canvas, checking something out.

"If my family was close, would I be getting back at my sister?"

David stands up and stretches. "OK, dude, I can't do this anymore. This is hard. And I can't sit on the floor anymore. Ouch." In the middle of his canvas is a robot-ish thing that looks suspiciously like Donna Russell.

"Excellent work." I lean his painting up against the wall next to Sid the Sasquatch, and I put my sea monsters next to Donna Russell in the field. It's a good collection. Too bad nobody wants to see it but us.

"It's eleven thirty." David checks his phone. "Too early to put out the ghouls?"

"Maybe not for a Sunday. Let me go scope out the house." Then I remember what's behind the garage. "I almost forgot the best part, too."

I prowl down the stairs. No sounds from Lou's room. I

skulk down the next set of stairs. No sounds from my parents' room. The back door squeaks, but I make it through and retrieve the gun from behind the garage. When I get back to the ballroom, David's rearranging the paintings along the wall. He turns around when I come in.

"How are you going to get the ghoulies to hold that?"

"Tape, I guess. Ghoulie Carter had a coffee cup at one point. Maybe I can get it jammed in one of their hands."

"Tape is ugly." He frowns.

"You gotta do what you gotta do for art. Ready for transport?" I get behind Ghoulie Sarah and motion him to get behind Ghoulie Brooklyn. "You kind of have to scoot them and carry them at the same time."

"Gotcha." He figures it out as we're going down the stairs, and there's only one loud clunk. But Lou's door stays closed. Then we both manage to make it down the second flight and out the door without any crashes or any movement from my parents' room. We tuck them into my truck, and I pray nobody hears it start.

I drive around the block a couple times when we get there, looking for suspicious vehicles, stakeout cars, anything like that. Doesn't look like anybody's paying attention. I send up a silent request: *Please, Universe, please don't let the cops arrest me and please don't let anybody steal the mannequins. I don't make a lot of money.*

Amazingly, Monster Matt and Ghoulie Carter's faces are

still there, along with all their offerings. Ghoulie Carter's purse has been stuffed full of flyers for an all-ages rave. In the shadows, they look like phantoms. In record time, we place the female ghoulies in a conversational group with the faces, then I tape the gun into Ghoulie Sarah's hand so it looks like she's just casually holding it there. I point it down, of course. No reason to be too confrontational.

Someone's put makeup on both Monster Matt's and Ghoulie Carter's faces, so now they kind of look like Andy Warhol's Marilyn Monroe screen prints. The boys' eye shadow is so blue you can see it in the dimness.

Miss Vixen tweets a photo: **A ghoulie crowd of pure awesome. Come see us sometime.**

David jogs across the street to survey the ghoulies. "Come on!"

"Dude, we have to get out of here. We don't know who's going to come by." I've been doing 360 sweeps of the environment every minute or so, and I do another one. Pretty much deserted.

"You have to see this!"

I'm dying to know, so I sprint over, and I'm amazed when I turn to look. Maybe even astounded, because they look good. Really good. Like actual, professional art, though very weird art. The girls look about a thousand times better than the guys did, back when they had bodies, because their clothes are David's clothes. But that's OK.

"What do you think?" David's grin is huge.

"Holy shit." I can't get over them. They're cooler than anything I've ever made. Ever.

ALL OF A SUDDEN, DAVID GRABS MY HAND AND HOLDS IT.

My mind flashes on the kiss he gave me when he came to my house. A car goes by us, on its way out of the lot, and they honk and yell, "Get a room!"

David's hands are smooth, soft, and gentle. Rory's hands are rough and strong.

He pulls his hand back and looks me square in the face. "Do you think . . ."

"You have nice hands." I almost say, *Nicer than Rory's,* but I stop myself.

"Thanks, but do you think we could go out?" He's holding my gaze.

"Probably not." I don't look away. He deserves the honesty. And I don't want to lose him as a friend. That fact is suddenly very clear to me.

"You know Rory's just going to hurt you. Even if she likes you, which I think she does."

My stomach jumps a little, hearing him say that about Rory. "She might. I can't quite tell."

"She's just not very nice." He turns to look at the ghoulies. "People say every guy is just a six-pack away."

"From holding hands with another guy?" I laugh and pick up his hand one more time, squeeze it, let it go.

"You know what I mean . . . It doesn't matter who's working on your dick, just that someone's working on it." He smiles, but he doesn't look at me.

"Oh. I'd never heard that."

"Remember it." He starts walking back to the ghoulies, and I follow.

Maybe he really is the better option. I can't say I've ever wished to be gay before tonight, but there it is. He'd be the best boyfriend in the world.

"Excuse me, gentlemen." A deep voice behind me.

I whirl around. "Who are you?"

A man is standing there in a sweatshirt and jeans. He's maybe a bit older than my dad, but not much, with wavy hair to his shoulders. He's got a notebook in his hand. "Do you know anything about those creatures in the parking lot? Is that what you were looking at?"

David grabs my hand again. "Nope. We were just admiring the moon. Romantic, you know." He points overhead, and there's a full moon, hanging low. "It's easier to see away from the lights." We're in a shadowy spot.

"Who are you?" I'm guessing I already know the answer.

The guy reaches in his pocket and pulls out a badge. "Officer Nelson. Those monsters have us a bit curious. Do either of you drive that white delivery truck? The one that looks like an old FedEx truck?" He points at my truck.

"Nope." David is an excellent liar. "Our car is over there." He points to one by the ghoulie end of the building. "We walked outside the store, and I noticed the moon."

"Right." I can't really tell if the guy believes us or not. "If you find out anything, would you please tell the Kwiky Pik clerks? They know we're looking for the artist. They told us it was someone named Mixt UP, but we're wondering if he's connected to Uncle Epic, if you know who that is." He hands David a card. "Or you can call us here." His card says OFFICER ROGER NELSON, HENDERSON POLICE DEPARTMENT, with a number.

"Sure thing, Officer. Never heard of Uncle Epic, but if we find out anything, we'll let you know." It's all I can to do keep my voice steady.

"You bet, Officer Nelson." David squeezes my hand again. "We're just going to look at the moon a little more."

"Enjoy, gentlemen." Officer Nelson fades back into the shadows, and I see him get into a car that's next to the building we're standing in front of.

"Just breathe. Breathe. Hold my hand. Breathe." David

is saying these things without moving his mouth while staring up at the moon.

"You're the world's best liar." I try not to move my lips.

"Lots of practice." He grins and squeezes my hand one last time, then lets it go.

Officer Nelson pulls out of the building's parking lot and merges into traffic. I let out my breath, which I didn't even realize I was holding. "Fuck. He didn't believe a word we said."

"Sure he did." David is confident. "They don't give you a card if they don't believe you. They take you to the station. You're still safe."

"But is Epic safe?"

"Listen." David puts his hands on my shoulders. "Epic will be fine. Trust me on that."

"I can't be the one to wreck Epic's reputation! Or his anonymity, or anything else!"

David laughs. "Trust me. He's not worried." He kisses me once on each cheek. "That's for luck. And for you being honest with me."

We cross to my truck. Ghoulie Sarah and Ghoulie Brooklyn are still looking fly, still talking to Ghoulie Carter and Monster Matt. All is well. But my heart's hammering so loud I can't hear anything.

• • •

2:51 a.m. My phone vibrates.

Why didn't you text me this weekend? Rory.

I didn't know if you wanted me to.

I did. Frowny face.

Oh.

Great.

V IS FOR

Vicious

When I walk to my first class on Monday morning, three things catch my eye. The first is Ronson Reimer, standing outside the chem lab, with a combination lock in his ear. Ronson normally has huge gauges in his ears, so the hole is there already, but a combination lock? His earlobe is pulled so long he looks like a basset hound. Ow. And he's totally mellow about the fact that some girl is spinning the lock dial, trying to get it to open while she's chatting him up.

"Ronson, why?" We're in at least two classes with each other every semester, so we know each other's names.

"I got inspired." He grins. "I think it's art."

The second thing I notice is that Ronson's wearing a skirt. It's closer to a utilikilt than one of Lou's tulle creations.

"The skirt is part of your art? Where'd you get it?"

"Some online shop of skirts for guys. I think it's called Represent."

I laugh. David must be advertising. "Pretty cool."

He nods and goes back to talking to the girl who's trying to open the lock.

The third thing I notice is how many people are pointing to their phones. Not just looking at them, pointing at them. I walk close to a group of girls to see what they're pointing at. One girl's showing the rest of her crowd a photo of the ghoulies outside of the Kwiky Pik and one girl's got a picture of the skirts, the one that David tweeted. They're deep in conversation, talking about who each ghoulie might be.

Good job, Miss Vixen.

I catch a glimpse of Lou when I'm going to lunch and she's going to class. She's wearing an old U of M sweatshirt, jeans, and tennis shoes—no skirt, no ballet slippers—and looking down, like she's going to get smacked by someone if she stops long enough. She skitters by Allison Lawson, who was also at the flash rob, and Lou's face lights up when she sees her. Allison turns her head away from Lou and rushes the other way. Complete burn. Lou's face clouds over as quickly as it lit up.

The almost-pain rockets through me again. Obviously I'm losing my cred as a rebel. You're not supposed to feel sorry for the object of your vendetta, are you? I need to get my vicious back.

Spanish class. Rory's sitting in front of me again, which is crappy. When Andie Braswell comes in, she rolls her eyes and flops next to me, back in the seat where Rory's been sitting. I shrug at her, since I don't know what's going on. She glares and opens her book.

Rory starts texting the minute Señor Gonzalez starts lecturing.

Still pissed you didn't text me. Frowny face.

My bad. Frowny face in return. **Did you have a nice weekend?** I want to reach into my phone and take it back a nanosecond after I send it. What a dumbass thing to say.

Lonely. Frowny face. **Want to repeat that last move sometime soon.**

Not gonna say no. Smiley face. And then I want to reach in my phone again—the smiley face was over the top.

We need you on Wednesday night at E's. Can I meet you at Pizza Vendetta?

Yup. I have to work anyway. **See you around 9?** Geno never makes me close on weeknights.

She turns around and gives me a look that's best described as steamy, glossy lips slightly apart, with one eyebrow raised and arched, like what you'd see in some dumb magazine ad.

Andie Braswell laughs.

"Señorita Carlson! Turn around and focus on me." Señor Gonzalez is not happy.

"Sí, señor." She winks and turns back to him. I close my eyes and will my boner to go away before the class is over.

When I'm stopped at the stoplight, waiting my turn in the rush hour that is after-school madness, the passenger side door opens. A body flings itself into the truck.

"Hey! Who the frak do you think—" Then I realize it's Lou. "Oh."

"Who were you expecting? The Easter Bunny?" She buckles her seat belt. "It's a family truck, butthead." She's breathing hard, like she ran to catch me. "Someday I'll get to drive it, too."

"Over my dead body." The light is green, so I proceed like the turtle I have to be through the intersection. People drive like fools after school.

"Shut up, dick." Her breathing is starting to slow down. "I don't need any more attitude."

"Why are you getting shit?" Let's see what she'll tell me.

"I'm not telling, because all you'd do is make fun of me."

"No I won't." I put on my best I'm-a-good-brother face.

"Yes, you would, because you're an annoying poseur who thinks he's above it all." She's getting pissed.

"You're a dilettante who thinks the entire world revolves around her."

"You're an asshole!" She's shouting now.

I shout back, "Suck it up!"

Then she's sobbing into her hands, weeping and wailing.

Instantly, shame sweeps over me. Lou carries on until we get to our house. Her big bushy hair covers her face, and her shoulders tremble like someone's shaking her. I try very, very hard not to listen. When we get home, she flings open the truck door and runs for the house. I grab her book bag from the floor and pitch it on the couch once I make it inside.

I may have pushed it too far.

After a ham sandwich, a Coke, and some yogurt, it's homework time under the watchful gaze of Donna Russell. But there's something rattling in my brain, something I can't quite grab. Then it hits me.

I go down and knock on Lou's door.

"Go away. I don't care who you are." She still sounds sniffly.

"I have a question for you."

"Ask it from there." A loud sniff.

"Why can't you just stop being friends with the people who are jerks to you?"

"None of your business!"

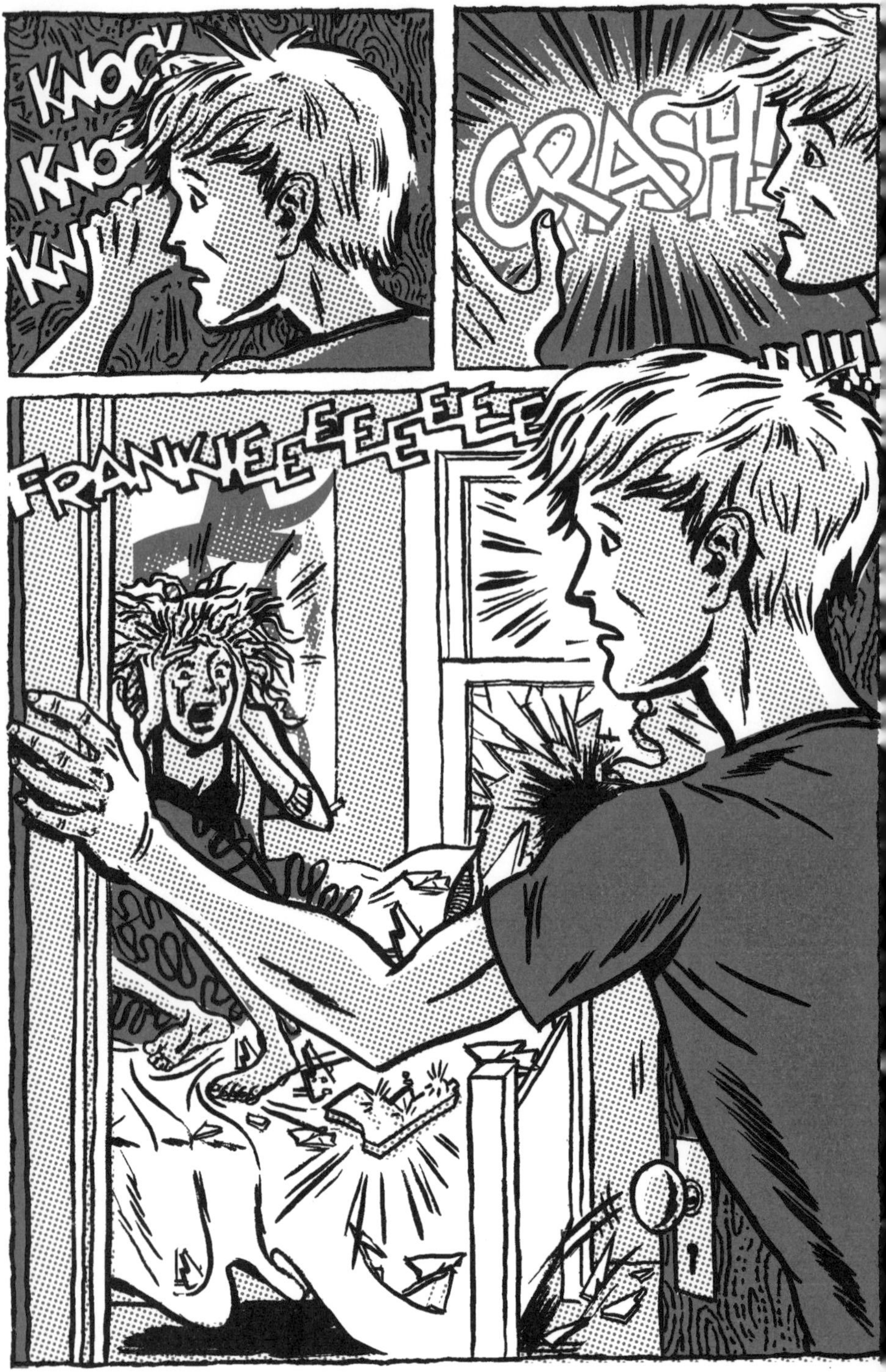
KNOCK KNOCK KNO
CRASH!
FRANKIEEEEEEE

What. The. Fuck.

"Don't move." I look at Lou, who's curled up on her bed with a very blotchy face and red-rimmed eyes. Of course she's barefoot. She always is, unless she's wearing ballet slippers. "Get some flip-flops now."

The fright is deep in her eyes, down to her core, but she's trying not to show me that. She hops off her bed and makes a wide circle around the glass to the garbage can underneath her desk, which she kicks to me because it's empty. "You don't have to help me clean this up."

"I know. Just get some shoes." She digs in her closet while I start putting the biggest chunks of glass into the garbage. I look out the window, too, to see if anyone's still out there. Of course they're not.

Thank god Mom and Dad aren't home. They'd lose their minds. Thank god Lou's window is at the back of the house so they won't see it. I wonder how much it costs to get a window replaced. Mannequins and windows. Good thing I never spend my Pizza Vendetta money.

Whoever sent the note with the cut-out letters isn't kidding. They know where she lives.

Once Lou's got some flip-flops, she approaches the mess. "What is this?" She picks up the chunk of sparkly gun and turns it over in her hands. It's only the grip and a tiny piece of the barrel.

"Good question." My face is probably the same color as the valentine on her bulletin board. "Go find me a broom."

I get most of the big chunks up with my hands. She brings back a full-size broom and a little whisk broom, plus two dustpans, which aren't entirely effective on carpet. Her garbage can is full of glass when we're done.

"Don't tell Mom and Dad." She's pulling the loose shards out of the window, so it's one big gaping hole without any jagged edges.

"Why? We should tell them. Who would do this?" I hope my face is as innocent as I try to make my voice.

"I have an idea." She drops a last piece of glass into the garbage can, and it shatters. "And no, we can't tell them. Just . . . no."

I relax a little bit. If she thought it was me, she'd be kicking my ass around the room right now. "What are you going to say happened to your window?"

She shrugs. "I kicked it, accidentally. Doing the choreography from some show because I was bored. They'll buy that. We'll tell them we went outside and picked up the glass in the yard. They'll believe us."

Of course they will. "Good plan. But we should tell them. What if these people hurt you?"

Snitches aren't popular people. Her fellow robbers might actually do something. I'm more than slightly freaked.

She grabs the garbage can and heads toward her door, but not before she's given me a death stare. "No. Don't say another word. Thanks for helping me." And she's gone, walking slowly down the stairs so she doesn't spill the glass.

The last ghoulie is a bad idea. I can't do it. Officer Nelson could be there. And what if they hurt her?

After supper I tell my folks I'm going to Pizza Vendetta, but I really go to the Kwiky Pik, to see how the girl ghoulies are doing. Amazingly, they're still there. I glance across the street to see if there's a car where Officer Nelson's car was. Nothing.

Someone's brought a few more candles and shoes for each girl—old and shitty Doc Martens for Ghoulie Sarah and football cleats for Ghoulie Brooklyn—plus each one now has a stuffed teddy bear peeking out of the top of her shirt. Someone's put makeup on their faces, too.

Miss Vixen tweets a photo of the newly added accessories: **Love that you love these ghoulies!** In the background of the photo, Monster Matt and Ghoulie Carter's faces float nearby, like guardians.

My heart is busting out of my chest with pride and love. The ghoulies are the coolest pieces I've ever done, except for Donna Russell. But Lou could be hurt. Like badly. And the cops could come back. A million billion thoughts swirl through me.

I can't finish them. It's too risky. I can't risk Epic's safety. Or Lou's.

I have to finish them. Have to. They matter.

Monsters or people: What are we? What am I?

A thought forms out of the swirl: They won't really hurt her, because they can't risk her actually going to the cops and ratting them out. They just want to scare her.

Someone please tell me I'm right about that.

Another thought forms out of the swirl: Epic is a grown man. He's done this forever. He knows the risks. He can take care of himself. If David is right and the cop believed us, then we're still OK.

@drseussisgod tweets back a photo of Monster Matt and Ghoulie Carter's bodies, with the crappy clothes I made still on them. **Soon I'll have two more.**

@ArtistMissVixen: **Stop harassing my ghouls, jerkwad!**

@drseussisgod: **Chill out.**

Now I'm just pissed, and I'm tempted to sleep in the parking lot, just to keep them safe, but I'm on truck restriction and I have a curfew, and I can't have the cops showing up again. I take one last photo of the ghoulies, far back so you can see the building and a little bit of the parking lot.

@ArtistMissVixen: **Leave them alone. They're happy.**

@drseussisgod: **Yes they are. You're a genius, @ArtistMissVixen.**

@ArtistMissVixen: **Stay away. Seriously.**

Miss Vixen better not ever find out who @drseussisgod is. It would not be pretty.

When I get back home, my folks are in the living room, watching some black-and-white musical from the forties. My mom's mending something big and fluffy in her lap. Something full of tulle. "Homework all done?"

"Yup." She's asked me that question maybe five times in the history of my high school career.

"Thank you for being home before your curfew." My dad smiles at me.

I try to smile back. "Yup."

When I pass Lou's room, I hear her yelling into her phone.

"Who the fuck threw a sparkly piece of wood through my window? If you know, you'd better tell me!" She's furious—her voice is two octaves above its normal pitch, and she's so loud I'm surprised my folks don't come ask what's wrong. There's a pause, then another Lou rant: "I am not Miss Vixen! I swear to you on a stack of scripts, I am not Miss Vixen. When I find out who is, I'm gonna lose my shit on their head."

What's she going to do, stomp on their foot and shake her hair at them? It's all I can do not to bust out laughing in the hallway. I'd kind of like to see her lose her shit at me. But my parents would be standing right behind her, waiting to lose *their* shit on my head if she finds out it's me. That part would be uncool.

One more ghoulie, and Miss Vixen retires, at least from outing flash robbers. She might still make some art. She's pretty good.

Then the stomach acid churns up in my throat.

What if they really do hurt Lou?

What if she's really in danger?

What if the cops take me in, and they make me confess to knowing Epic? Or at least knowing where his garage is?

I grab my pillow, then go up to sleep with Donna Russell. She doesn't care when I get home. She's just happy to see me.

She doesn't even think I'm an asshole, even when the possibility is pretty real.

I have to finish my piece. It's my art. I have to.

Don't I?

V IS FOR VICES

When I make it to my truck on Tuesday after school, which I drove because it was supposed to rain today, but it didn't, Rory's propped herself up against the door, looking like she does this all the time and aren't I happy to see her? And of course I am, even though I just left her in Spanish class about five minutes ago.

"Can I come to your place?" She hugs her bag to her chest. "I want to see where the magic happens."

"The magic?"

"You know, with the monster zombie creatures." She smiles like she wants in on the joke and lowers her voice.

"I know David helped you with the last two ghoulies, because I recognized his skirts. Can I help you too?"

"You can't tell people it's me. Not anyone." I'm close enough to smell her again. I spent all of Spanish class catching whiffs of a spicy, musky perfume that's new. Now there's leather mixed in, from her bag, and the smell of spring on the wind. It's a bit head-rushy.

"Hey! Frankie! Hey! I need a ride!" A voice that's like a sharp stick in my ear bounces off the truck and makes Rory look up.

"Then get your ass in here." I sigh. "Rory, this is my sister, Lou."

Lou arrives, out of breath, and gives Rory the look she reserves for those who just don't understand how phenomenal she is. She's obviously recovered some swagger. "Nice to meet you." She reaches around Rory and opens the door to the passenger seat, then climbs in.

To say that Rory is stunned is an understatement. "Where am I supposed to sit?"

Lou hooks her thumb over her shoulder. "Plenty of space back there."

I slide into the driver's seat, keeping my eyes down, not making eye contact with anyone. The Rory/Lou bomb could blow any second.

Lou clicks her seat belt shut. "We have to go to Target. I need stuff."

"You don't get to order me around."

"Look." She fixes me with a stare, and I hear a cough of amusement from behind my seat. "I need to go to Target, so take me to Target." She turns to face the front again. "Please. Now." She's straight and proper in her seat, just waiting for the truck to move.

"Be a good brother, Frankie, and take Lou to Target. I'll keep you company while she's in the store." I can't see Rory's face, which is probably a good thing. I'm grateful Lou's looking out the window.

I pretend to be pissed. "Whatever." We fight the stupid traffic out of the parking lot. "Where are Mom and Dad? Why can't they take you?"

Lou sniffs. "You know they're working. You can take me."

We turn a corner, and there's a big thump from the back.

"Hold the straps on the wall. It helps." Lou's voice is cheery.

"Yeah. Thanks." Rory's not appreciative of the advice, judging from her voice.

"Don't blame me. I told you that the last time you rode back there, when David was with us." I make a mental note to be more careful.

"You pulled away too fast for me to grab on." She is not happy.

Lou snorts.

Silence for a while. Then we're at Target. Thank god it's close.

"I won't be long." And Lou slams out the door.

"Take your time, drama girl. We'll be right here." Rory says this loud enough that Lou hears her through the window, and I see Lou flip her the bird as she walks away.

Rory comes up front and stands between the two seats. "You really bounce around back there."

I swivel around, point to the strap on the wall, and give her a "duh" look.

"Never mind that right now. C'mere." She grabs my hand and pulls me into the back of the truck.

"What?" I let her pull me back there, of course, but I'm also just a little concerned. And also very, very happy that nobody can see in.

"Just . . ." She turns to face me. "This." And she kisses me, full force, grabbing me and pulling me to her.

I pull away. "You want to make out? Here?"

She sighs. "I want to make art. Right here. We're kinetic sculpture." And she kisses me again.

It's intense. Immense. And all I want is a couch.

"Look, Rory, we're in a parking lot. We can't be doing this." I can barely get the words out in between kisses.

"Nobody can see. And she'll get lost looking at a pair of sparkly ballet slippers or something." Her mouth is so hot on mine. On-fire hot. Soft and wet and hot. I'm gonna fall down.

"Can we . . . are there blankets in here?" Rory pulls away and starts looking around.

"Nothing but that." I spot the towel I used to wrap the ghoulie gun in. It's still got gold glitter from the paint in it. When I pick it up, the towel flakes gold onto the floor.

"Never mind, then." Rory pulls me down to the truck floor, and I can't get there soon enough. She is my vice. My hand is up her sweater and her breast is so warm, so squishy but firm and warm, and I am squeezing and moving and feeling, and her hand is on my jeans, I hear the zipper go, and then her fingers close around me and I almost lose consciousness.

"Oh. Nice. Let me help you with that." Her hand is squeezing and moving, and I am a limp noodle and a razor-tight wire all at the same time. I cannot kiss her hard enough and I cannot find where my hands should go, because I know nothing about what to do when the hottest girl on the planet has her hand on you and it's so amazing that all the world is exploding supernovas.

Rory is instantly up and I scramble off the floor, zipping up as I go in the hopes that my jumble of getting-up noise covers the sound. Rory sits down on the floor and grabs a strap. I hobble to the driver's seat.

Face redder than I've ever seen it before, Lou stares straight ahead in the passenger seat with her Target bag on her lap and proceeds to fill the silence.

"You'll never guess who was at the cash register. Remember mean old Mr. Larchmont, the guy who used to live next to us when we were little? He was there, in a wheelchair, and his daughter was with him, and they started talking to me. I have no idea how they recognized me, but they did, and . . ."

It takes about ten years to get to our house, and I work on restoring my breathing and my heart rate while I drive and Lou talks, which sort of works. When we get there, Lou bolts inside as quick as she can go.

I turn to Rory, not exactly sure what to say. "So. This is my house."

"Where I'm assuming you have a bedroom?" The smile is back, the one that says she's not embarrassed that my sister caught her with her hand on my dick. Me? I'm embarrassed. But not enough to take her home.

"Um, yeah, of course, but . . ."

"Let's not talk." She kisses my lips like she's the breeze in the trees. "Let's go find your room and pretend we're doing Spanish homework." She holds up her schoolbag.

She doesn't have to ask again. We sneak past Lou's door, then we creep up the stairs to Donna Russell, where she'll have blankets and a big floor waiting for us. Nobody will interrupt.

Maybe an hour later we pull apart, and Rory finally looks around to see where I've brought her. "This is your bedroom?"

"It's a storage room. It used to be a ballroom."

She's on her feet, straightening out her clothes, buttoning and zipping. "There's so much to play with." The pile of fabric catches her attention, and she starts digging through it. "Some of this stuff is super old. And so cool." She holds up a piece large enough to make a dress—at least I'd guess it's large enough to make a dress. "This is from the seventies, maybe even from Europe, judging from the pattern. Maybe Sweden. Can I have it?" She spins to look at me.

"Sure, I guess." I fix my clothes so it doesn't look like we just had the world's most intense mash session, which would have been different if a person could make condoms appear out of thin air. "I don't know who else wants it." What can it hurt to give her some fabric?

Rory puts it into her bag, which is lying at Donna Russell's feet. Then she sees the stack of photocopied face pieces. "What's this?" She starts sifting though them.

"Those are the flash robbers' faces. Pieces of them, anyway."

She pulls out the life-size face for Lou and puts it over her own, then starts talking. "Hi, my name is Lou. Do you know me? I'm so self-involved, I created Facebook, Instagram, Tumblr, Snapchat, and Twitter profiles for myself for good days AND bad days! I don't need castmates when I do a play, because I do all the parts myself! I'm so awesome I shit rainbows and glitter!" Rory is giggling, but I'm not.

"Put it back, all right? I need it." I'm the only one who gets to say bad things about my sister. A thought suddenly arrows through my brain. "You're not the one taking the ghoulie bodies, are you?"

She levels a look at me. "What would be the point of that? And what are THESE?" Suddenly Rory is across the room and down on her knees, getting close-up to Sid the Sasquatch and the sea monsters. "Did you do these?"

"David did the one with the robot in the open field." My mind's still processing what she said. I think she's telling the truth about the ghoulie bodies.

"Epic would love these. You should bring them over sometime and show him." She reaches out and touches Sid. "I'd hang this one over my couch, no problem."

A large BANG echoes up the stairwell.

"What the hell was that?" Rory looks at me. "Someone's blowing off hand grenades?"

"I have no idea." I move as fast as I can down the stairs.

Lou's door is wide open. When I look in her room, she's by the window, looking out. The mirror on her wall is shattered, and there's another glittery piece of wood on the floor. It's the second half—the barrel—of Ghoulie Sarah's gun.

"You OK?" I move toward her, watching where I'm stepping, because my shoes are up with Donna Russell and Rory.

"Assholes!" She gasps through her tears. "They almost

hit me in the motherfucking head!" And she dissolves onto her bed.

I cross carefully to the window and look out, too. It must have been Carter—Mr. Football himself—who threw it, because Lou's window isn't that big, though it's easier to get things through it since there's no glass. Carter made a huge hole in the plastic Dad covered it with. My folks weren't too pissed about the window—they believed her story about accidentally kicking it out—but they're making her pay for the glass replacement. She didn't complain when they told her, which is a miracle.

"You should tell Mom and Dad someone's trying to hurt you." This is bad.

"No!" She sits up on her bed. "They can't know. Just . . . just help me pick up the mirror."

"Lou, this is serious. Really serious. You have to tell them." My stomach is in knots.

"Just shut up, Frankie. You don't know what you're dealing with." She's still crying, but she's pissed, too.

Yes, I do know. The knots get tighter.

"Let me go get my shoes." I turn around and take the stairs two at a time. Rory's back to shuffling through the ghoulie face pieces.

"Someone threw a chunk of wood through Lou's window, and it broke her mirror. I need to help her clean it up." I find my shoes over by the stack of fabric. I don't even remember taking them off. "Can you do your home-work for a while?"

"I guess." It's clear she's not happy I'm deserting her.

"I'll be back soon." I lean down to kiss her, since she's on the floor, but she moves away.

Max Ledermann, the kid she left sobbing in the caf at school, is suddenly front and center in my brain. *This is how it goes, buddy. Just wait.*

Lou and I get the mirror picked up and pitched into the trash can behind the garage. My folks still aren't home, which makes me wonder why they're working late, but I'm more concerned about Rory in the ballroom. I sprint back up to Donna Russell, and Rory is plopped in the middle of the floor, working on a couch painting. She's got a Godzilla-ish guy coming out from behind a very peaceful country cottage, and there are sheep and people running in all di-rections. It's the canvas I was going to paint next.

"Excellent monster choice." I sit down next to her. "Run out of homework?"

"I never do my homework." She gives a sheep another fluff of white wool. "Well, I never do it until after sup-per and after I've done everything but homework. I hate school." She paints one last flourish on Godzilla's head, one last point, and she hands me her brush. "There are a million interesting things in the world, and I intend to try them all. That's why I love hanging out with Epic. I've been to seven different countries because of him." Rory stands up, grabs her painting, and leans it on the wall with the other ones. "Mine is way better than David's. My Godzilla is actually scary. His robot's just dumb. But really, what's not dumb about adding monsters into thrift-store paintings?"

"I think it's pretty hilarious, actually." She can't just insult Sid like that, or David's robot.

"I didn't mean it that way. I just meant . . . well, never mind." She turns to me again with one of those I'm-the-sexiest-girl-on-earth smiles. "Today was fun. We should do it again sometime. Soon, in fact."

She's more beautiful than Miss America and Miss World combined, and I can smell her again. Slightly sweaty. A little flowery, a little spicy, with undertones of my after-shave. My heart does a little jump-hop when I smell it.

I am going to be chewed up and spit out. I know it. But when she leans in to kiss me, of course I kiss her back. This moment may never come again.

V IS FOR

VICTIMLESS CRIME

Wednesday night at Pizza Vendetta. Geno's been after me to make Zambonis, so I make twelve of them, in between all the other pizzas and pizza tasks I've done, and wrap them for the freezer. We should have enough for two months. People don't order them all that often.

At nine, Geno tells me I can go do my homework, but I go out to my truck and of course Rory is there.

"Epic's next piece is going to be amazing. AMAZING." She does a funny little dance, then leans over to kiss me. It's still like an exploding supernova, and just as quick.

"Let's go. I have a curfew now, and I'm only allowed to drive to school and work." I start the truck and she gets in.

"A curfew? What are you, twelve?" Even in the shadows, I see the smirk on her face.

"Yes, didn't you know?" I glare in response to her smirk.

I don't ask her for directions to get to Epic's—I remember most of it, and I want to see if I can get there by myself, landmark to landmark. I only blank one time, but Rory gets me started again.

When we arrive, she hops out and keys the code for the garage door, then motions me inside. David materializes and we bro-hug when I get out of the truck, clasped hands with a shoulder bump, not a real hug but it's something. We haven't talked much since he asked me out.

"Very masculine of you, young man in the skirt, to bro-hug with such authority." I give him a fist bump for added emphasis.

"I'm only a six-pack away from dating girls and wearing pants." He's got on a short frilly skirt that looks like a Hawaiian vacation, the flowers are so bright.

"Maybe a few six-packs."

He tosses me a construction worker's measuring tape. "Help me measure the inside of your truck."

"Why do you need to know that?" I open the back doors and push them wide, leaving space for both of us to climb in.

"Epic's got to know how many pieces your truck can handle."

"No live animals, right?" You can still catch a whiff of sheep if you breathe deep enough.

"Nope. Just papier-mâché. But a lot of it, and some of it's really big."

I go stand by the front seats with one end of the tape measure, and he stands at the end of the truck bed, by the doors. It's about eighteen feet long, and eight feet wide. Plenty of room for whatever Epic's got going on.

Then David holds out his hand. "Now give me your keys."

"My keys? Why?" That's a weird request.

"Just give them here and quit asking questions."

I drop them into his hand. He climbs out of the back of the truck.

A huge THUMP-whack-THUMP-whack-THUMP-whack noise start up somewhere in the garage.

"What's that?" I jump off the back deck of the truck and walk around to see.

Rory's in the far corner, presiding over this huge machine that's making the big noise. It kind of looks like a copier, but it's a little more mechanical than that. "Epic's printing press. He needs more money."

"Where'd he get it?" It's not like anything I've ever seen.

"Not sure." Rory shakes her head. "I think he bought it when a magazine was going out of business. He never buys anything new."

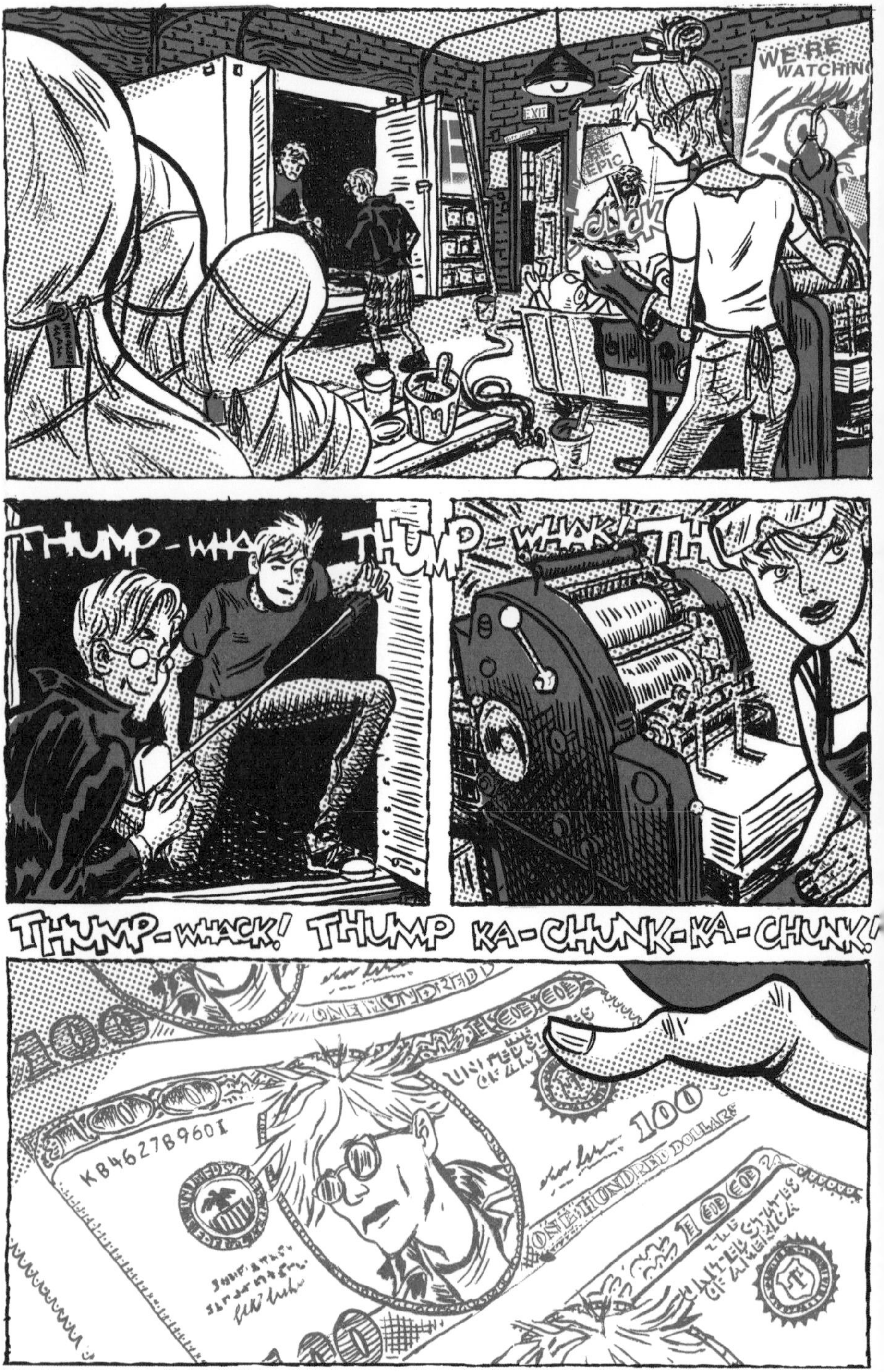
WE'RE WATCHIN
EXIT
CLICK
THUMP-WHA
THUMP-WHAK! TH
THUMP-WHACK! THUMP KA-CHUNK-KA-CHUNK!
ONE HUNDRED DOLLARS
KB46278960I
100

Every time the machine gives a ka-CHUNK, a fresh print slides out and you can smell the ink. Each sheet has a few rows of what looks like hundred-dollar bills, except that where Ben Franklin is supposed to be, there's a guy in Ray-Bans with really funky straightened hair and a feather boa around his neck. Probably can't use them to buy smokes at the Kwiky Pik.

"Is that Warhol?"

Rory points at the wall, where there's a replica of a Campbell's soup can painting. "Who was more against consumerism than Warhol?"

"It might be funnier if it was Donald Trump."

"Tell that to Epic." Rory gathers up the sheets and carries them over to another table, where there's something that might be a paper-cutting machine. There are stacks of money next to the machine, and she hands me a stack as she points toward another table. "Just cover the forms in this glue, then smooth the bills on."

"What are they?" I peer at the thing on the table, and it doesn't make much sense. It looks kind of like an airplane, long and rounded, but with big bumps on one end, on either side of the long rounded part.

Rory's on the other side of the table, and she rolls her eyes, because I don't get the joke. "Come stand over here."

When I move closer to her, I understand—it's a penis.

Balls and shaft, all laid out in glued-on newspaper, ready for its final coating of cash. It's maybe a foot long.

I need to process this information. "Epic is making penises, and we're covering them with fake money that has Andy Warhol in a feather boa on them. Then what?"

"Then we lay them around Nicollet Mall, in front of various places, on Friday night. And they get one of these stuck on top." She reaches below the table and comes up with a sign on a stick. The sign says CONSUMERISM CAN SUCK ME. "Each penis also gets two stickers." I notice squares on the table that say BE EPIC and NOT A FELON. Obviously Epic reads the paper, too.

"And he thinks we can just lay these out on Nicollet Mall? With all the security cameras everywhere?" My mind flashes to a picture of my face on TV in my living room, my parents' heads exploding. Though at least they'd understand where I've been. "We're gonna get caught for sure."

"Ski masks, of course, just like we did with the ATMs. I still have ours." Rory leans close. "We're penis ninjas." She kisses me, and I hear a throat clear from somewhere close to the printing press.

"Don't rub it in." David, coming back from the far corner of the garage.

"Sorry, cuz." But her tone of voice tells me that she is nowhere near sorry. "Get your glue stick on, Frankie." Rory hugs me, then slaps me on the ass, and I frown. She grins.

I send David some thought vibes: *Sorry, dude. We're still bros, though.*

"Does Epic give us instructions in case we get caught and taken in? What do we do then?" I open a jar of glue, and my hand cramps from gripping the lid so hard.

Rory laughs. "That doesn't happen. Relax."

David hands me my keys, and he shows me another set, which he pockets.

"Epic has a key machine? How cool is that?"

David nods. "He bought the remnants of a mom-and-pop hardware store years ago. When we were in London, we did a piece that was about three blocks long, and the person who was supposed to drive the getaway truck lost their keys when he got chased by a dog. We had to walk three miles back to the hotel. Considering how big Nicollet Mall is, and the cop possibility, I think it's good to have two sets."

"David, you're a smart dude."

"A six-pack away from being the president of the United States." He nods.

I start smoothing glue on the penis and plastering the Warhol money on top of the glue, and David shapes small penises over at another table. Rory disappears through a door in the back of the garage.

David holds up a penis for me to see. "Did you read the article in the *Pioneer Press*?" That's St. Paul's newspaper.

"How could you miss it?" It was another two-page spread of Uncle Epic's art during the time he's been home, the eyes and the sheep, plus a bunch of little pieces Epic did in the last few years. The reporter talked about how Epic was one of the most important artistic voices of his age, how you don't get a show at the Walker if you're not somebody important, and no, Epic's not a felon, haters gonna hate, street art is a victimless crime, and shut up. Sounds like Marta did her PR work.

"What did Epic say about it?"

David shrugs. "All press is good press. Read the sticker."

"But why the hell is he doing something as public as Nicollet Mall?"

"Do you think he'll be there with us? Who'll be caught and who won't?" He gives me a look and goes back to shaping his peepee.

"So he lets his crews take the fall for him?"

David gives me another look. "That's part of the usefulness of crews."

I let that sink in for a second.

"Look, it's not like I resent Epic for that fact. We know it's part of why he needs us, and we do it because we're cheap labor and we're family. But we keep him making art, and that's important." He shrugs again. "Epic's work isn't the same old crap. It's direct and blunt. It's also not online, either, where you could just pass him by. People can't ignore him when he's plastered penises across a pedestrian mall. So we help. Though my mom's not happy the cops are watching more than usual." David smiles. "But she believes in him, too. She's his sister."

"The family that makes art together stays together?"

"Something like that." He's working on another penis.

"How many little peepees does Epic want?" There are three on my table that I'm covering in money, and David has three more on his table, plus one that he's working on.

"Probably ten. He's going to put them in front of doors and stuff like that. Casual, like they belong there. And not for every business, just for some. Then there are some bigger dicks that will go to bigger businesses." He points at a huge table by the door that Rory went through. The penises on that table are probably four feet long. "Those two go by the Target and the Macy's. They're big ol' consumer dicks."

"Nothing wrong with being straightforward. And I suppose we need to make some more CONSUMERISM CAN SUCK ME signs?"

"That's my job for tomorrow." David points to a pile of wood and cardboard, next to a small can of paint. "Right now we've got to get the little dicks covered in money so we can work on the big one."

"The big one?"

He makes some this-high and this-wide gestures. "There's got to be at least one big dick, right? It goes in front of the WXXO studio window, propped up on a board so it's visible to the entire viewing population." WXXO is a TV station that does a big morning show on Saturdays, and one of their studios looks out onto Nicollet Mall.

"I wonder how long it will be before someone notices it."

"No idea." David grabs a big white piece of foam board that's leaning against the table leg. "I also have to make the BE EPIC sign for the Giant Sausage." He waves the sign around. "Be epic, ladies and gentlemen. Have some of this here giant weenie!"

Rory comes back with some beach balls. "OK, boys, here's your scrotum for Minnesota's Big Wang. Get going so the glue can dry."

David and I bust out laughing so hard that we can't do anything but fall all over ourselves and the balls Rory handed us. "Scrotum" may be the funniest word ever, and we're tired and punchy. Just when we're finally stopping, one of us will say "scrotum" and the other will say "Minnesota's Big Wang" and someone will say "it needs to dry," and we're back laughing again. Then David chokes out, "Look at Epic's one hundred percent Minnesota beef stick!" and I can't even stand up anymore.

After we get our acts together, we start working on ways to cover the beach balls with papier-mâché. It takes us a little bit, but we get it figured out, and the balls look good. Kind of like real testicles. Once everything's covered, we get some glue and money plastered onto the wet paper. Rory started up the printing press again, and there's more THUMP-whack-THUMP-whack-THUMP-whack in the background, followed by the occasional ka-CHUNK when the press cuts the money. It's really too bad we can't print real money.

David lays a huge PVC pipe on the table. "Here's our shaft." And he cracks up so bad he can't talk for a while, and that gets me going, but we make ourselves stop and we build a penis shaft over the pipe.

My practical brain kicks in before too long, and I look at David. "Where's the board for this thing? If we don't get it on something flat, it'll break when we move it."

"Over there." It's leaning by a random TV, and he brings it back to where we're working. "Let's slide the balls on first." We get the scrotum settled, and then we carefully move the shaft onto the board.

Finally it's done, and it looks really, really good, for something that's six feet long, with balls that are four feet wide, total, and everything's covered in fake money. As long as your expectations are reasonably low, this is a piece of art.

David and I marvel for a while, then we count the little dicks that are still to be covered in money: six. There are six dicks that are already finished. And David has to make some more CONSUMERISM CAN SUCK ME signs, plus the BE EPIC sign that will go on the Great Minnesota Bratwurst.

"We've still got a lot of work to do." David yawns. "But it's three."

Holy shit. I pat myself, looking for my phone, but it's nowhere. "Show me." David flashes me his phone. It's 3:05, to be exact. I sprint for my truck and start it up before David gets to the door control. It gets stinky really fast from the exhaust. "My kielbasa is in extreme danger. Open the damn door."

Rory shouts from somewhere, "Nobody needs carbon monoxide poisoning, Frankie."

"Sorry, Rory. Sorry, David and Epic." I holler it out the window. And I back out of the garage like I'm on fire. The

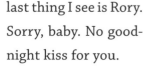

last thing I see is Rory. Sorry, baby. No goodnight kiss for you.

It's at least fifteen minutes to get home from Epic's garage, and when I get there, the entire house is blazing, though mercifully the ballroom lights at the top of the house are still dark. Nobody's been up to visit Donna

or all the ghoulie materials, thank god. I park, take a deep breath, and open the door.

My mom and dad are asleep in the living room, one on each end of the couch. I tiptoe through the living room and almost make it to the stairs when I hear a "Get back here, young man, before you make it any worse on yourself than it already is."

I go back.

My mother is standing up, nudging my dad's legs as she goes so he'll wake up, too. "Did you notice all the texts you had?"

I check. Ten. "I was busy with David and Rory. My phone was in the truck. I wasn't paying attention. I'm sorry."

"Do you not realize that it's a school night, which also happens to be a work night?" If her eyes were laser death rays, I would be dead right now. Her bathrobe's open, and she pulls it around her pajamas like she's just as angry at the robe as she is at me.

"Yes. I'm sorry, Mom."

"You're grounded. And your truck is gone."

I can't process it. "You mean I can't drive it?"

My dad's finally awake and in the game. "No more driving until you start respecting us and the limits we've set for you."

It's like a hammer blow. "But I need it. I need to haul stuff."

"What would you ever need to haul?" My mom's eyes are

still blazing, even though she's yawning. "It's not your job to haul stuff. All you need to do is get to school and work."

"That bitch Rory—you hauled her around." Now Lou's in the doorway, hair looking like she stirred it with an outboard motor, yawning to match my mom's yawns.

"What does she mean?" My dad's wide awake now.

"Just . . . never mind." I don't want them to know Rory was here or anywhere near my truck. "Please don't take it away. Please." How will I get the next ghoulie down to the Kwiky Pik? How will we get the dicks to Nicollet Mall in two days? They can't destroy my life. "Please don't do this."

"Too late." My mom holds out her hand. "Keys, please."

"Please don't do this." I am so close to crying.

"Think about it the next time you stay out until three thirty on a school night."

I drop them into her hand. "When can I have it back?"

"When hell freezes over. I have no idea. Right now, everybody's going to bed. Nobody thinks well at this time of day." She swats Lou on the butt. "Shoo." Then she points at me. "You're our slave for a while. Just know that. Now go." Her face softens, and I see the tears in her eyes. "We're worried, Frankie. You used to be such a good kid."

"I was a fucking bored kid. I just didn't have anything else to do." I stomp up the stairs to my room. When I hear Lou go into her room and close the door, I slide out of mine and sneak up the stairs to Donna Russell, who would never take my truck away.

First I text David: **Asshole parents took my truck away. Hold tight to those keys. Don't tell E. Will work out a plan.**

Then I set the alarm on my phone, since I have to get up in three hours for school. They'll chuck my ass down the street if I don't get up.

Then I can't help it—I sob into Donna Russell's soft blanket legs.

V IS FOR VOLUNTEER

Thursday is the longest day of my life. Three hours of sleep isn't good for anyone. Everyone is practically sliding into their soup on Thursday at supper, we're all so tired from last night's fiasco, and my parents are still royally pissed at me. No gratitude ritual tonight, which probably hasn't happened for three years. They don't remember because they're so tired. While my mom and dad give me death glares, Lou ignores me. She's pissed she doesn't have a ride to school anymore. But I still have Ramona. And Donna Russell, for that matter. She's never pissed at me.

Probably around nine, I go to the kitchen to find an apple or some peanut butter or something, but I am stopped by the sound of my parents' voices in the living room. I sneak a look around the corner.

Mom, sitting on the couch and mending another skirt: "We'll get through this. The good kid will come back."

Dad, pacing: "Bullshit. Staying out all night . . . e-mails from his teachers . . . next thing you know he'll be skipping work, too. And I bet he won't go to college. From what it looks like, he's going straight to the Kwiky Pik to get a job."

Mom, composed as can be: "He'll be fine. He's got a year to get his head on straight." And she sews. Dad paces. Nobody says a word. The TV blares.

I've never heard my parents disagree, first of all. And second of all, I'd never guess in a million billion years that they'd disagree about me.

For the record, I'll cut my arm off before I take a job at the Kwiky Pik. And thanks a lot, Dad, for assuming that staying out all night and forgetting some homework means I won't go to college.

I make no noise when I slide past the living room doorway into the kitchen. Ramen is sounding quite excellent all of a sudden. By the time I come back through, seven minutes later, my mom is slumped over her mending, sound asleep, and my dad is sprawled out at the other end of the couch, sawing logs.

Being a parent must suck. You try to keep your kids out of trouble, and they mess with you every chance they get.

Something hard hits me in the chest when I come out of the bathroom after I brush my teeth.

I look down and see Lou's flip-flop on the floor.

"What's your freaking issue?"

She's standing in the doorway of her room. "Did you take my necklace?"

"What necklace?" I have no idea what she's talking about.

"My drama mask necklace. I can't find it anywhere."

"Why would I take your necklace?" I pick up the flip-flop and chuck it back at her. It hits her in the side of the head.

"Ow, you jerkface. You're a stupid-ass cock licker who only causes his family trouble. You suck, you know that?" And she slams her door closed.

"Lou!" My mother yells up the stairs from their room. "Cut that out!"

"You're a freaky dumb twat who only thinks about herself! I hope your necklace is gone forever!" I pound once on her door, a very solid THUMP. The door shakes.

"Frankie! Quit that!" Mom again.

I go to bed. They can all suck it.

Friday night at Pizza Vendetta. This is the first Friday I've worked that I haven't had a truck. This is the first Friday I've needed a truck, too—like really NEEDED it. My hands won't stop shaking, because I'm alternately pissed and nervous by turns. Plus my parents are coming to get me at eleven thirty. How freaking embarrassing is that?

All night I get pizzas wrong, and one even gets sent back. They wanted sausage, green olive, and onion, and I gave them hamburger, black olive, and garlic chunks. Geno grabs me by the scruff of my neck and drags me to the back room. His wiry gray hair is poking out from under his pizza man hat, and his face is redder than usual. His white T-shirt is smeared with sauce. "What the hell is wrong with you, Frankie? You never get stuff wrong, and this pizza is a total mess. What's wrong with you?" He lets me go, which is good, because he's strong and my arm hurts where he grabbed it.

"I, uh . . ." I think fast. "I had a bad day at school." Which it was. Rory alternated between giving me the stink eye and licking her lips all sexy-like when she caught me looking at her. She's pissed I ran out the other night without a good-night kiss.

"Well, make it un-bad, right now. You can't be screwin' up on the orders, Pepperoniangelo. Got it? Or you're outta here. I mean it." He points at me, but I can see he doesn't mean it. It's in his eyes. He needs me.

"Promise, boss. I won't screw up anymore." I hold up my hand in an I-swear gesture. "Everything perfect from now on."

He frowns. "It better be. Now get out there and get to work."

"You got it, boss." I will myself to focus, and I get every other order right for the rest of the night. No more complaints.

When I take a break, I check Miss Vixen's Twitter feed, and I see a picture of four faces on the wall of the Kwiky Pik. No ghoulie bodies anywhere. Then there's another shot of the faces with their shoes and their mementos. Someone's stuck a glow stick into each ghoulie's candle, so it looks like the candles are lit. I have to admit the faces and their shoes look cool, but cool will not buy me back the parts I have to replace for Epic. I do a quick Google search, and at this point, it looks like I owe Epic about six hundred bucks. I can't get fired now.

If I ever find out who @drseussisgod is, I will come unglued. Who wants mannequin parts except weirdos like me and Uncle Epic? I think Rory was telling the truth—it's not her. But I have no idea who else it could be.

At 11:20, everything's done and I walk out back. My dad's standing there, next to the truck, and he's smoking. I slide in the passenger seat without saying a word. I don't even want to know why he's messing with his pipes before a show.

He stomps out his butt, picks it up, puts it in his coat pocket, and gets in. "How was your night, Frankie?"

"Same old same old. You watch people, you make pizza, Geno yells, it's all good."

He laughs. "Geno's a good yeller." They've seen him in action.

He seems less icy, less pissed. This is good, but it may be the nicotine talking. He's wearing his bustier under a trench coat—the show hasn't even started yet, and he's going to have to hustle to get back to the theater by the time he goes on, which is usually about twelve fifteen. He's driving fast. If we get pulled over, it'll look like a crossdresser is stealing kids in a big delivery truck, and they'll never believe that I'm his son.

We drive in silence for a while.

"So. Dad." I clear my throat, just to get ready. "When can I have my truck back? And why are you driving it?"

"Your mom has the car, and I don't want to drive the work truck if I'm not cleaning." He doesn't look at me. "We haven't decided yet. Maybe soon. Maybe not. It depends on how willing you are to follow the rules we've laid down."

"I'll be better. I promise."

"Not just better. You need to get your act together and keep it together. No question."

"No question."

And we're home. Dad pulls into the driveway, I get out, and he screeches away so he can get to his show on time. I pray he gets back before I need it.

Two thirty a.m. I've been making couch-painting monsters. Lou is asleep in her room. Mom's back from her show, Dad's back from his, and they're asleep, too. I text David to be here as soon as he can be, and I'll meet him outside. If I get caught, I'm volunteering myself for a firing squad. On the bullet side.

My parents aren't just asleep—they're snoring louder than jet engines. I can hear them all the way in the hall, because their door is open. My dad starts talking in his sleep when I walk by.

"You didn't really . . . did you?"

My mom answers. "I did."

"Well, that guy is just the worst." Snort snuffle snorf.

She turns over. "Cucumbers never make sense."

My heart's racing about a million beats per minute, and I'm trying not to laugh, but I freeze, just in case they wake themselves up by talking. I wait for approximately a year, which is probably only a couple minutes, then continue slinking through the house.

The moment I've got my hand on the front doorknob, my mom screeches "KITTENS!" at the top of her lungs, like they're chasing her. I hit the floor with a WHUMP, I'm so freaked, and I can barely contain my yell because she scared me so much. But then I can't control my laughter. That may have been the funniest thing she's ever said. I wait another year, then slowly slowly slowly open the front door.

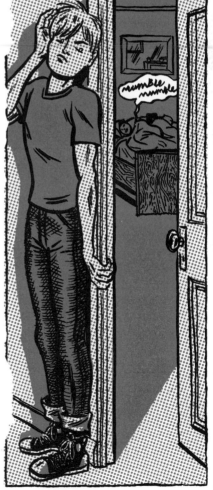

David's standing on my porch, out of breath from long-boarding so fast. "I just got here." He holds out the keys. "Let's go."

I'm still laughing when I get in the truck. "Kittens! All you fucking kittens, back off! Woo-hoo!"

"What the hell are you talking about?" David's getting into the passenger side.

"Forget it. We can't be late." I roll down my window. "Watch out, stupid-ass kittens!"

"You're cracked." David rolls his eyes.

By the time we get to Epic's, Rory's waiting for me outside with a stack of sculptures wrapped in black garbage bags. She gives me a big hug and a smooch on the mouth. "We thought you'd never get here." Obviously she's done ignoring me for a while.

"Relax with the kissing." David gives Rory a glare. "We don't have lots of spare time. People come into the studio around four thirty, and the show starts at five. We gotta move."

David loads a flat cart with a handle into the truck, which is going to be useful, because Nicollet Mall is twelve blocks long. Next to go in is the Minnesota Man Meat and its signs, then the medium-sized dicks, then the small door-decoration dicks. David drilled holes in the penises—penii?—so the signs would be sure to stand up. It all fits in the truck, but there's not much room to spare.

Rory hops in the passenger seat and David sits among the man jerky. We hustle to downtown Minneapolis, but by the time we get there, it's three fifteen. We've got a lot of ground to cover.

Before we leave the truck, which we park kind of close to the middle of the mall, Rory throws us two plain black ski masks, and she puts on a third. "Now we're ready."

We all touch fists. We have to work fast.

David and I load up the cart with the little dicks, and we skate it like a longboard down to the other end of the mall, leaving Rory to set up the medium-size Manly Slim Jims in front of Macy's and Target. We leave a few randomly around, constantly scanning for movement and people, but we make sure to get one in front of the library that's there.

Once everything is all set with the small penises, it's time for the big show. David and I glide our way back to the truck and to Rory.

"Let's do this!" She's almost hopping, she's so excited. "This is even more fun than sheep!"

David and I get the Minnesota Hot Beef Injection out from the truck, sliding it onto the flat cart. Its beefy goodness overpowers the small space and the small wheels, but it's all we've got.

Rory's already in front of the studio window of WXXO, scouting for the best place to put the sculpture, something not obvious but still visible. There are two skinny trees and a planter full of flowers, so Rory opts to lean the Major Peepee up against the planter and kind of drape the plants around it. She gets the signs arranged next to the piece, then we stand by the studio window to check the effect. The signs should catch your eye first, and the signs are turned toward the TV station, so people in the studio looking through the window to the mall will see the signs first, and read them right along with the viewing audience. Then they'll realize there's a big old penis propped up in the scenery. At least that's what we hope.

It's 4:10 a.m., which means we should get the hell off of Nicollet Mall. Things will start waking up, especially at coffee shops, though we didn't leave a Little Dingle at any of them.

Rory's in the truck first, and she's honking the horn. "Here's your penis drop, Minneapolis! Hello, penis delivery!" She's shouting and laughing like a wild woman.

"You're gonna get us arrested, fool." David knocks her hand away from the horn and points. A rent-a-cop has just come out of City Center, looking around for the source of the noise.

I turn to hide my face and whip off my mask. "Sit down." Now is when I wish my truck was covered in camouflage.

While she scrambles across to the passenger side, I get in, calm as can be, and start things up. David shuts the back door once he's heaved the cart in, and we drive away, smooth and easy.

"David, what's the cop doing?"

David looks out the back-door windows. "Nada. He looked around a little, and he saw us, but we must've just looked like delivery people. He's going back inside."

Rory's still cackling. "That was amazing!" She leans out of the passenger seat and gives me a huge kiss on the cheek. "We have to do that more often!"

"Hate to tell you, Rory, but papier-mâché penises are a one-shot deal. You can't repeat that shit."

David laughs. "One shot. With dicks, that's a pun."

Then I laugh. Then we all laugh, and then we're back at Epic's by the time we've made as many penis jokes as are humanly possible.

Rory jumps from the passenger side to punch in the code to get the garage door up. David hops out the back and yanks the flat cart with him. "See you, Frankie."

"You rock, Skirt Man. That's your superhero name."

"I like it." And he's pushing the cart into the garage.

Rory's come back to my window. "I want to see you soon." She's whispering. "A lot of you. In a horizontal position."

She is not saying this.

"Well . . ." And that's all I get out, because she's kissing me, full on, making my head blow apart while my body fuses together into one hard knot which is not made of papier-mâché. And she smells like night air, adventure, and something that might be glue. When she finally pulls away, I'd swear I wasn't on Earth anymore.

"Better go." She licks her lips. "Text me, OK?"

"Uh." I can't think. "Yeah."

And she's gone in the slam of the side door.

"Bye," I croak, even though she can't hear me.

I drive home in a daze, so it takes me a couple seconds to notice that the entire house is lit up like a Christmas tree, including a light in Donna Russell's ballroom, holy shit. My stomach falls on the floor of the truck, and I metaphorically scoop it up and swallow it again.

I know what's coming, but I wouldn't have missed that for the world.

Almost before I've shut the truck door, my mother is out of the house and in the driveway. She's got on a sweatshirt and pajama pants. No kittens anywhere to be seen. "Franklin Brett Neumann, you are not going to see the outside of this house for the next ten years. Do you understand me? You are grounded until the end of time."

If a person could light someone else on fire with their eyes, I'd be in flames, and her hair would be smoking. She is so angry I can't step any closer to the house for fear of being incinerated in her aura.

"You screwed up big-time, son. Really big-time." My dad is right behind her, but even he's keeping his distance from her fury. He's got on boxers and a T-shirt, no pink bathrobe.

"It's just . . . I know I messed up, but my friends needed me." I sound stupid, but it's the truth.

"Your friends aren't the boss of your life. We are, and when we say no driving, we mean no driving." Her face is the color of a fire truck. "You are in extra trouble because you made another set of keys. Give them here now. You won't see that truck until you graduate." She opens her palm, and I drop them in. "Get inside. Don't talk to me for a while." She won't even look at me.

I shoot a glance at my dad, and he just nods his head, letting me know he agrees with her.

I look at my phone. It's 5:12. How did they know I was gone? All I want is to get upstairs and check on Donna Russell.

When I go by the living room, Lou's wrapped in a quilt on the couch.

"What's wrong with you?" She looks like she's five again, all tiny and bundled up.

"You don't want to know."

I don't. She's right. But the guilt is suddenly thick in my stomach. "Tell me anyway."

"Just a nightmare."

"So why is everyone up?"

Lou sighs. "I was screaming. Mom and Dad came busting upstairs, and then we wondered why you didn't wake up, and then they realized you were gone."

"When was this?"

She shrugs. "Maybe half an hour ago. Where were you?"

"With the friends that everybody thinks are imaginary. What was the nightmare?"

Why didn't they text me when they realized I was gone?

"I don't even know now. There was breaking glass. And some body parts running after me." She curls deeper into the blanket. "It was just scary."

My body is icy cold. "But you can probably go back to sleep now. Can't you?"

"Maybe." Then she smiles. "Will you come sleep with me? Like we used to do when we were little?"

My mind speeds back to a big blanket fort we set up in her room. We must have been six and eight, something like that. We used to make blanket forts all the time, and we'd make Mom and Dad bring supper in there so we could all eat in the fort. Then we'd spend the night in it, just me and Lou, and we'd read books by flashlight and tell silly stories. It was cramped and cozy, and I remember feeling

OK, like I actually did belong with them. Like my family understood me, even just for a little bit.

That stupid guilt arrow slices through me and hits a bull's-eye right in the pit of my stomach. "Meet me on your bed. But I'm not staying."

Lou throws off her quilt and gives me a whack on the head on her way up the stairs.

I hear my parents in the kitchen—they must be planning to behead me now—but I race up both sets of stairs before they catch me. Donna Russell's still there, watching over the ballroom, and it doesn't look like anything's been taken or moved. Nobody touched the couch paintings—they're still lined up against the wall. Luckily the only ghoulie stuff lying around is the sewing machine. The face photocopies, the mannequin parts, and the fabric are all in the closet. Once I reassure myself that my kingdom is still intact, I shut the light off and go back downstairs.

She's got a bunch of pillows and blankets on her bed for me, which is queen-size, so two teenagers fit all right. I throw my shoes in my room and flop on the unclaimed half of her bed.

Lou's under the covers and yawning already, so I start yawning, too.

"Thanks, Frankie." She closes her eyes.

"You are a basket case of a girl who has too much imagination."

"You are an egregious error of a guy who has too much ego." She closes her eyes.

"Bonus points for alliteration." I close mine, too.

And then it's noon, and Lou is gone. I'm alone in her nightmare drama club room. But she was nice enough to cover me with a blanket and shut her door.

V IS FOR VENI, VIDI, VICI

Sunday morning. I'm watching a news clip from WXXO's Saturday morning show for about the ninetieth time. David texted me yesterday afternoon: **Go to YouTube and search for "WXXO penis prank." I didn't put it there.** Of course I forgot to set our TiVo to record the morning show, but the video tells me all I need to know.

Five a.m. The conversation goes like this:

HOST LADY: Good morning, Minnesota! Welcome to your weekend.
HOST DUDE: Welcome to Saturday, and . . . [squints off camera] What? There's a what? A penis? [looks in the camera] Friends, they're telling us there's something unusual outside our window. [turns around]
HOST LADY: [looking off camera] Did you just say there's a dick out there? [turns in chair]

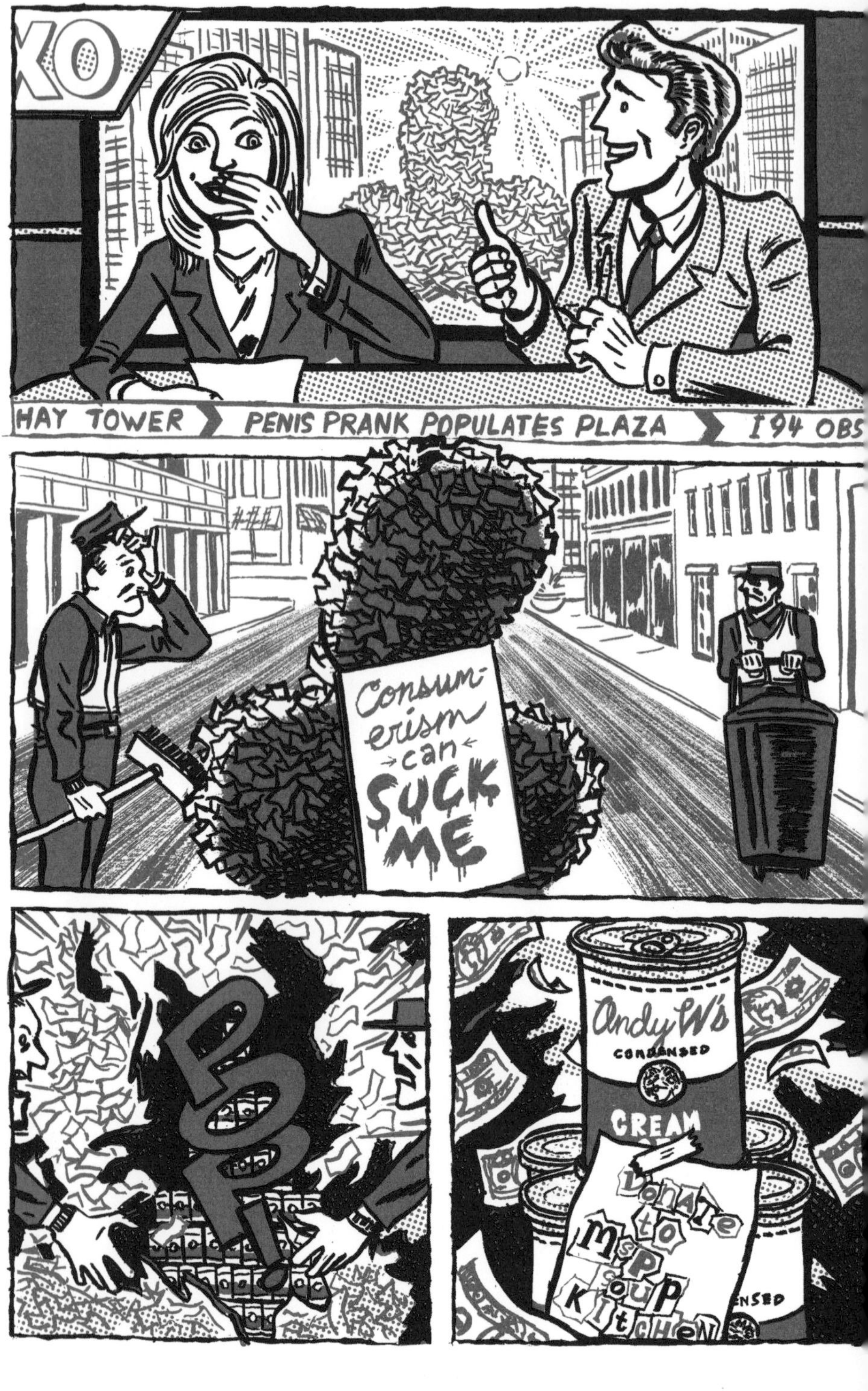
XO
HAY TOWER
PENIS PRANK POPULATES PLAZA
I94 OBS
Consum-erism can SUCK ME
Andy W's
CONDENSED
CREAM
Donate to msp soup kitchen
ENSED

HOST DUDE: Well, friends, someone was busy last night.

HOST LADY: [uncontrollable laughter, leaning out of her chair and crying]

HOST DUDE: Uncle Epic, my hat's off to you. [stands up and bows deeply]

You can hear the laughter off camera, and the camera bobs just a little, like someone's bumped it. Then it goes black.

There was an article in the Minneapolis *Star Tribune* this morning, complete with pictures, but they didn't show any of the man meat, just a close-up of the Warhol money and a side view of part of the Big Kielbasa at WXXO. The article made it sound like Epic was both a genius and a public menace, which seems fair. The reporter said nobody had proven a definite connection between the flash robs and Epic, but police were convinced it was there. The Walker refused to comment about whether or not Epic's show was still on.

Even if David thinks Epic will be fine, I'm not sure.

When I check Miss Vixen's Twitter feed, there's a tweet from @drseussisgod. It's a picture of one of Epic's penises with a note on a piece of paper next to the dick. The note says *Why don't you do something funny like this?*

Dear @drseussisgod, you can suck my Minnesota Man Meat.

I try to spend the day doing homework, but since my folks are still uber-pissed at me, they make me clean out their truck. Just as I'm sneezing out the last of the Ajax powder I had to sweep up from the truck floor—they really need to find a better place for it, since it dumps over so much—I get a text from David.

When do we do more ghoulies?

I sneeze. **Might be done. Haven't decided.**

NO. Frowny faces times twenty. **We have to do at least one more. I'm coming over.**

David shows up at seven, wearing his saggy black grandma skirt, and my parents welcome him at the same time they remind me that I'm grounded and I have no truck privileges so have fun in my room, since that's the only place I can go. But of course we sneak up to Donna Russell as soon as we possibly can.

"It's like a room full of treasure." David's looking around again. "Fabric, sewing machine, paint, whatever. It's the jackpot."

"If it was somewhere else, it would be treasure. Right now it's just sanity."

"Now it's time for the lecture." David puts his hands on his hips. "This is Skirt Man talking to you. You can't quit now."

"My sister's having screaming nightmares, and people are throwing shit in her window. She got kicked out of her

Macbeth scene because girls refused to work with her, and she's lost all her friends. That cop was watching when we put out Sarah and Brooklyn, and we don't want to give the police any more ammunition to be looking for Epic." That bull's-eye in the pit of my stomach where the guilt arrow hit starts to ache. "Another ghoulie wouldn't help anyone." If I don't watch it, I'm going to sob. "I . . . really should quit. Yeah."

David can tell I absolutely don't want to quit. "Miss Vixen has to say good-bye, and Epic can handle himself. He's Epic." He points a finger at me. "The haters don't have any more tricks for Lou, and she can make new friends. She made her own decision to be part of that flash rob. The last ghoulie doesn't have to be about Lou."

Last ghoulie, last hurrah. Miss Vixen really should say good-bye. Leave Lou out of it. Epic is epic.

Say something that matters. What matters?

Art matters.

"OK, but if something weird goes down, you have to help me fix it."

He smiles. "Fine. But nothing's gonna happen. Nobody cares anymore about the ghoulies—they're old news, after five flash robs and three huge Epic pieces, one of which included penises. You just need to finish your work. As your friend, I want to help you do that."

"Are you insulting Miss Vixen?" I give him the finger. "Five flash robs? I thought there were four."

"Latest one was yesterday at a Kwiky Pik by the airport. Robbers were dressed as flight attendants with Barack Obama masks." He rolls his eyes.

"Good lord. No wonder the cops are pissed at Epic, even though they're wrong. Do they know who's doing it?"

"Not that I've heard. But don't worry about that. Shut up and get busy." He turns and starts rummaging in the closet. "All your fabric is stupid."

I try and decide who the last ghoulie should be. "Do you want to make a guy ghoul or a girl ghoul?"

David thinks while he digs around. "Mixtape monster?"

"Brandon Anderson and Allison Lawson could go together." I survey the mannequin parts. "I hereby christen the next monster Brallison. Can you make me something that looks like a Greek toga, but a little simpler? And the skirt could be shorter?"

"Sure thing." David holds out a couple curtains that were in the pile, the gauzy thin kind. "Can I make it out of this? It's pretty girly."

"Perfect." I sort through a bag of clothes in a corner—old clothes that never got donated to a thrift store—and pull out a pair of my dad's cuffed dress pants, from his office days. "Brallison can wear these under her skirt. I also need you to make a sash, like Miss America would wear. And do you think Epic will be mad if I alter just one torso?"

David shakes his head. "He kind of owes you, doesn't he? He never pays you for gas or anything."

"Good point, except for the fact that someone's stolen four ghoulies' worth of mannequin parts, so now I owe him. Hang on while I find some tools."

"Can I take some fabric for skirts?" He's already sorting through folded scraps.

"You just told me my fabric was stupid."

"I didn't mean it." He starts making a pile of fabric he likes.

"Knock yourself out." And I go slow and quiet down the steps.

When I get to the next floor, the coast is clear. I hear Lou in her room, on her phone.

"No, I'm not Miss Vixen! I've said it a million times!" Her voice is high and frustrated.

Someone must still be talking to her, but they're not talking about rainbows and unicorns.

I try to act casual when I get to the main floor. My parents are in the living room, nodding and asleep over their books because it's eight thirty and that's late for old people like them. Quiet as a mouse, I let myself out of the house and find a handsaw and a file in the garage. Quiet as a mouse, I let myself back inside, and take a quick detour through the kitchen for one last prop. By the time I pass the living room again, they haven't moved.

When I get back up to David, he's made a stack of fabric that's obviously his bounty, and he's sewed a ruffle made of purple tulle onto his black grandma skirt.

"I want this." He lays his hand on the stack, like he's protecting it from me.

"Take it. You're a six-pack away from opening a dress shop."

"You know it, brother." He sighs. "Whatcha gonna do with that manly saw?"

"Just watch. And for the record, the purple ruffle isn't going to help that skirt. It's just ugly. Hold this." I clear a spot on the floor.

David holds the torso down so it won't move, at least not much, and I do a horrible job of hacking off one breast.

"I feel like the apprentice to a serial killer dismemberer guy." He frowns while I saw.

"What's your point?" Sweat trickles down my forehead and into my eye.

Finally I get the plastic mound off the chest, and there's a huge gaping hole, which makes me just as uncomfortable as mutilating the torso. David goes back to sewing while I work on the body. The file helps some of the raggedness, but then I cover the hole with tape and paper. It's just too much to look at.

"Are you up for the challenge of Monster Brallison's features?" The stack of copied face pieces are closer to David, and I point to them. "We need to really mix it up this time. Boy, girl, monster craziness."

"I need to finish three seams." He bends over his toga, which is looking quite light and fluffy.

I spread the faces out on the table the sewing machine sits on. When David's done, we pick Allison's blown-up face as Monster Brallison's base, and we leave Brallison her lips. Then we get Luke Holdrege's nose out, and one of Matt Havelock's eyes, on the side of the face above the breast. Sarah Taylor's eye goes on the side above the hole in Monster Brallison's chest. There's a pile of pipe cleaners that got left out from David's Mood Bag of Craftiness, so I twist them into interesting shapes and tape them on the back of Monster Brallison's head for hair.

"It's balanced." David stands back to look, once we've

got Monster Brallison's face and body attached, and the toga and pants are on. "I like it."

"Did you do the sash?" Nothing like footballs or test tubes or lions this time around—just a sash, like she's the Ghoulie of the Year winner. And no tulle. This is not about Lou.

"Right here." David hands me the sash, and I paint ART MATTERS on it in huge letters, then drape it over Brallison.

He smiles, but it's sad. "It's a shame we have to say it at all."

I stick a Popsicle stick from David's bag into the bottom of a Styrofoam cup, then tape the stick in place in Brallison's hand. Then I rip down the sides to about an inch high, so the cup and stick are kind of like a torch. Finally I impale the unpeeled banana I grabbed from the kitchen on the Popsicle stick. Even though this is about Miss Vixen, I want a final homage to the zip-up banana bus.

My brain is running a total of all the things that could happen if we take this ghoulie to the Kwiky Pik. What if Lou can't find new friends? What if Officer Nelson arrests us? What if Epic gets in trouble? What if I get grounded until I'm thirty?

David moves around Monster Brallison. "Best ghoulie yet, hands down." He checks his phone. "It's eleven thirty. How the hell are we going to get this to the Kwiky Pik?"

"Help me take Monster Brallison apart."

"Why?" He frowns. "We just got him—her—put together."

"We can't carry it like this. We're going to need pieces."
I take off Monster Brallison's clothes and arms, and I un-
attach the head piece from the torso.

"How do we get it out the door?"

"Carefully. Quietly." I go to the top of the stairs and
listen. "Pick up everything you can carry." I gather up as
much of Monster Brallison as I can, and David grabs the
rest of it along with the mannequin stand. We go really,
really slow down the stairs, and we don't drop anything.
All's quiet from Lou's room. We're just as quiet going down
the next set of stairs, and we ease ourselves out the back
door. Then we realize David's longboard is inside the front
door, so I sneak back and grab it.

Getting to the Kwiky Pik takes a long, long time. Longer than I wish it did. We drop Monster Brallison's pants
once, and once David loses the face but we don't discover
it until a few blocks later, so we have to go back and find
it. Finally we're there.

David and I put Monster Brallison back together at top
speed, just in case the cops are lurking someplace. S/he's
one lonely creature all by herself. The ghosts of the ghoulies on the wall make her seem even more alone. But maybe
that's OK for the last one. All of the ghoulies' stuff is gone,
too: the shoes and the candles and the old glow sticks. The
only thing left are faces on the wall. Even so, *veni, vidi, vici*:
we came, we saw, we conquered. Art wins.

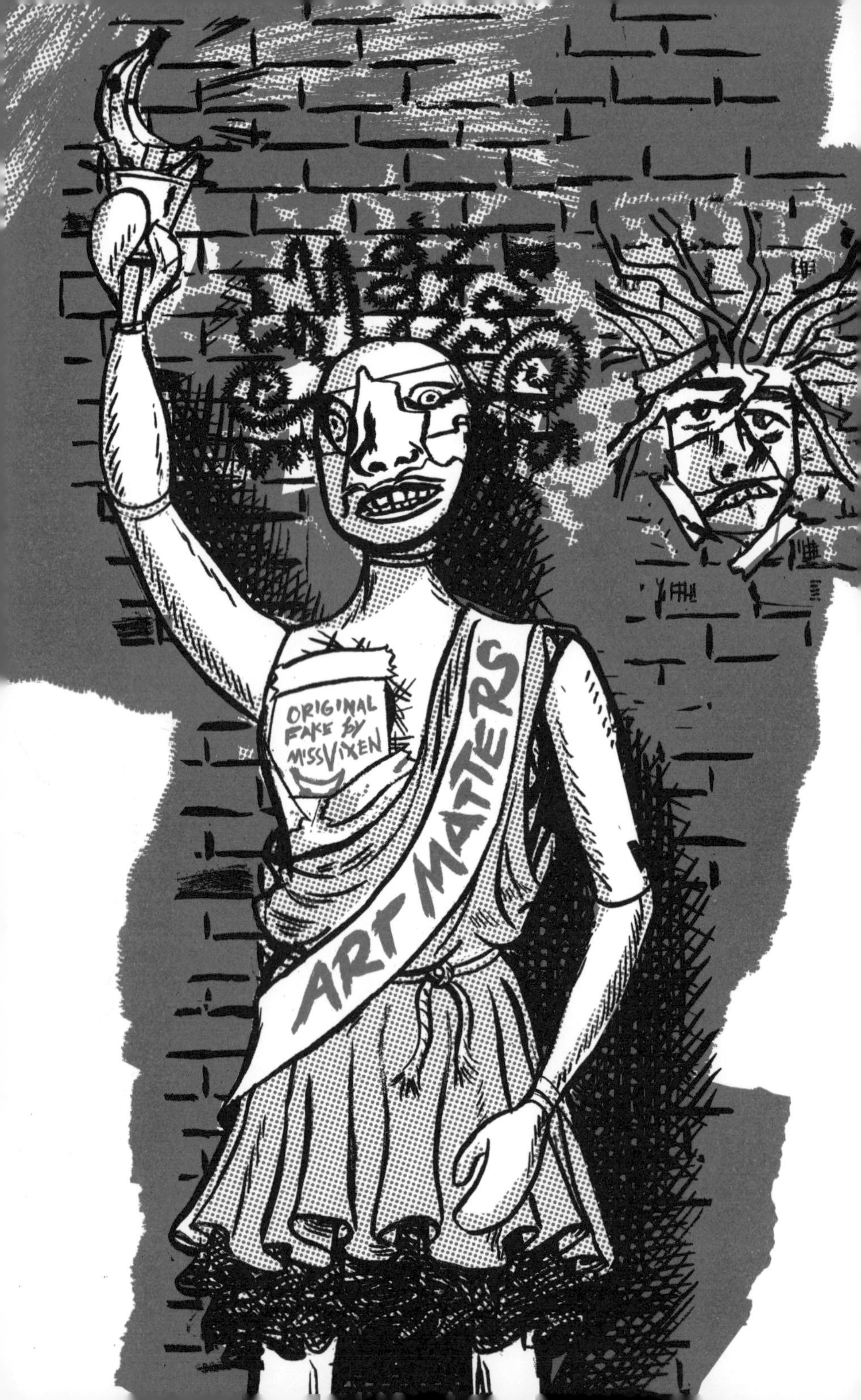
ORIGINAL FAKE BY MISSVIXEN
ART MATTERS

Miss Vixen tweets a photo: **The last ghoulie with her ghostie friends. Last Original Fake. Thanks for the memories.** Then a special photo of Monster Brallison for @ drseussisgod: **Stay away from this one. Please.**

David leaves, then I glide home, going slow because I'm tired. It's beautiful, with an almost warm breeze and newly bushy trees in the faint moonlight. You can smell that spring is definitely here. If Rory smelled like spring, I would be in deep trouble.

It's awesome to be out in the middle of the night. There are so many things I could do. I could set bombs off in other neighborhoods and nobody would see. I could go to the grocery store and buy food and set out a buffet to feed all the homeless people and nobody would have any idea it was me. I could set fire to the school. I could make an enormous pile of trash cans. I could take soap and write UNCLE EPIC IS GOD on everybody's car. It's a rush, to be anonymous in the dark.

And parents—my parents, David's mom, anybody's parents—are ignorant if they think they know what their kids are doing.

I slide into the dark house, silent as a shadow. When I get to my room, there's a note on my bed: *YOU DON'T EVEN KNOW HOW MUCH TROUBLE YOU'RE IN. MOM.*

OK, then. So much for stealth and them not paying attention.

I don't brush my teeth, because if they all fall out, it's fine. Nobody's going to see me ever again, since I'm going to live upstairs with Donna Russell for the rest of my life.

3:42 a.m. Text from Rory. **Wake up, sexy.**
I'm here. Kind of.

See you tomorrow. We should meet up. I have a surprise for you!

OK. I doze off.

Still there? There are three messages that say that by the time the phone's vibration shakes me awake again.

Sort of.

Dream of me, OK? And she's gone.

I do dream about her. And it ends up the way you think it might.

VULNERABLE

Mondays must be the most boring days in the history of America, and this Monday is no exception. Turns out Rory's not here, so I have no idea what her surprise is. Also, Spanish class smells a lot less excellent without her.

Mom didn't say a word to me before school. She wouldn't look at me, either. I guess she's saving up her anger for suppertime, when we talk about what we're thankful for. She'll tell us she's thankful she gets to rip me a new one.

After school it's time to glide by the Kwiky Pik and check out Monster Brallison. I heard a few comments in the hall, which is good. I want Miss Vixen's last ghoulie to be the one people talk about for a long time.

From a distance I can see there's a crowd, which is cool, but maybe not good. And then the cops pull up, which is really not good. Once I get close enough, I can hear yelling. It's a high-pitched "No! Fuck you! No!" Each yell is followed by a ripping sound.

I glide a little faster.

By the time I get there, the shouting and ripping have stopped. Once I push my way to the front of the crowd, I see Lou swinging a mannequin stand. Monster Brallison is in tatters on the ground, clothes and mannequin pieces everywhere, along with a bunch of ripped-up paper. Lou's face floats on the top of the rubble pile, her photocopied face, approximately the same size as the photocopied faces I used to make the ghoulies. The face that used to be in my pile of photocopies at home.

And who should be standing on the edge of the crowd but Rory, looking highly amused.

Lou sees me, drops the mannequin stand, and screams, "Frankie! She stole my necklace and she framed me and GET AWAY FROM ME!" The cops are reaching for her while she points at Rory. Lou bursts into tears. My stomach shrivels up.

"Miss, you need to come with us. You need to calm

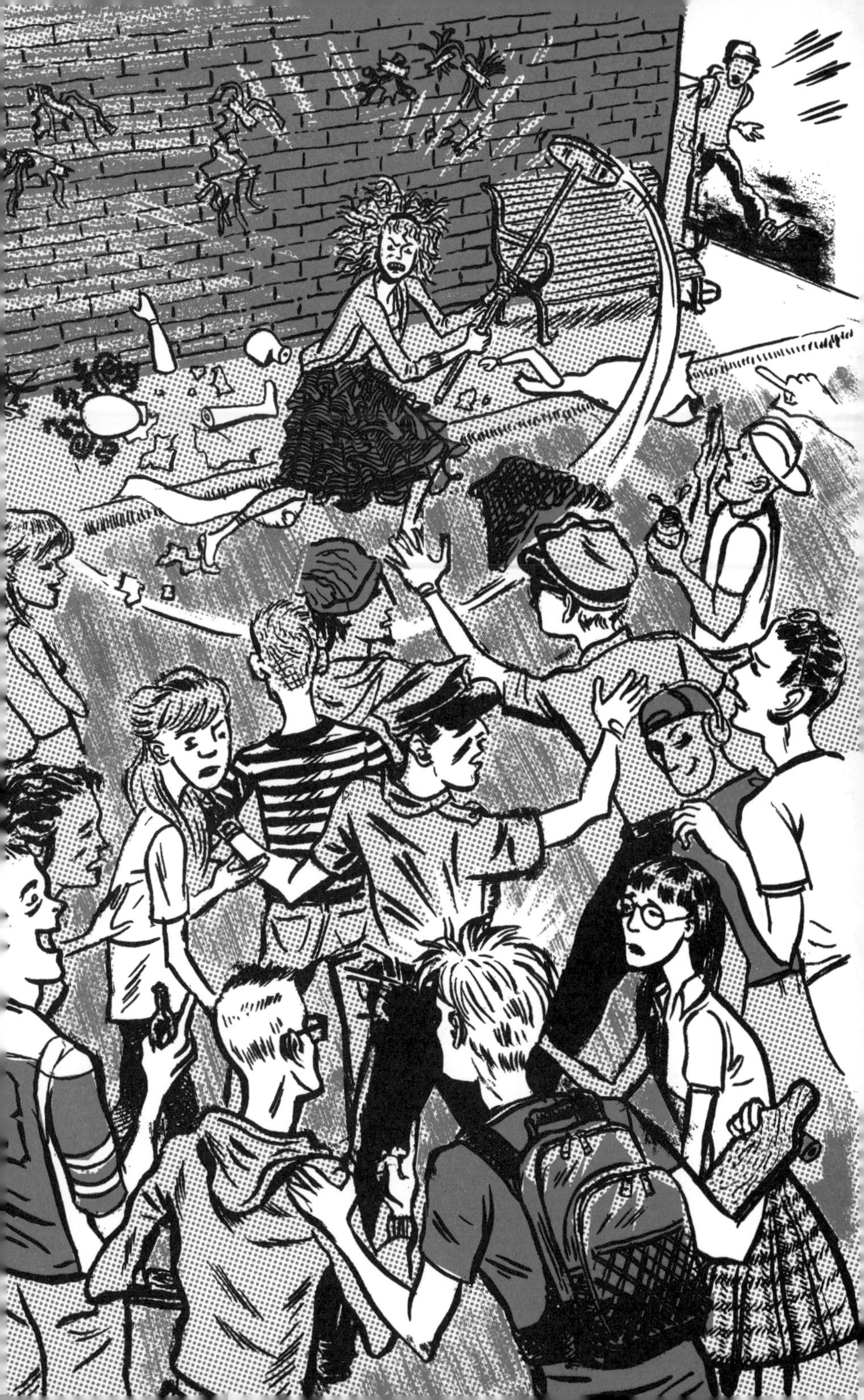

down and come talk with us at the station." A police officer has his hands out in front of him, looking like he wants to make peace while he's actually reaching for her arms.

"I haven't done anything!" Lou shrieks at him and looks at me. "Frankie, help!"

"We're going to talk once you calm down, miss, and we're going to do it at the station." The officer grabs her, not all that gently, while she tries to shrug him off. They put her in the back of their car and zoom off. My throat closes up when I see Lou's face framed by the cop car window. Everyone watches them go, and then, when the car is gone, like one person's head, they all turn to look at me.

I look at Rory. She's grinning ear to ear. "Surprise!" She claps her hands like I'm supposed to join her in celebrating.

I see a glint of gold underneath Monster Brallison's carnage. When I look closer, I realize it's Lou's drama mask necklace, so I dig it out and put it in my pocket. "This is my surprise? You stole her necklace? And her face?"

"Small details." Rory gestures to the paper scattered around. "You should've seen it. She had a complete meltdown."

"And now she's been hauled off in a cop car!" My chest is tight, and the guilt arrow is stabbing me everywhere.

"I thought you wanted to make her feel bad." Rory's face is mean.

"That's my biz, not yours. Jesus, Rory, what did you do?" I grab things, picking up the remains, so nobody can see how close I am to tears. A girl hands me one of Brallison's arms. Out of the corner of my eye I see a few flash robbers— Carter, Matt, Allison, and Sarah. When I turn to them, they glare and walk away in a group, muttering to each other.

Once I really look at the pieces of paper, what happened starts to make sense. Rory made a big paper doll and taped it on top of Brallison. It's a drawing of a girl wearing a tulle skirt, with Lou's photocopied face on the top. The girl's shirt says I'M MISS VIXEN, AND I'M GOING TO THE COPS. FLASH ROBBERS, GET READY.

"You are a complete and utter bitch."

"Don't tell me you aren't happy she freaked out." Rory's got her feet planted and her arms crossed, glaring at me.

"Who called the cops?"

Rory smirks. "Probably the people inside. I don't know."

"I bet you did that, too. The people inside can't even see this end of the building." I keep gathering Monster Brallison pieces, stacking the mannequin parts by the wall and grabbing paper before it blows away. "You're an asshat, you know that? You fucked with someone who's never hurt you. Why do you shit on people?"

I need to get to the police station, and I'm picking up litter. What the hell is wrong with me?

"I thought you'd be happy." Her arms are still crossed.

"This is between Lou and me." The more I think about it, the angrier I get. "Do what you want with your knitting and with Epic, but the ghoulies are mine. And my sister is off-limits." The garbage can isn't bolted down, so I drag it over to the pile of pieces I've started. I can't help Lou anyway.

A hand rests on my lower back, and it feels like a hot coal. "I didn't know she was going to bust stuff up. I just wanted her to . . . I don't know . . . be mad. She was the fool for being at the flash rob. She should have expected something like this."

I shake off her hand. "You wanted to do a flash rob, too. What if someone decided to rat you out? What would you do if you saw yourself made into a giant paper doll, after people had threatened you with violence to keep quiet? Wouldn't you want to beat the crap out of everything?"

Of course I've just described what I did to Lou. Now the guilt arrow has moved from the pit of my stomach to my heart, and it's stabbing me into little pieces.

If I say anything more, I'm going to lose it, so I just keep shuffling the remains of Monster Brallison and the paper doll into the garbage can. All the other ghoulie faces are still tacked up on the wall of the Kwiky Pik. They're a pretty stern jury, even with their makeup on.

"I've got to go find Lou. Don't ever talk to me again." If I could make my words into poison spears, I'd pin her ass to the parking lot.

"Do you even know where the police station is?" There's a hint of laughter in Rory's voice. She points. "About six blocks that way, then take a left."

I grab Ramona and push fast toward the cop shop while I try calling my folks. No answer.

When I get there, I'm out of breath. The woman behind the counter glares at me like I'm going to contaminate her by breathing on her too hard. She's short and slightly lumpy, with aggressively red hair that complements her stern demeanor.

"I need to find Tallulah Neumann. Can you help me?"

The woman is unmoved. "Is she a minor?"

"Yes. She's my sister."

"You'll have to wait there for her—your—parents." The woman points to a couple rows of chairs in the ugliest waiting room I've ever seen. It's an excellent place to feel hopeless, so I take Ramona into the corner and kick my own mental ass for a while. Why did I ever start with the ghoulies? Why did I ever think it was a good idea to mess with Lou? Why didn't I just tell my parents about the flash rob like any other big brother would? Why the hell was it more important to make art? And why why why did I ever get close enough to Rory to smell her? Why couldn't she smell like a sewer? None of this would have happened if she'd smelled like crap.

I text Lou: **I'm here but they won't let me come see you. They said wait for folks.**

No answer. I'd bet they took her phone.

And now I have no fucking idea what to do.

I twirl Ramona's wheel until the woman gives me a death stare, because it's not particularly quiet to spin a longboard wheel. But there's no sign that says I have to be quiet.

I text my dad first, just for the calm factor: **Please come to the police station near Henderson High. Don't freak out. Nobody's dead.**

I can't think what to do next, so I text David. **Rory is a bitch and I'm never doing anything with E again if she's there. Lou's at the police station because of her.**

He texts back immediately. **I told you it might end poorly.**

He did tell me. **Always listen to a bro. My mistake.**

Six smiley faces. **6-pack away from being a bro. Where are you?**

Cop shop, duh, trying to think of a way to spring Lou. Can't get my folks to answer.

Be cool. No worries. Easy for him to say.

I text my mom, since Dad hasn't texted. She's gonna blow up anyway. **Call me as soon as you get this. Lou is in trouble.** Then I put Ramona down on the ground and push her back and forth with my foot. Counter Lady gives me another death stare. But seriously, what can I do? I've never been so helpless in my whole life.

Fifteen minutes go by. No text from either parent.

IN LESS THAN 10 SECONDS, I AM GOING TO SCREAM, CRY, OR THROW UP. MAYBE ALL THREE. INSTEAD I CLOSE MY EYES.

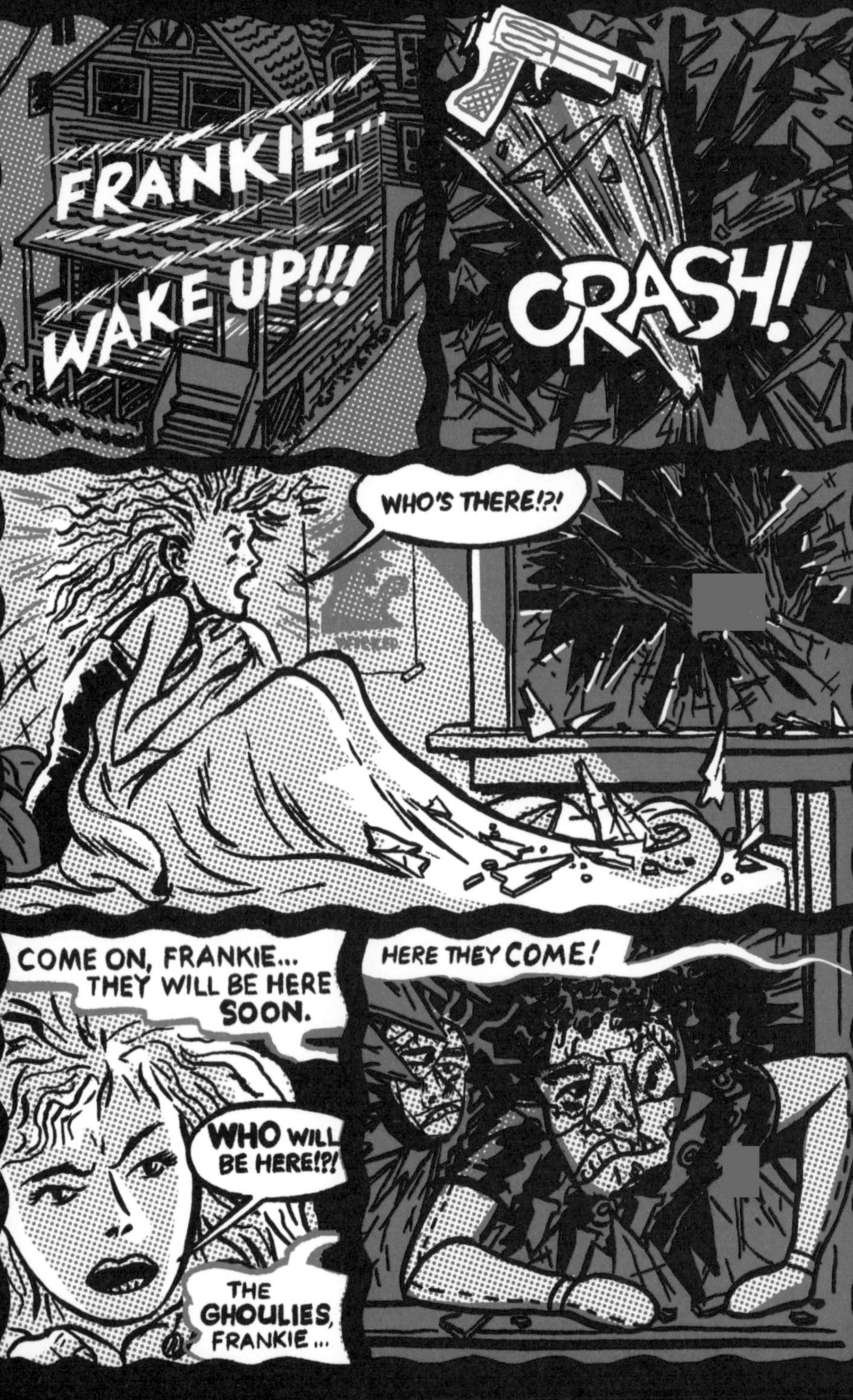
FRANKIE...
WAKE UP!!!
CRASH!
WHO'S THERE!?!
COME ON, FRANKIE... THEY WILL BE HERE SOON.
WHO WILL BE HERE!?!
THE GHOULIES, FRANKIE...
HERE THEY COME!

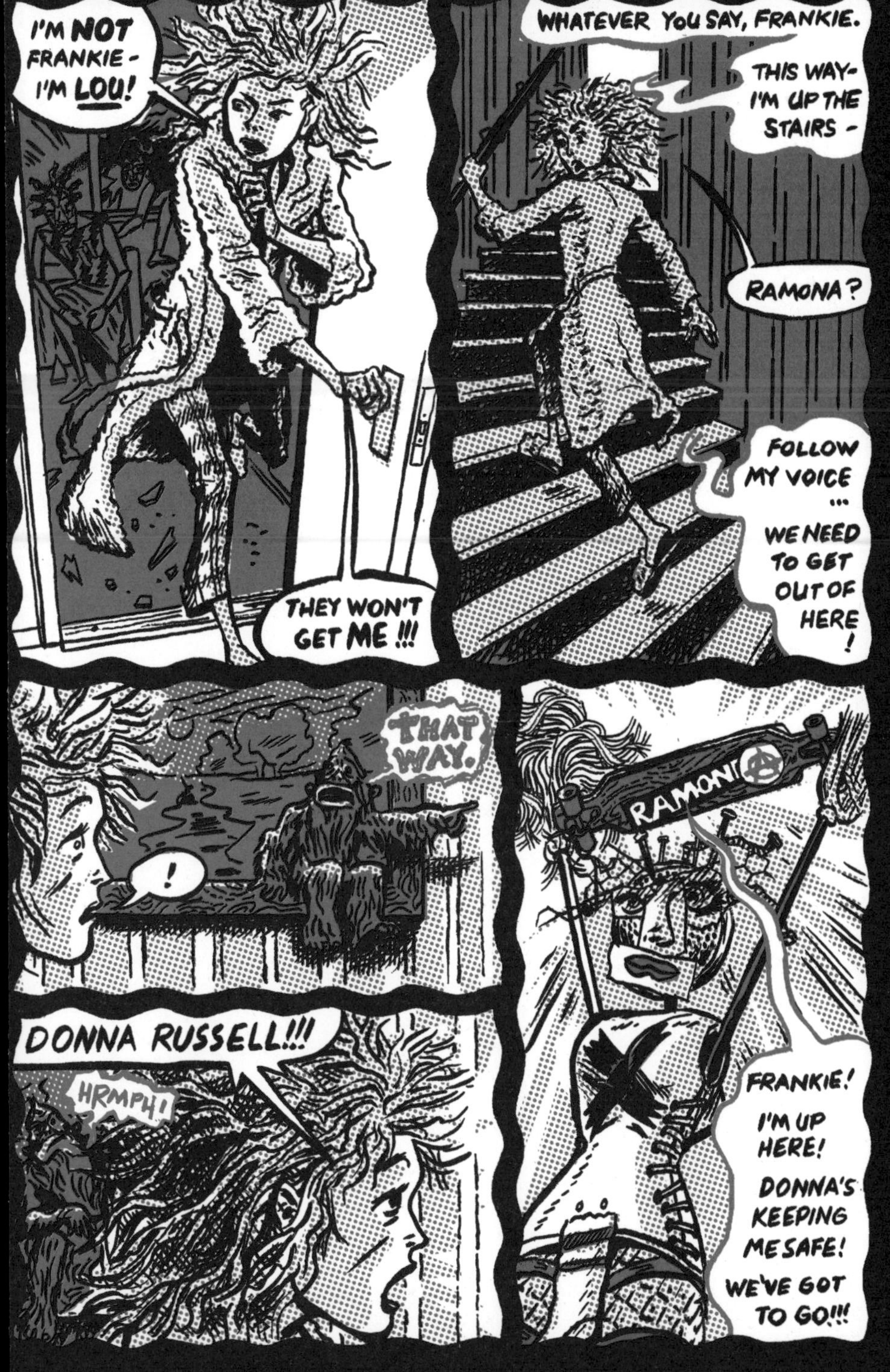

I'M NOT FRANKIE - I'M LOU!
THEY WON'T GET ME !!!
WHATEVER YOU SAY, FRANKIE.
THIS WAY- I'M UP THE STAIRS -
RAMONA?
FOLLOW MY VOICE ... WE NEED TO GET OUT OF HERE !
THAT WAY.
!
RAMON
DONNA RUSSELL!!!
HRMPH!
FRANKIE!
I'M UP HERE!
DONNA'S KEEPING ME SAFE!
WE'VE GOT TO GO!!!

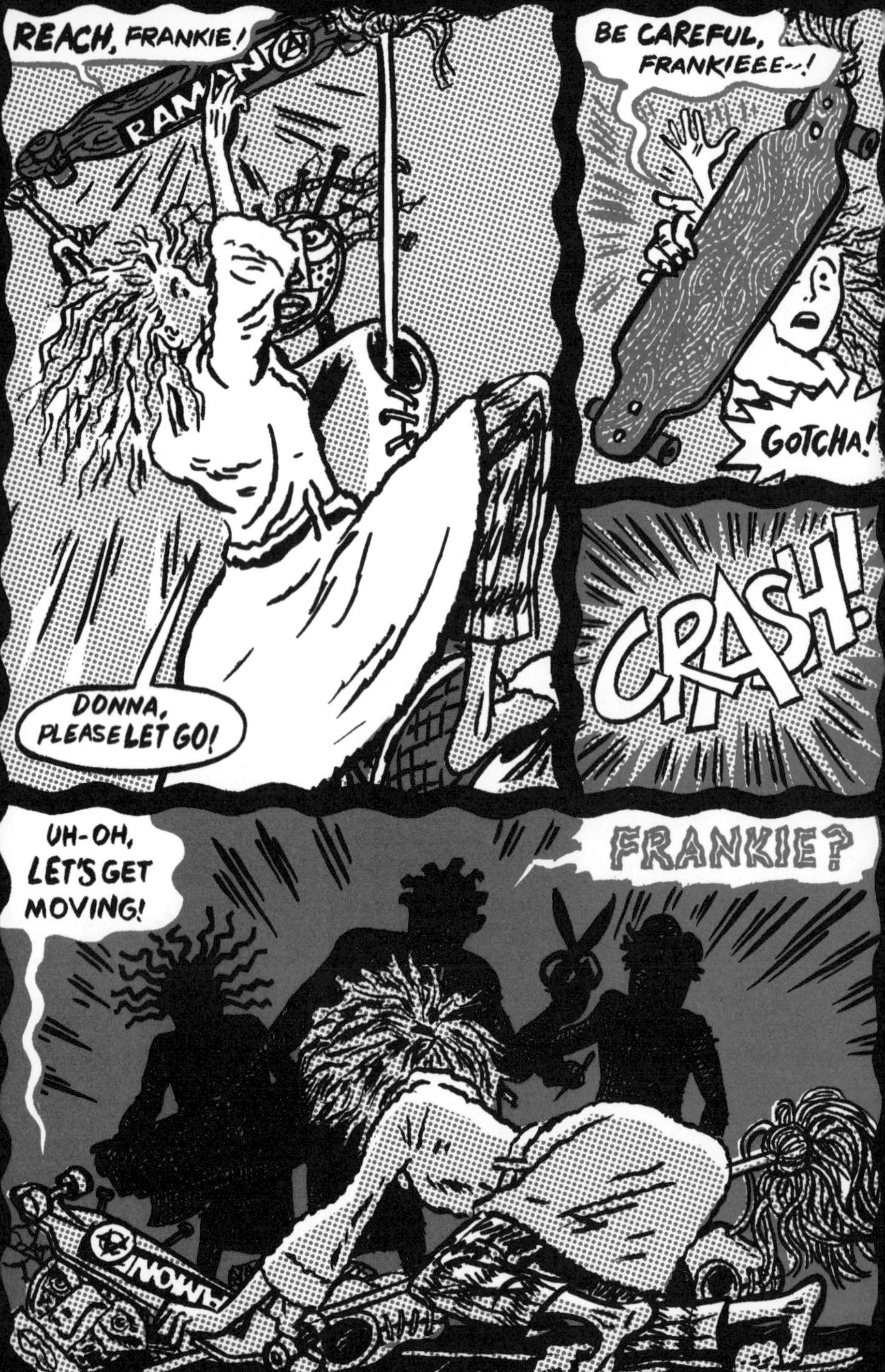
REACH, FRANKIE!
RAMONES
DONNA, PLEASE LET GO!
BE CAREFUL, FRANKIEEE--!
GOTCHA!
CRASH!
UH-OH, LET'S GET MOVING!
FRANKIE?

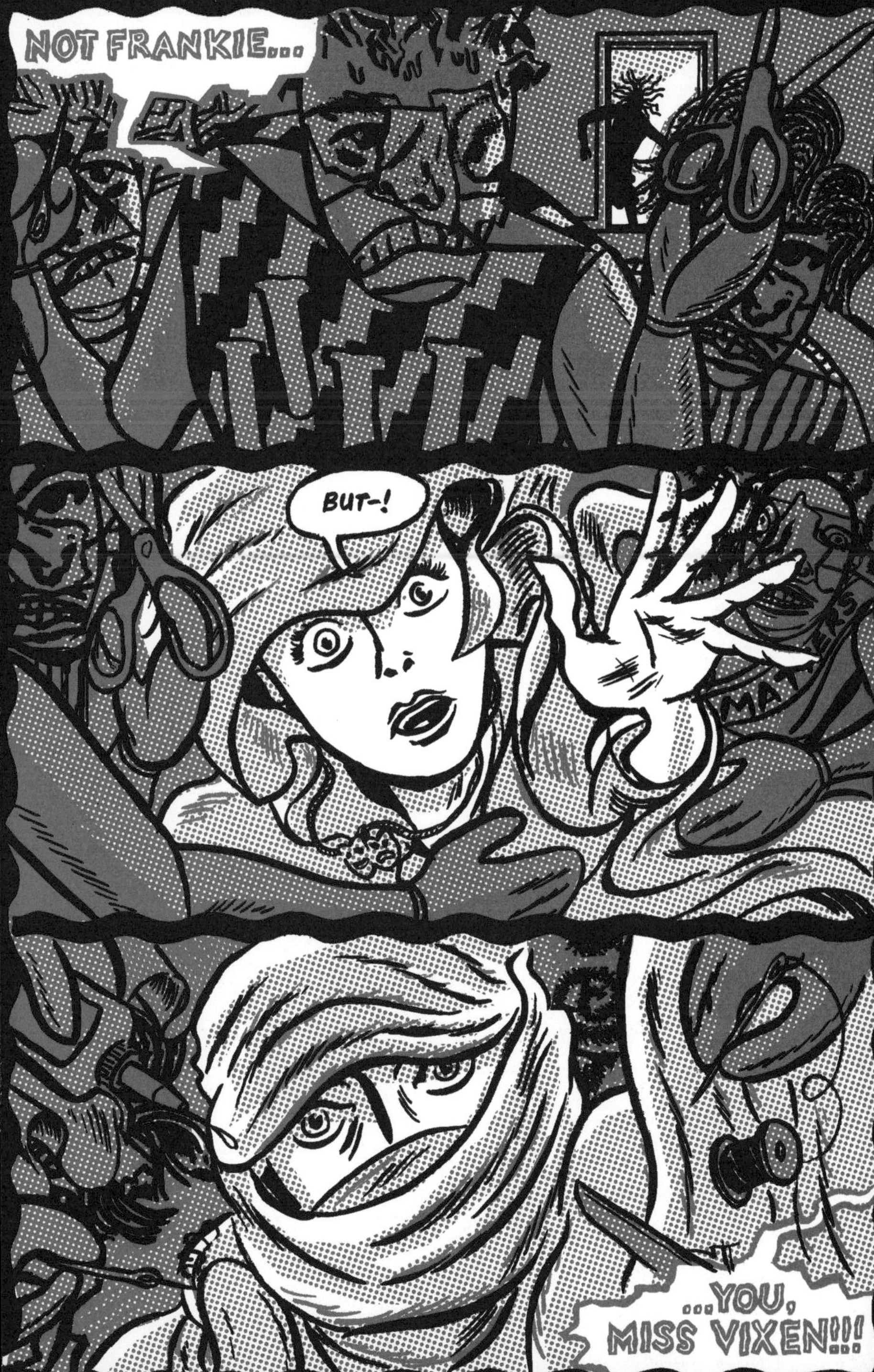
NOT FRANKIE...
BUT-!
...YOU, MISS VIXEN!!!

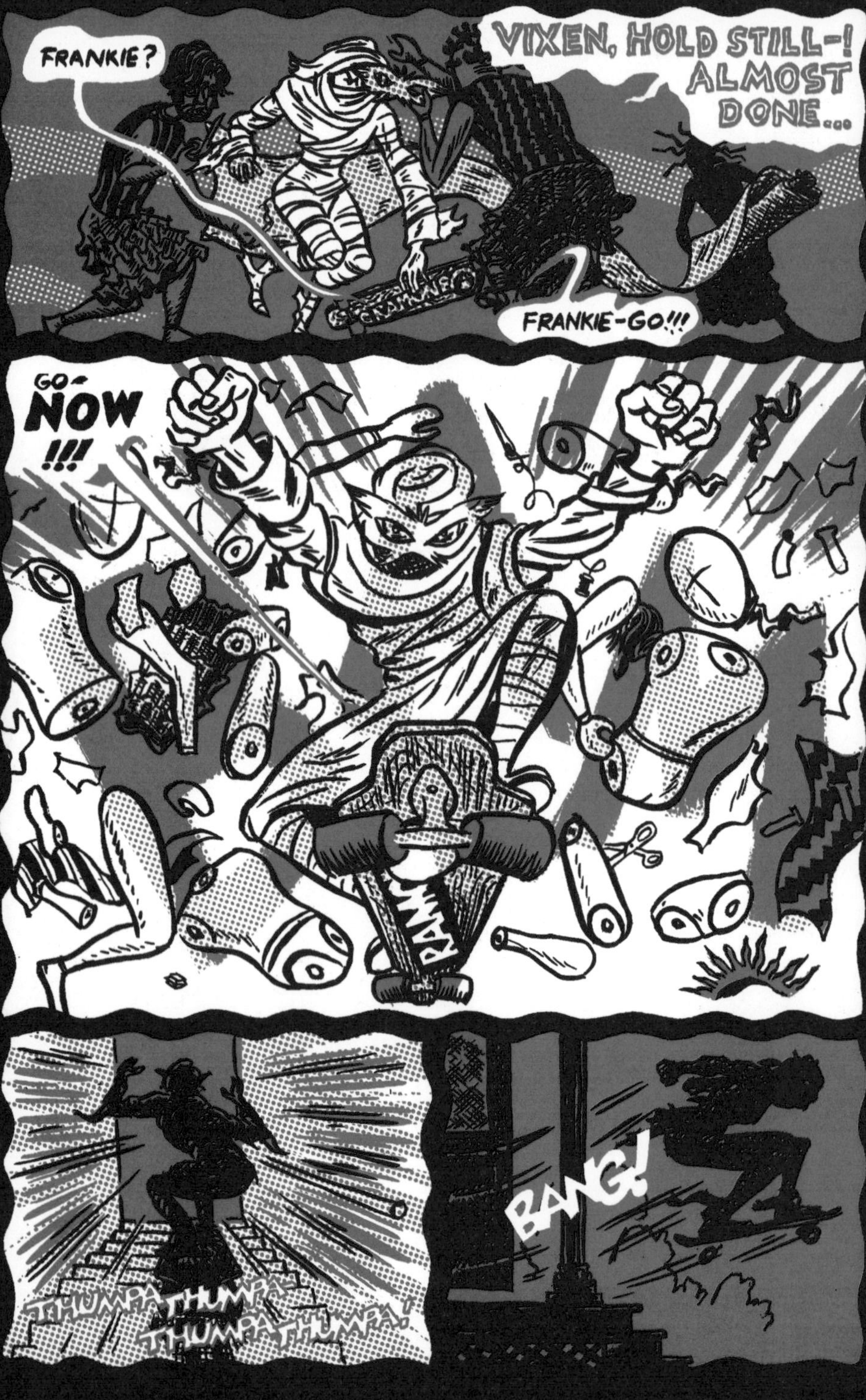
FRANKIE?
VIXEN, HOLD STILL-! ALMOST DONE...
FRANKIE-GO!!!
GO-NOW!!!
THUMPATHUMPA
THUMPA THUMPA
BANG!

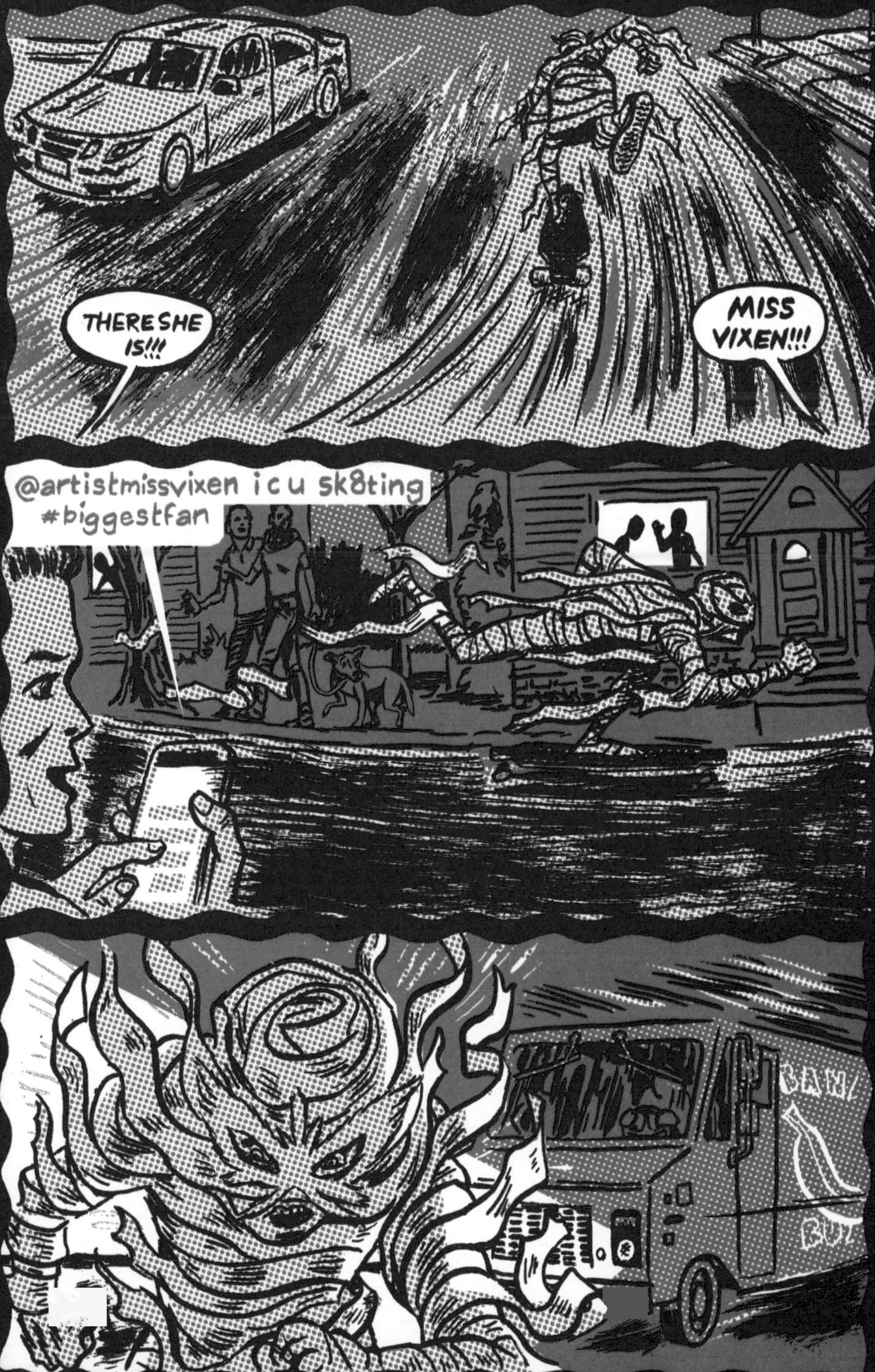
THERE SHE IS!!!
MISS VIXEN!!!
@artistmissvixen i c u sk8ting #biggestfan

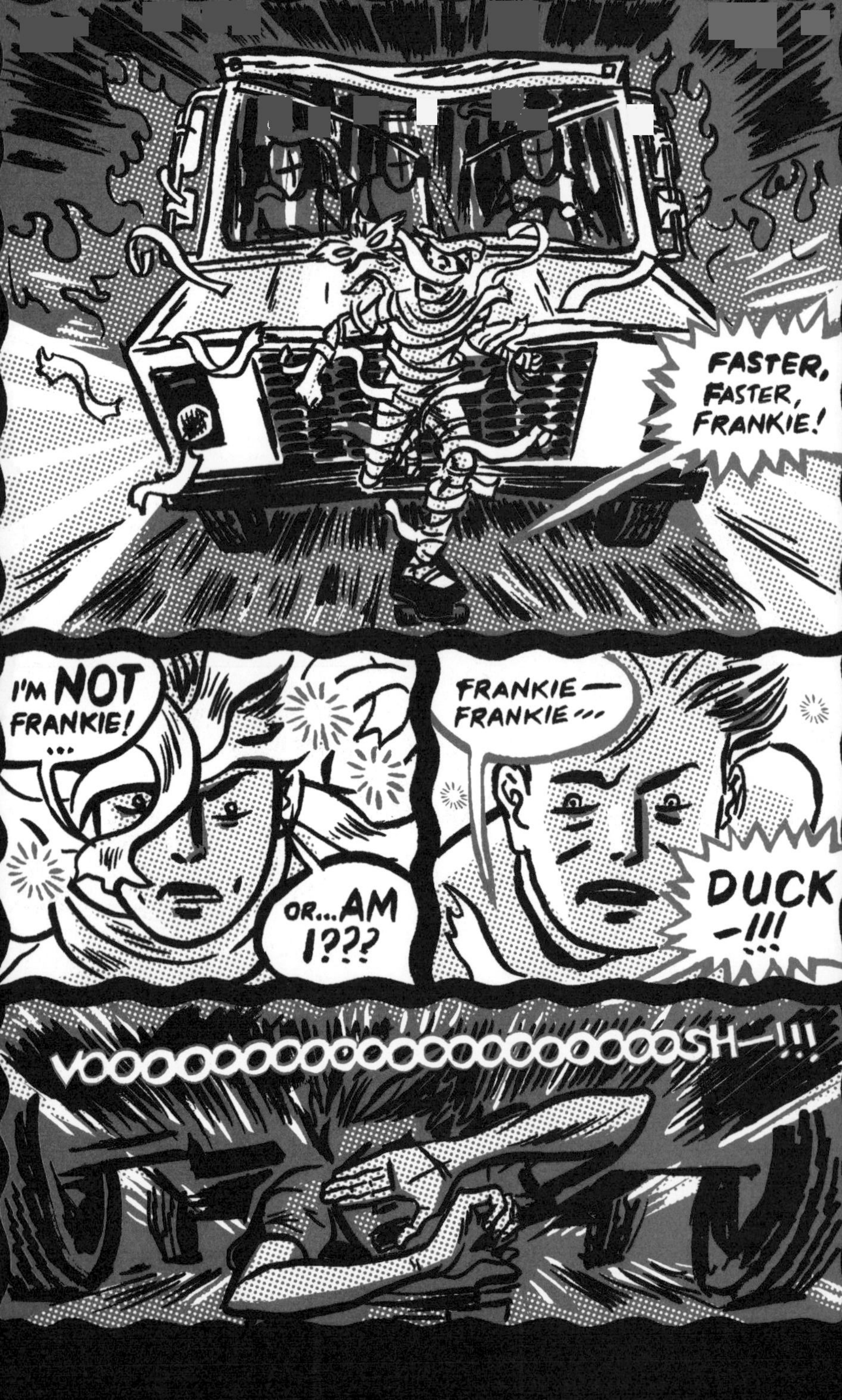

FASTER, FASTER, FRANKIE!
I'M NOT FRANKIE! ...
OR...AM I???
FRANKIE— FRANKIE—...
DUCK —!!! ...
VOOOOOOOOOOOOOOOOOOOOOOOOOSH—!!!

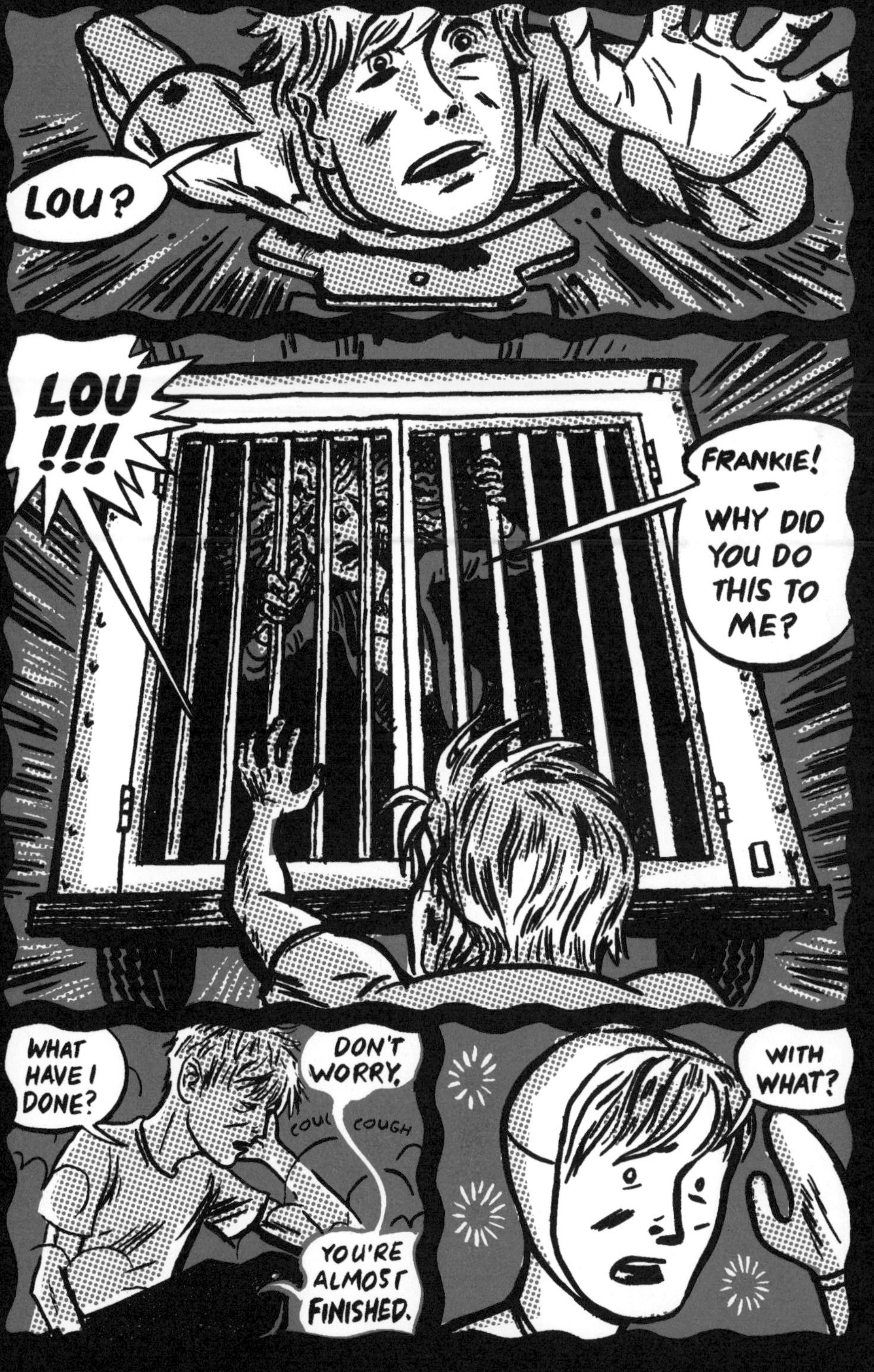
LOU?
LOU!!!
FRANKIE! — WHY DID YOU DO THIS TO ME?
WHAT HAVE I DONE?
DON'T WORRY,
COUGH COUGH
YOU'RE ALMOST FINISHED.
WITH WHAT?

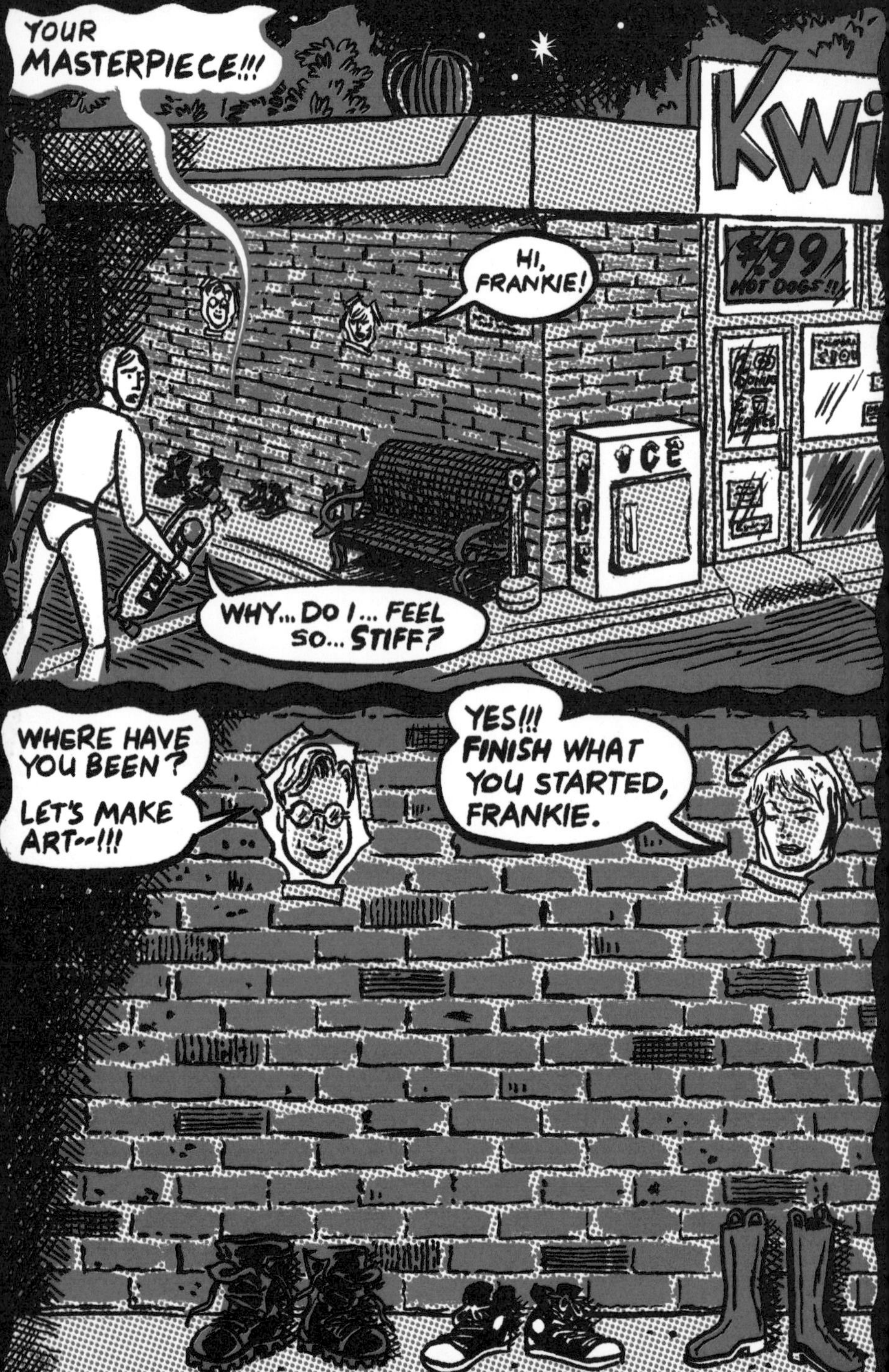
YOUR MASTERPIECE!!!
HI, FRANKIE!
$.99 HOT DOGS!!
ICE
WHY... DO I... FEEL SO... STIFF?
WHERE HAVE YOU BEEN?
LET'S MAKE ART--!!!
YES!!! FINISH WHAT YOU STARTED, FRANKIE.

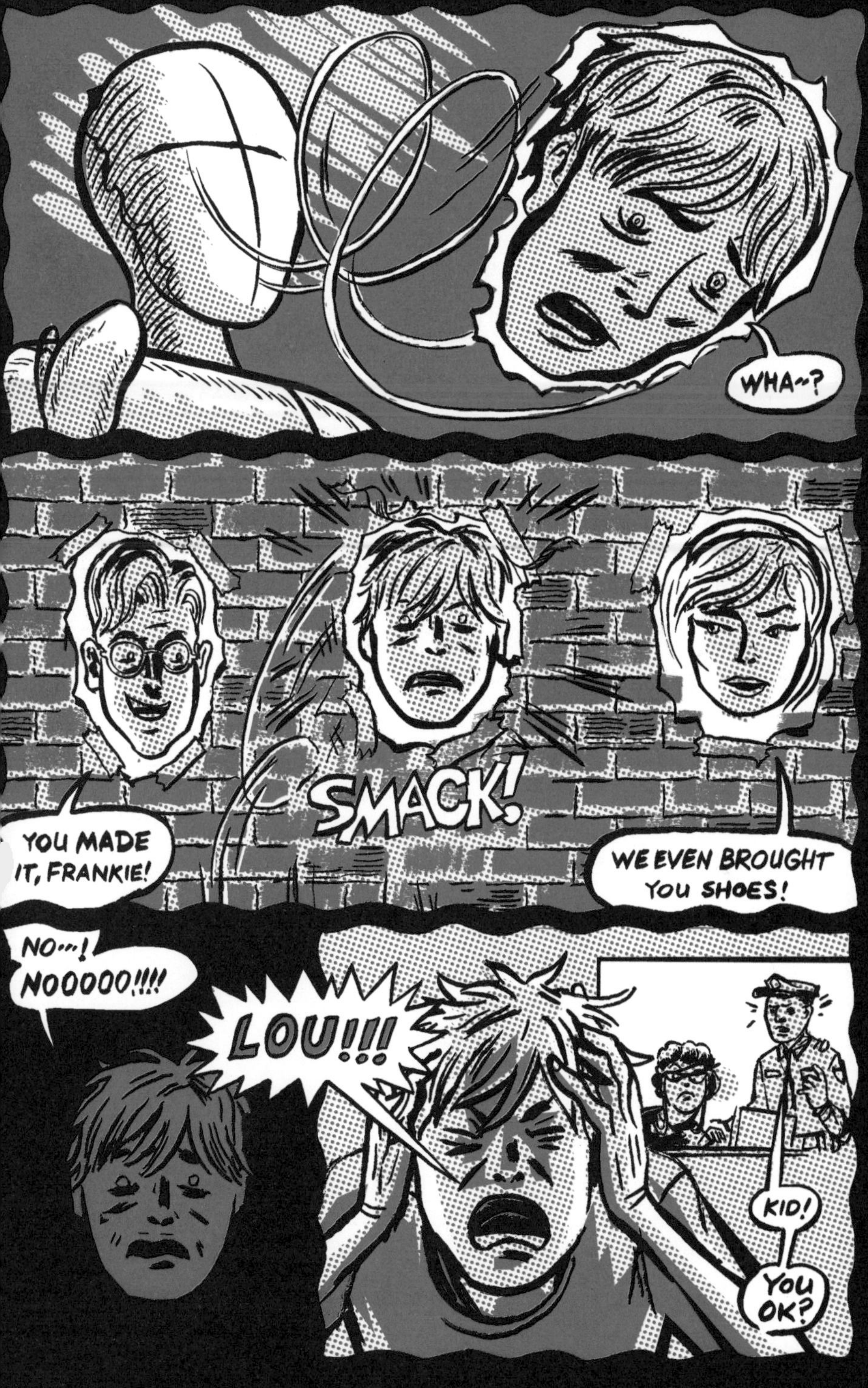
WHA--?
SMACK!
YOU MADE IT, FRANKIE!
WE EVEN BROUGHT YOU SHOES!
NO...! NOOOOO!!!!
LOU!!!
KID!
YOU OK?

"Yeah." Can't believe I drifted. Still going to throw up.

A guy comes into the station, an average-looking guy with honey-blond hair and green eyes, kind of handsome, medium build, not too tall, dressed in pants and a tie and a white shirt. Once he spots me, he makes a beeline for the chair next to mine and sits down.

"Dr. Seuss is god." He says this calmly, like the entire world understands this fact.

"Whatever you say." I stand up and move three chairs down. Not interested.

His eyes are asking me to get what he's saying. "I love Dr. Seuss." He takes a piece of paper from his pocket. It's a folded-up Andy Warhol hundred-dollar bill.

So much goes bouncing through my brain. "It's so not safe for you to be here." The man's been anonymous longer than I've been alive. He can't blow that because of me. "You need to leave now."

His voice is low and composed. "I'm sorry it took me so long. Let's go find your sister, shall we? This is all you need to know." He shoves the paper into my hand. The Warhol bill has an address written on it. "Memorize it." His eyes are laughing, but they're also asking me not to blow it. Epic Is more vulnerable right now than he's ever been in his life. "Tallulah's birthday is May 9, 2001, right? There are so many of you kids, I can't keep you straight." Big grin.

"How'd you . . ." How does he know that?

"So many, I need my own department at the Bureau of Vital Records." He's almost laughing outright now.

"You're so funny, Dad." I read the address about ten times. Once I've got it, I stand up, grab Ramona, and move to the counter with Epic. "This lady can tell us where to find Lou." I pray my real parents don't show up. I'm sure the cops called them, too.

"You're the father?" She gives me a suspicious look. "He's not old enough to be your dad."

"My parents were high school sex fiends, and they had me when they were sixteen. This is my father. We'd like to see my sister." I try and give her a nasty look in return, for her rudeness.

"Could we please see Tallulah? She's probably very scared." Epic is nowhere near rude. In fact, he's pleasant, like he's talking about our lovely spring weather. The lady actually gives him a faint smile.

Then it hits me full force: Uncle Epic—THE Uncle Epic— is standing next to me. His only disguise is my silence.

My knees give a little, so I prop myself up on the counter.

Epic's charm gets some action. She picks up the phone and presses a few buttons, then says, "Juvenile female." Then she listens. When she hangs up, she gives me another death stare and another faint smile to Epic. "All right. Back through the gate, turn to your right, third door on the left."

"Thank you, ma'am." Epic nods. I move through the gate and practically run to find Lou. Epic walks with all the confidence in the world, like he's not aware that every single cop in the place would tackle his ass in ten seconds if they knew who he was.

She's sitting at a table in the middle of a big room, all by herself. It's obvious she's been crying, because her face is blotched out, though the enormous Kleenex pile on the table is a good clue, too. When she sees me, she jumps up so fast she knocks the chair over as she throws herself into my arms.

"Hey! It's OK! Really, you're all right." I don't know what to do besides pat her back. "Maybe we can go now."

She raises her head to look me in the face. "They want to know what I know about the sheep."

"What?"

Epic coughs.

Lou breaks away from me and gives him a scowl. "Who's that?" Epic smiles.

"That's Dad, of course." I kick her foot, warning her to play along. We sit back down again, me and Lou on one side of the table, Epic next to Lou at the end. The cops' chairs are opposite me and Lou.

I'm scared.

The door opens again. Two cops come in. Both are young-ish, somewhere between my age and Epic's, and neither looks particularly mean. One of them addresses Epic. "My name is Officer Travas. Sir, is this your daughter?"

He nods. "Yes, this is my Tallulah."

"Could you give me her birthdate?"

"May 9, 2001." He says this like he was in the room when it happened. Thank god for whoever he knows in Vital Records.

The second cop shakes Epic's hand. "I'm Officer Kaiser, and we're concerned your daughter is involved with Uncle Epic and the flash robs he's been conducting around the city." He puts a clipboard on the table.

"Uncle Epic isn't a felon. He's not involved with the flash robs. At all." The words tumble out of my mouth.

They ignore me. "Was your daughter a part of these incidents, sir?"

Epic's face goes crimson as he speaks. "Lou is not involved with Uncle Epic, and Uncle Epic isn't involved with the flash robs."

They have to hear me. "I know who did the first flash rob. It wasn't Epic. I'll tell you what I know."

Epic's face starts to clear, but Lou hunches her shoulders into her ears.

Officer Travas pounces. "That's a start. Did you orchestrate the others as well? We've been watching your ghoulies. What's your name, young man?" He produces a notebook from his back pocket.

"Me?" My whole body feels like it's been stuck into a fire. "Frankie. Franklin Neumann. I didn't do the flash rob. Any of them."

"But how would you know about the first flash rob if you weren't there? And what do you know about a guy named Mixt UP?" Officer Kaiser looks smug, like he's got it all figured out. The tops of his ears are red. "We also know you were part of at least two of Epic's pieces, because your white delivery truck was in the vicinity of his eyes at the capitol and the sheep in Loring Park. We figure you must mastermind the robberies under Uncle Epic's direction. If you were involved in Epic's work, why wouldn't you be involved in the flash robs?"

"He's an artist, not a criminal, and I didn't mastermind anything!" I'm going to vomit on the table. I look at Epic, which he must take as a cue, because he starts talking.

"Officers, could you please tell me why you assume that Uncle Epic is involved in the flash robs? Do you have proof of a connection between him and the robberies?"

Officer Kaiser's ears are still beet red. "We're working on it."

"But you don't have any direct proof." Epic's not smiling, but he's not frowning either.

"The only thing we have right now is the presence of a white delivery truck at two of Uncle Epic's pieces and at the Kwiky Pik, the site of the first flash rob. That truck is registered to you, Brett Neumann. We also know that there were sculptures in the parking lot of the Kwiky Pik that referenced words like 'I know who did it.'" Officer Kaiser looks a little less intense, because he knows he's just laid out some pretty weak connections.

"Do you have proof the white delivery truck was actually involved in the art pieces or the robberies, or was it just present?" Epic seems to know this line of questioning.

"We know it was present." Officer Kaiser glares, and Epic smiles.

Officer Travas shakes his head and turns his attention back to Lou and me. "Let's focus on the flash rob for a minute. Do you understand the penalties for aggravated robbery? Especially one where the clerk almost died as a result of the robbery? If that had happened, we'd be talking about manslaughter. Instead, how does twenty years strike you? That's what you get when you commit robbery with a gun in Minnesota."

All the air in the room is sucked up. Up to twenty years for Lou, who's staring daggers at me, because she now understands who Miss Vixen is. I am dead.

But I'm also an asshole. Yes, Lou made a huge mistake, but I'm the jerk who capitalized on it.

I can't believe I'm going to say this.

"OK. I did it. But Epic didn't do a thing. I'll tell you who robbed the first Kwiky Pik if you believe me that Epic had nothing to do with it."

"Would you sign a legal document stating Uncle Epic has nothing to do with the flash robs? A document that includes penalties for lying?" Officer Kaiser is making notes. His ears look like they're going to explode, they're so red. Officer Travas is watching all of us, trying to figure out if anyone's being shady.

"Yes. Of course."

"You can't confess to something you didn't do, Frankie." This from Uncle Epic. "I'm glad you can defend your artist friend, but you can't confess to a crime you didn't commit."

"No, you can't." A very small voice from my left.

"Tallulah, we need to get you a lawyer if you want to talk about this." Epic again.

"Shut up, Lou. I know who robbed the Kwiky Pik."

"And so do I, so let me tell it. You don't know everything. I do." She's determined.

This gets the officers' attention. "Start talking, Tallulah." Officer Kaiser gives her a no-nonsense look as he passes the clipboard to Officer Travas, who immediately starts writing.

"What night was it and where was it?" Officer Kaiser is making sure.

"April 22, at the Kwiky Pik near Golden Valley Boulevard and Highway 12."

"And how were the flash robbers dressed?"

She looks defiant and angry. And a little bit relieved. "We had on costumes like the court of Louis XIV that we borrowed from the community theater located at 84th and Locust. Matt Havelock's mother works there, and he took the key to the building from her key ring. We all wore masks. The gun came from Elijah Bush's house. Nobody fired it. Only a few people actually took things, maybe Brandon Anderson, Carter Stone, Matt Havelock, and Brooklyn Smith. I don't know for sure. I watched, and I touched the gun, but I handed it off to someone else right away." And she bursts into tears. I reach over and hug her as tight as I can. Epic comes over and pats her on the back, looking as concerned as he can for a girl he's never met before.

"Could you make a list of the people who were there?" This request from Officer Travas, who's still writing things on the clipboard.

"Yes." Lou reaches for the Kleenex again. Officer Travas passes over the clipboard and a pen after he moves the top piece of paper. She starts to write. Epic gives her one more pat and goes back to his chair.

"Young man, do you know what Uncle Epic looks like?" Officer Kaiser is focused on me again.

"I'm a huge fan, but no, I don't know him personally." I keep my eyes strictly on Officer Kaiser, because if I look at Epic, I'm dead. At the same time, I want to shout, *He's sitting right in front of you!* My mind seizes on the address Epic handed me. "I can tell you the address of a place where I heard Uncle Epic lives. But it's just a rumor."

"Do you know where the sheep came from?" Officer Travas is looking intense again. He takes a piece of paper from his breast pocket and pulls a pen from the same place. "Write down that address here, please." He slides the paper and pen over to me. Lou is still making a list. I have no idea what Epic is doing, since I can't look at him. I hear him clear his throat.

"You mean the sheep in Loring Park? The owner's

phone number was on the bottom of the sheep. Didn't you see that?"

Oh shit. What if they didn't see that? Ohshitohshitohshit.

Officer Kaiser makes a note on the clipboard. "We did see that. How did you know about it?"

Ohshit.

"A friend took a picture." Which isn't a lie, because David did text me photos.

"The sheep's owner came and took them back pretty early the next day." Officer Travas crosses his arms. "And his grandson goes to your school, so I'm wondering if you know him. Jess Wistrom?"

"My friend was there before the sheep were gone, around seven a.m. the morning after Uncle Epic did the piece. Running." David wouldn't run unless a zombie was chasing him. Maybe not even then.

Officer Kaiser raises his eyebrows. "I see. You're saying you didn't help with the sheep, even though we saw a truck just like yours close to the scene. And the eyes at the capitol—you weren't there, either? How about the penises on Nicollet Mall? Are you prepared to pay a fine for illegal dumping?"

I don't raise my eyebrows back at him, even though I want to. "Why would I have to pay a fine when you can't prove my truck was involved with the pieces? And what does Epic's work have to do with the flash robs? Isn't that what really matters—armed robbery in five different places around town? Or is ruining Epic more important than public safety?"

"Son, watch your tone. Respect matters." Epic's making sure the cops know he's the dad, but I think he also doesn't want me to get too carried away.

I write down 7100 Nicollet Avenue and pass it over to Officer Travas. That's the address that was on the Warhol money.

"You're sure this is where he is?" Officer Travas reads it and tries to stare into my soul to see if I'm telling the truth.

"That's the only address I know that's connected to Uncle Epic." Which is also not a lie, because I have no idea what the address is for his shop. All I know is that it's on 34th Street.

Lou pushes her list back to Officer Travas. "Will I get twenty years in jail?" She looks so little and scared.

"No. When people cooperate, we give them lesser charges." He holds up the list. "We'll have to see what these individuals say, to see if your story checks out, that you didn't do anything but watch."

Lou sags and closes her eyes. "OK." The stone lifts off my heart. My parents will still flip out, but it's better than aggravated robbery.

"Did your flash robbers have anything to do with the other robberies in town?" Officer Travas directs this question to Lou.

"No. We only did one. I have no idea who did the others. I didn't even know there were other ones until you said there were." Her eyes are still closed.

"So what was up with the monsters in the parking lot of the Kwiky Pik, Franklin?" Officer Travas turns to me again. "What do you know about Mixt UP?"

"It's a long story." One I don't really want to tell right now, because they'll arrest me for being the shittiest brother on the planet, which Lou is confirming with every nasty sideways look she gives me.

"But you do claim them."

"Yes."

"You realize we can fine you for leaving them there. Even though their bodies disappeared, their faces didn't."

ZING. The lightbulb goes on. Their bodies. Dr. Seuss. Epic took his ghoulie parts back.

Thank god I don't owe him any money.

Back to reality. "That's fine." I just want this nightmare to be over. I just want Epic to walk out the doors of this place with his freedom and his anonymity.

Officer Travas finally looks satisfied.

Officer Kaiser looks at Epic. "We can release Tallulah to you today, but we have to process her first. And we'll write Franklin a ticket for illegal dumping."

Epic nods. "I understand."

"I'll wait for you both in the lobby, but I have to go back

to Kwiky Pik first." I stand up. "Am I free to go, Officers? I don't have any charges, do I?"

Officer Travas shakes his head. "We don't have anything to charge you with, but you'll pay for leaving your monsters around. And from here on out, I'd suggest you keep your nose clean. If we ever see your delivery truck close to one of Uncle Epic's pieces, we'll ticket you on the spot. Even if he doesn't do flash robs, he's still annoying as hell."

A snort from the end of the table.

"I'll send your ticket with your dad." He leaves the room.

Officer Kaiser stands up, too. "Tallulah, will you and your dad please come with me? We should be able to process you within an hour. Then you'll be free to go until your court appearance, which should be within a couple days. Make sure you have a lawyer when you come to court."

"Yes, sir." Epic has on his best serious-dad face. Lou is crying again, but very silently. The tears trickle down, one by one. I move to hug her, but she shoves me away with a black look. They leave the room, and I pray like I've never prayed before that they don't ask Epic for any ID, or to prove he's her dad. We have an hour to go in this charade.

I push back to the Kwiky Pik and make sure all the paper and scraps are picked up. I don't know how Lou managed to rip Monster Brallison's clothes, but she did. Someone's put Monster Brallison's face up with the others, so now there are five ghostly ghoulie faces in a row on the wall. I take a picture of all of them, and Miss Vixen tweets it: **The last act of the ghoulies. Love these creatures. Thanks to Miss Vixen's fans.**

The mannequin parts and the stand are gone. Maybe Rory took them back to Epic. But why would she do something nice?

I glide back to the police station and wait in the lobby. The counter lady looks less pissed at me, because I keep my wheels quiet this time. Still no texts from my parents, which is incredibly strange, but I'm more worried about getting Epic and Lou out of the police station with Epic's cover intact. I sweat so much I can smell my armpits after about ten minutes. I'm gross. And petrified.

Epic and Lou come out from behind the counter about fifteen minutes after I get back, and I leap to my feet. Lou looks composed. She's stopped crying, though her eyes are red and puffy. Epic looks cool as frost in October.

"Ready to get home?" Some impulse makes me hold out my hand to Lou, but she swats me away.

My phone vibrates. **WHERE THE HELL ARE YOU AND WHY IS LOU IN TROUBLE?** My mom. I text back: **Be home in ten minutes. Stay there. Will explain then. Lou is OK.** Vibration. Text from my dad: **Things OK, Frankie?** I text back: **Be home in ten minutes. Stay there. Will explain then.**

Epic leads us to his car, which is a red '88 Honda Accord with more rust on it than paint. I know it's an '88 Accord because my dad had one just like it in college and I've seen pictures.

I blurt it out. "You can afford a better ride than this."

He laughs. "This is my disguise car. For when I want to look like a nerdy computer programmer or a Dungeons & Dragons player."

When we're in the car, me in the front and Lou in the back, she finally lets it fly: "Who the fuck are you? I mean, thanks for pretending to be my dad, but seriously, who are you?" She points at me. "I know exactly who you are, you lowdown fucking jerkoff. You asswipe. You cocksucker."

Epic answers like she's not just breathed fire in his presence. "I'm a friend of your brother's. My name's Jamie Carlson."

"How'd you know my birthdate?" She frowns.

"I have a friend at Vital Records." He smiles. "Thanks for pretending I was your dad."

"Are you kidding? I'm in so much shit, I didn't want to add on some charge of impersonating a dad or something like that. Could police actually charge you with that? I have no idea." And that's all she says. She stares out the window.

"You were a godsend . . . Jamie. Thanks for helping us. It was crazy stupid for you to do it, but thank you."

"Thanks for defending Uncle Epic." He chuckles.

I now know one of the greatest secrets in the world—well, two, if you count birth name and facial recognition as separate secrets. It's all I can do not to holler like I've just won a million dollars. But I keep it cool. Then it also hits me that Rory and I just had a horrible fight. Like a friendship/relationship-ending fight.

"Um, Jamie . . . Rory and I . . ."

He nods. "She told me. You're still in my crew. She just won't do the projects you and David do."

I didn't even realize I'd been holding my breath until I let it out in one long whoosh. "OK. Thanks. Thank you a million times."

He points to the dashboard of his car. There's a HIPPOS: ADORABLE DEATH MACHINES sticker there. I completely missed it when I got in. "I've admired your work for a few years. Glad to have you on board."

I almost faint. "From—"

"Drastic Plastic, on the rack with all the free stuff. Bet you thought nobody ever took one." He smiles the kindest smile anybody's ever smiled at me. Then we're home, so it saves me from more conversation.

Lou looks at Epic. She's been crying again. "Thanks again for helping, Jamie. I won't tell." And she's out the door and into the house.

I will murder her for real if she does.

I climb out of the backseat and come to the driver's

window to stick out my hand. "Your name and your face are safe with me. And I'll keep Lou in line."

He grins. "David was right about you—that you're a quality guy—and I'm sorry you were right about Rory." He salutes me and zooms off in his car, which farts some ugly exhaust as he goes. I'm left standing there with my hand out, looking like a dumbass.

As disguises go, it's a pretty good one.

Mom and Dad are sitting at the table, where hamburgers, baked beans, and salad are laid out for us. Lou's nowhere to be seen. It's all I can do not to put my arms in front of my face, to shield me from the shouting that's sure to start any second.

My mom points at my chair. "Sit. Lou went to wash up. She said there's a lot to talk about. And we probably don't want to know." She pours me a glass of milk while she gives me the eye.

Lou comes back in, and my mom looks between us, her face as stern as I've ever seen it. "So. Spill it. You were both at the police station. Are you both in trouble?"

Lou glares at me. "Frankie got a ticket. I, on the other hand, need a lawyer because Miss Vixen ratted me out."

I'm pissed. "This has nothing to do with Miss Vixen, you idiot. You need a lawyer because you were part of an armed robbery! Even though Miss Vixen ratted out the flash robbers, Miss Vixen didn't make you go to the Kwiky Pik dressed like a fancy French lady!"

My mom's mouth is hanging open. My dad manages to get the words out. "Armed . . . robbery?"

"But I'm not being charged with it. It'll be something less, they said. So we have to go to court in a few days."

"Why didn't we know this?" My mom is on her feet and furious. "Who was with you while the police were talking to you? You're a minor, Lou! You need an adult with you for legal stuff." Mom's voice is high and tense.

Lou points at me. "Frankie's friend Jamie came, and he sat with us while we talked to the cops, and then while they fingerprinted me and all that. The police didn't ask him for ID, so they never knew he wasn't my dad."

"Is this the robbery where Marvin had a heart attack?" Dad's still trying to process.

"Yes. Nobody meant for that to happen. It was just a bunch of stupid theater people who wanted to do something risky for the thrill. I didn't take anything, and I only touched the gun once. It was dumb, and I'm sorry. They'll call us when they have my court date. And we need to bring a lawyer. That's all I know." Lou's eyes are locked on mine. She's not done.

My mom has nothing to say to this. Nor does my dad. They just look from one of us to the other, then to each other, like their children have been replaced by aliens.

Lou tries to cut me with her stare. "Your girlfriend is going to pay for that paper doll. I don't know how yet, but she will."

"Who's your girlfriend?" My dad's confused. "What does she have to do with armed robbery?"

"Ask Frankie." Lou scowls. "Her name's Rory. They make out in the Target parking lot."

My mom raises her eyebrows at me. "You were making out in the Target parking lot?"

"Rory's not my girlfriend. At least not anymore. Probably never was. And we weren't out in the open. We were in the truck." I don't want my parents to know any of this.

Lou scowls some more. "Doesn't matter if she's your girlfriend or not, she was a complete bitch to make that paper doll. But it's nothing compared to how you framed me with the monsters, Miss Vixen."

The guilt arrow twists in my gut.

My mom leans in. "What did you say, Lou?"

My dad's looking between us again. He can feel the heat in Lou's glare of pure hatred. "Who's Miss Vixen?"

"Is she someone you both know?" This from my mom.

"In a manner of speaking." Lou stands up, and her composed voice scares me more than anything she's ever done. "You're going to regret this. So much." She turns around and goes to a kitchen drawer, takes something out that I can't see, then marches up the stairs.

My dad isn't sure what's just happened. "Explain all of this, please."

I can't look at either of them. "When I found out Lou was in the flash rob, it was just . . . too tempting. She's done so much shit to me over the years, it looked like a great time to get back at her for some of it. Miss Vixen—that's me—made some art that got her in trouble with her friends, and I guess it went too far." That's the understatement of the world.

Mom shakes her head. "So she was an idiot, and then you were one too?"

"Something like that."

Dad frowns. "Has she ever done anything that mean to you?"

I think before I answer him. Might as well say it. "She stole you guys from me. I'd say that's pretty shitty."

My dad stares at me. My mom frowns with her whole face.

BUMP. I hear it again. BUMP. And then I see Lou at the bottom of the stairs.

I jump up. "That's not yours. Off-limits."

How does she know about Donna Russell?

"Oh yeah? My life is off-limits, too. So just suck it, Frankie." And she shoves Donna Russell out the door.

My parents look at me. I look at them. It takes a second for my brain to work.

Oh no.

I sprint from my chair. "Don't hurt her!"

Lou's gotten the gas can from the garage, and she's put it and Donna Russell on the lawn. She's shredding Donna, piece by piece, pulling her apart and off the mannequin stand.

"Stop! Stop it!" I screech from the bottom of my gut while Lou pours gas on my best girl. "Don't do it!"

"See how it makes you feel." There is venom in Lou's voice. "Just see how you like it." Then she clicks the fire stick she took from the kitchen drawer, and the pile of junk that is Donna Russell is in flames.

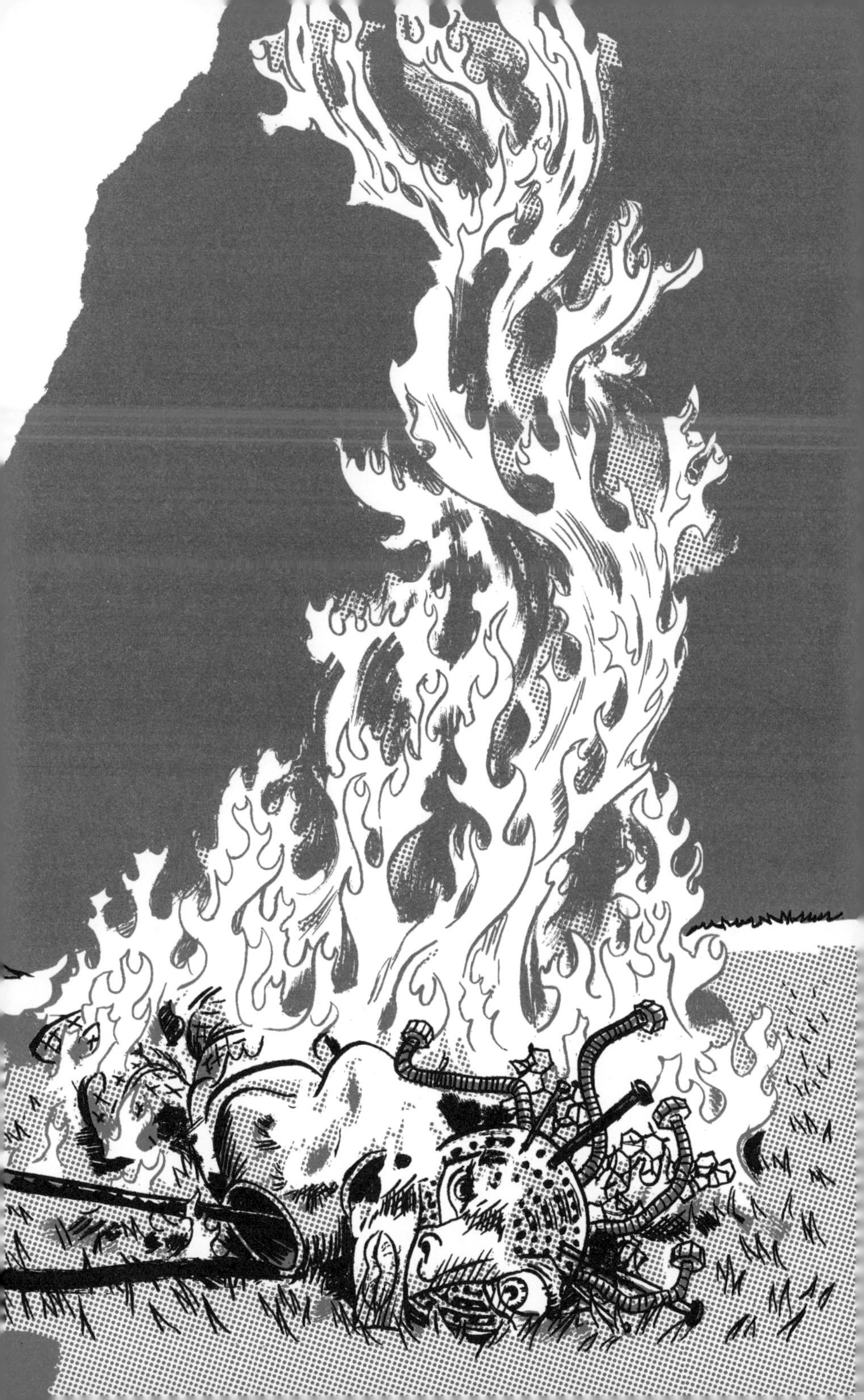

All the strength runs out of my legs, and I'm on the ground, just like Donna.

"Lou, what are you doing?" My mother arrives in time to see the flames get a little taller. "You can't light a fire on the grass!"

My dad just turns and runs around the corner of the house.

"HOW DO YOU LIKE THIS, FRANKIE?" Now Lou's screaming at the top of her lungs. "HOW DO YOU LIKE IT WHEN YOUR LIFE GOES UPSIDE DOWN?"

I can't talk. I just watch Donna burn. The tears make the whole scene blurry, so the fire looks like it's made out of watercolors.

SPLOOSH. My dad is there with the hose, and then Donna Russell is a smoking pile of wire and metal and plastic and fabric, stinking like crazy.

My best friend is gone.

"All of you. In the house." My mom's voice is barely controlled, and she has one very firm hand on Lou's shoulder. "Get up, Frankie."

I try, but my legs still aren't working. She was the only one who understood.

"Come on, Frankie." My dad's voice is soft and gentle. He puts an arm around me and helps me up. "Let's go inside."

It's almost dark, and Donna is destruction personified on the front lawn. It's hard to walk.

My mother sends Lou to a chair, ~~and~~ my dad guides me to another. Then they both sit down.

"Too much, children, too much. You can't do this stuff to each other, not to mention to the lawn." My dad sighs.

Lou crosses her arms. "He's done way more harm than I have."

I stand up so fast I almost knock the table over. "YOU DESTROYED THE ONLY PERSON WHO UNDERSTANDS ME. YOU CAN HAVE ANY FRIENDS YOU WANT AND YOU TOOK AWAY THE ONE PERSON WHO LOVED ME FOR ME." I yell it from my toes. "ALL I WANTED WAS TO BE HEARD. FOR ONCE IN MY GODDAMN LIFE I WANTED SOMEONE TO HEAR ME." I am an insane yelling machine.

"Frankie, sit down." My dad is amazingly serene in the face of my screaming. "Can we talk like civil people?"

"NO. SHE KILLED DONNA RUSSELL. You aren't supposed to know about Donna anyway!" And then all the intensity drains away, just like that, and I'm a sobbing puddle on the floor. My mom gets me some Kleenex and pats my shoulder until I can get up. It's a long time—or at least it feels like it to me—before I get back up on the chair.

"I'm not apologizing for killing Donna Russell. Frankie killed my social life." Lou's arms are still crossed.

"You were with people who robbed a store at gunpoint. You are going to be charged with crimes because you were with those friends. You really want people like that in your

life?" My mom's voice is cool and steely. "Do you understand why Frankie's angry at you? And at us?"

"No." She acts like she's never done a thing wrong in
her life.

I fill in the blanks for her. "Let's see, how about that
stupid camp poster, and Pepperoniangelo, and maybe you
owe me a skateboard and a bike, and the million other stupid shit things you've done to me. Which is all just petty
stuff, of course. But you're the real Frankie, remember?
It's so clear they love you more than me, and THAT FUCK-
ING HURTS. ALL RIGHT? IT HURTS." My throat aches
from all the shouting.

Nobody says any-
thing for a while. My
mother comes and puts
her arms around me.
When she moves back,
her face is wet. So is my
dad's when he comes
and hugs me after she's done.

Lou breaks the silence. "OK, fine, but that stupid
zip-up banana bus was a long time ago, and I didn't mean
anything by the Pepperoniangelo thing, but you're an ass-
clown, Frankie, plain and simple."

"Doesn't mean you weren't shitty to claim the banana
bus as yours."

My mom is stern. "Did you steal his poster, Tallulah?"

She sighs. "Yes, all right, yes, I did. The poster was his."

"I'm sorry I messed up your dumb social life, and I'm sorry Rory was mean, and I'm sorry they threatened you and threw the ghoulie gun in your window. But you just burned the one person who understood me. I'll never forgive you for that." An icy stillness has settled over me. On my heart. Ice will freeze out the grief. I am so cold I start to shiver.

My mom reaches out her hand to me. "Why do you think we don't understand you? That we don't love you?"

"You don't. How could you? All of you are the same. You sing, you dance, you're talented and people love to watch you. It's a thousand times easier for you to love Lou, because she's like you. But I'm not interesting. I'm boring. Not like you." Iceberg. I'm an iceberg.

"We love you the way you are." My dad's face has never looked more sincere.

"You like her most, though. That's always been obvious."

"Don't be an ass, Frankie!" My mom never cusses at us. "You will NOT suggest that I love one child more than the other. That is NOT how it works in this house. We love Lou because she's Lou. We love you because you're you. THAT'S ALL." She slams her hand on the table for emphasis.

"All right then." I don't know what else to say. She's never been like this.

"All right then." She's still pissed, but it's fading out and something else is replacing that idea. She's putting the pieces together. "So all the crap that Lou's done to you over the years became the reason why Miss Vixen made art about the flash rob."

"Something like that." I see an immediate crack in my iceberg, but I ignore it. I have to stay cold.

"I will always hate you for that." Lou honks her nose into a Kleenex and pushes her hair out of her face. "You still suck for Miss Vixen."

"I don't care." And I don't. "I'll always hate you for burning Donna Russell."

Another long silence. Then I remember Lou's necklace, and I take it out of my pocket and shove it across the table to her. My parents just watch. I don't explain.

Lou sighs as she puts the necklace on. "Your monsters were cool, even if you're a jerk."

"They're ghoulies, and it's not my fault you gave me perfect revenge material."

"Whatever." The necklace gleams, and she pats it into place. "Your girlfriend better watch herself."

I wouldn't be surprised if some paper doll of Rory ends up somewhere Rory won't like it. "I already said she's not my girlfriend. And you're a bushwhacked stupid thief of a Barbie doll with dumbass friends."

She stands up. "Can I go now?"

"No. Sit." My mom sighs. "We still have to eat."

Lou frowns and sits back down. "I don't wear tulle every day."

"You used to. Almost every day, anyway." I frown back at her.

"Do we have any big boxes?" Now it's my turn to stand up. "I know we have to eat, but I need to do this first."

"In the garage." Dad gives me an odd look. "What do you need a box for?"

"I've got to put Donna Russell in something." I can't say any more, or I'll cry, so I just leave. When I get out to the front yard, my dad is there, and he helps me gather up Donna's remains. The iceberg inside me melts a tiny bit. Her pieces are still warm, and I'm afraid the box will smolder, but nothing happens. My chest is tight and achy, and my throat hurts from holding in the tears. My dad helps me carry her behind the garage, and he gives me a one-armed hug when we get her back there. Even though I don't want it to, the iceberg cracks. I feel it go.

Dad gives me a funny half smile, though I think he wants to be more serious than he is. "Did Miss Vixen document her work while she was tormenting Lou?"

The iceberg crumbles into ice cubes. I'm still shivery, but maybe I'll warm up.

"All good artists document their work." I show him Miss Vixen's tweets, from the very first ghoulie up through the last. It's been three weeks since I met David and Rory. Three weeks since Lou's flash rob. Two and a half weeks of ghoulies. But it feels like it started a million years ago.

Then we go inside and eat. My parents talk about lawyers, how long Lou's going to be grounded, and how camp has to wait. Lou scowls. I don't talk.

Before she goes to bed, my mom kisses my cheek. "If you give us some of your art to put up, you won't have to draw on the wall by Lou's photos."

"You saw that?"

She laughs. "I like the Sasquatch painting. He'll look good over the couch. Good night, Frankie."

I brush my teeth and go to bed with a book about Uncle Epic, written by this guy who's done profiles of all sorts of street artists. Then I realize that the next book about Epic will probably include photos of pieces I've helped him with. Me. Franklin Brett Neumann. I helped Uncle Epic.

And I was Miss Vixen. And she might not be done yet. There's a lot to talk about in this big dumb world.

Soft knock on the door.

"Yeah, what?"

Her bushy head pokes around the door. "Can I come in?"

I don't answer.

"Please?"

"Whatever." I pretend to read.

Lou moves a few feet inside my door. She's got a blotchy red face again. "Am I right about who it was that dropped us off?"

I don't even flinch. "You asked him his name. He's Jamie Carlson. Just a friend."

"You don't have friends, remember?" She frowns. "Especially not friends older than thirty."

"I have exactly two friends—David and Jamie. I used to have three."

"Yeah, right."

"If you ever tell, I will cut off all your hair while you sleep. And hide all your ballet flats. And then murder you."

She knows I'm serious. "Fine."

"Fine."

"Look, I know I've been a shit to you over the years. But you messed with me really bad."

I don't say anything.

Her voice is small. "I know it was wrong to burn Donna. People shouldn't hurt other people's art. Or steal it, either." A tear spills down her cheek. "I'm sorry."

The guilt arrow twists so hard in my stomach I almost gag.

So I say it. "I'm sorry, too. Miss Vixen just . . . got away from me, I guess. I wanted someone to hear me."

"Yeah." She's quiet for a minute, looking at the floor. "I'll probably find new friends."

"I'll probably make more sculpture."

"She really was cool, you know." Lou smiles.

"Miss Vixen or Donna Russell?"

"Both, actually. So . . . good night." She picks up a shirt on the foot of my bed, wads it up, and chucks it at me. "You're a stupid asshole but not a completely horrible brother."

I chuck it back at her, but she dodges it. "You're an insensitive hag but good at apologies."

"Whatever, Frankie." She rolls her eyes and leaves.

"Whatever, Lou." The door clicks shut.

I read until my phone vibrates. It's two pictures, both from @drseussisgod. The first one is the first four ghoulies, minus their faces: **Waiting for you at the garage. Come see us sometime.**

That picture's going in the scrapbook.

The second photo is another pyramid of TVs, with the words BETTER LUCK NEXT TIME painted on them. They're in an empty room with windows—it looks kind of like another garage space. The caption on this one says **Surprise for the cops at 7100 Nicollet Avenue.**

After a while, I get out of bed and bring Sid down to the living room. It takes me a while to get him placed, but I hang him over the couch and square it up.

MY MOM'S RIGHT.

HE LOOKS AWESOME.

V is for VICTORY LAP

Tuesday nights at Pizza Vendetta are pretty damn slow, so I make six Pepperoni Zambonis for the freezer. And I sweep and mop and scrub countertops and make sauce and do every stupid thing I can to keep out of Geno's way. Things get tough when Geno notices we're not doing anything, because then we end up doing stuff like dusting ceiling fans. I'd rather mix pizza sauce.

I'm filling Parmesan cheese shakers behind the counter when David comes in, looking panicked.

"She's coming for you." He's panting like he's run five miles to warn me. She wasn't in school today, which was

OK with me. I wasn't sure what I'd say to her, but I guess I'll have to figure it out. Yesterday sort of seems like a dream, between busted ghoulies, the police, Epic, Lou, and Donna Russell. I forgot about Rory.

"Slow down, crazy man. You're two seconds from a heart attack."

He frowns at me while he recovers. "She's really, really angry. I'd watch yourself."

"I didn't do anything."

"She's mad that you're mad at her about the paper doll."

"Oh, well, that makes perfect sense. I shouldn't be mad that she's picking on my sister?" I throw David a pepperoni from the toppings container, and he catches it in his mouth. Hopefully Geno didn't see that.

"Nobody said she made sense. Can I have another?" And he catches the next one I throw.

Then the door opens and Rory is there. And she's doing her best to be sure I'm sorry.

She's dressed to make me remember all the good stuff, of course—tons of cleavage and a very tight skirt—and she comes in with Matt Havelock, Carter Stone, and Brandon Anderson, who you'd think would be in jail, but they're not. Maybe their folks bailed them out. All of them cut me to ribbons with their murderous stares while they walk to a booth. I'm sure they figure I'll crumble at the sight of their wrath.

David watches them. "I think you're supposed to crawl back to her now, dude. Or at least feel a little bad."

"I'm sure." I go back to filling Parmesan cheese shakers.

Jen comes over with their order. "They want to know if anyone else can make their pizza." She rolls her eyes. "I told them I'd ask."

"Let me check." I go in the back, and Geno's in the can, so I knock. "Geno, can you make a pizza?"

"Not now, Frankie. My gut's acting up." Which means he's in there smoking. I can hear the fan.

"OK." I go back up front to Jen. "Nope, just me. Geno's in the can."

David laughs. "You tried."

Jen goes back to their table, and they frown and make noise, but Jen eventually writes something down and brings it back to me. "Large pepperoni."

"Easy enough." I start slapping things down, and dig out the best-looking pepperoni Zamboni I've made, just to give them something extra. Why not be nice? Turn the other cheek, all that. But when I'm laying down the pepperoni V, I also make a big F and a big U.

David can see what I'm doing from his side of the glass barrier, and he smiles. "Think they'll notice?"

"I have no idea." I shove the pizza in the oven.

He nods. "Text me when you're almost done with work. Let's skate." And he's out the door.

I start cleaning up, because we're only open for another half hour. When I come up from putting the flour under the counter, Rory's standing there.

"Your pizza's almost ready." I try for cheery but I sound like a dick, so I point a spatula at her. "It was really, really shitty to steal Lou's necklace, not to mention her face."

She sniffs. "You don't even like her. Why are you sticking up for her?"

"Because even if I don't like her, she's still my sister."

"You're a hypocrite."

"Maybe so. But *I* get to mess with her. Not you." And I turn my back on her to carry a stack of dirty dishes to the sink.

When I come back, she's at the table with Matt, Carter, and Brandon. Their pizza's ready, so I take it out of the oven, slice it up, and have Jen deliver it, with another pitcher of pop on the house. I put the money for the pop into the till, so I don't forget, and then I finish cleaning up.

They don't stay long to eat their pizza, and they don't see the F U because they'd have started throwing the pizza if they had. When they're leaving, Rory comes close to the glass partition.

I try and smile. "What do you want?"

"You're a sucky kisser." Her face is scrunched up like she's eating a lemon.

I burst out laughing. I can't help it. "Is that the worst you can do?"

She's flustered, like she can't believe I didn't burst into flames or tears at her insult.

But I'm not Max Ledermann.

"Whatever, Rory. See you later." I wave, and she turns around in a huff. Matt, Carter, and Brandon form a little posse behind her, like they're her slaves. She's never hung out with theater guys before. I predict it will last three days.

I text David: **Done in about ten minutes. Glide on by.**

And he does, and we go, and the night smells good.

AND

WE'RE

FREE.

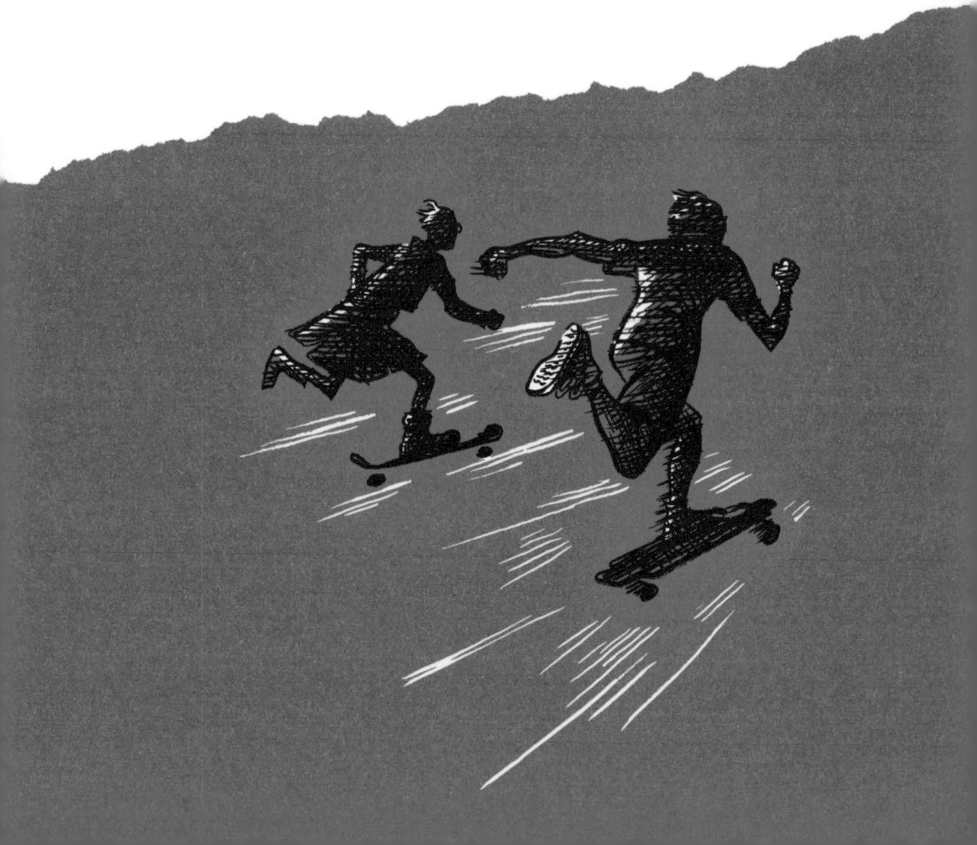

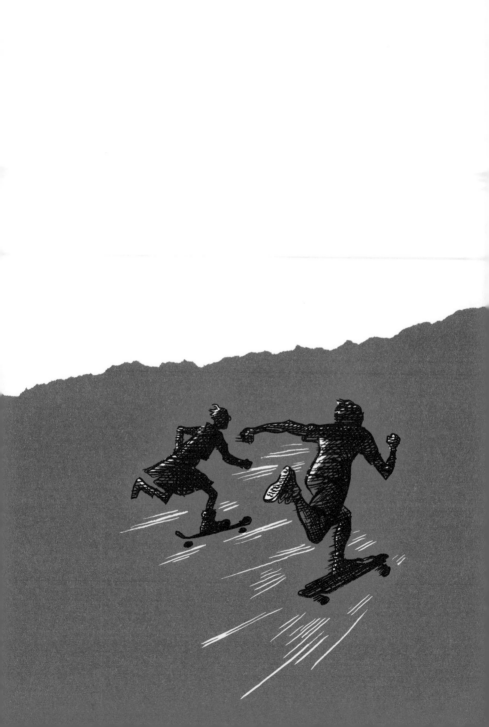

ACKNOWLEDGMENTS

All books need a village to keep them going. Some books have more villagers than others.

I first need to thank the Minnesota State Arts Board, the State of Minnesota Legacy Amendment, and South Central College, for support in finishing earlier drafts of this novel.

I definitely need to thank Inspector Travas and Sgt. Shawn Shanley for help with police details. Many thanks also go to Mary Altman, Public Arts Administrator with the City of Minneapolis, and Kirstin Wiegmann, with Forecast Public Art, for help with understanding how a city might approach street art.

Of course, I always have to thank my agent, Amy Tipton (couldn't do it without you); my Sisters in Ink, for much writing support and cheerleading (never want to do it without you); Dan and Shae, for support, love, and putting up with me (definitely definitely couldn't do it without you); E. Eero Johnson, for the IN-CREDIBLE ILLUSTRATIONS HOLY WOW I LOVE THEM THANK YOU SO MUCH (there'd be no book without you); and the friends I've had over the years who had no idea I was just punting, the ones who've never questioned my labels of "artist" or "poet" or "writer." Because you didn't doubt me, I let myself create. Thanks a million for that. Finally, thanks to my excellent brothers, Kjell and Chris, for being the best parts of my childhood—no rivalry required.

—KIRSTIN CRONN-MILLS

I would like to thank the brilliantly creative Kirstin Cronn-Mills, who pitched me the irresistible idea of collaborating for a Midwestern, punk rock, high school novel/graphic novel hybrid; and to the talented illustrators Christina Rodriguez and Stephen Shaskan, who helped her to make our introduction.

Our son, Liffy, was delivered on the same weekend that G. P. Putnam's Sons picked up the book (a dream publisher for this penguin-obsessed little boy). Thanks to agent Amy Tipton, who took me under her (other) wing; to Tammy and Emmett, for holding down the fort while I disappeared night after night into drawings; to any friend or acquaintance who politely nodded their head when I tried to describe this crazy project; to comic book pioneers like Jack Kirby, Harvey Kurtzman, Will Eisner, Moebius, George Herriman and Winsor McCay, and *RAW* magazine for lighting my inspiration; and to friends like CSA Design, Uncivilized Books and Nozone for keeping those flames going.

Finally, thanks to Speedball Super-Black India Ink for always living up to your name, and to parents like mine, who never paused to question their child's artistic aspirations.

—E. EERO JOHNSON

We both want to thank Stacey, Cecilia, Ryan, Kate, and all the folks at G. P. Putnam's Sons who believed in our story and the unusual way it would be told, and then made it look so easy when all the pieces finally fit together into the joyous, funky, fun book you're holding in your hands.

—KIRSTIN CRONN-MILLS and E. EERO JOHNSON

KIRSTIN CRONN-MILLS

is a self-proclaimed word nerd who secretly wants to be a street artist. Her first young adult novel, *The Sky Always Hears Me: And the Hills Don't Mind*, was a 2010 finalist for the Minnesota Book Award for Young People's Literature. Her second novel, *Beautiful Music for Ugly Children*, won ALA's Stonewall Book Award in 2014 as well as an IPPY silver medal for Gay/Lesbian/Bi/Trans Fiction. She writes a lot, reads as much as she can, teaches at a two-year college, and goofs around with her son, Shae, and her husband, Dan.

E. EERO JOHNSON

(Erik T. Johnson) is a Minneapolis-based illustrator, graphic designer, and comic book artist. His illustrations have appeared in *GQ*, *The New Yorker*, *Newsweek*, *Wired*, and *The New York Times*, and on several book covers. His comic book projects, *The Outliers* and *Kozmo-Knot*, have gained a growing interest from the indie comic world. He lives with his wife, Tammy; sons, Emmett and Eilif; and a crazy Boston terrier.